Nights *of the* Red Moon

Milton T. Burton

Minotaur Books

A Thomas Dunne Book
New York

This is a work of fiction. All of the characters, organizations, and events portrayed in this novel are either products of the author's imagination or are used fictitiously.

A THOMAS DUNNE BOOK FOR MINOTAUR BOOKS.
An imprint of St. Martin's Publishing Group.

www.thomasdunnebooks.com
www.minotaurbooks.com

Library of Congress Cataloging-in-Publication Data

Burton, Milton T.
    Nights of the red moon / Milton T. Burton.—1st ed.
      p.   cm.
    "A Thomas Dunne book."
    ISBN 978-0-312-64800-8
    1. Sheriffs—Fiction.   2. Spouses of clergy—Crimes against—Fiction.   3. Texas—Fiction.   I. Title.
PS3602.U77N54   2010
813'.6—dc22

                                        2010035346

First Edition: December 2010

10   9   8   7   6   5   4   3   2   1

Fondly dedicated to the memory of

Claire Craig Budd
1948–2004

ACKNOWLEDGMENTS

Numerous acknowledgments and thanks are in order.

First to Stanley Haskins and Nancy Thomas-Haskins for their financial support and other favors too numerous to mention, and especially to Nancy for her endless hours of unpaid proofreading and many valuable suggestions.

To David Hudson, Terry Cowan, Rabbi Steve Fisch, Jim Graham, Joe Prentis, and Debbie Lageman—some of whom have helped keep me afloat financially and all of whom have been unstinting in their enthusiasm and encouragement.

To retired Texas Ranger Sergeant Steve Black, retired Texas Ranger Captain Jack Dean, retired FBI Special Agent Dennis Murphy, former Bullard, Texas, City Marshall Connie Vaughan, and Texas Adult Parole Officer Alice Alexander for patiently and generously giving of their time to answer my numerous questions about law enforcement and police and parole procedures.

To Joe Prentis for his early reading of the manuscript and his encouragement and faith.

To my agent, Ron Goldfarb, for staying the course.

To my editor, Kat Brzozowski, for being everything an editor should be.

To Tom Dunne of Thomas Dunne Books for seeing some value in me as a writer.

To David Thompson and the staff at Murder by the Book in Houston, to Ed Kaufman at "M" is for Mystery in San Mateo, California, and to Barbara Peters at the Poisoned Pen in Phoenix, along with numerous others in the book business who have given their support and encouragement.

To Lise Kim Horton for her help, encouragement, and just being her enthusiastic self.

To my children, Seth, Samantha, David, and Thomas, to my son-in-law Elton, and to my daughter-in-law Laurie for giving my life a depth of meaning that no literary accomplishment could ever equal.

Aside from stories gleaned from my own personal acquaintance with such former Texas sheriffs as Esten Ray, Frank Brunt, Roy Herrington, and Nathan Tindall, I have drawn heavily on *The Texas Sheriff: Lord of the County Line* by Thad Sitton of Austin. Mr. Sitton is a professional historian who writes like a first-rate journalist with a keen eye for character and story.

Nights *of the* Red Moon

CHAPTER ONE

S hortly before sunup on a hot, dry morning in early September of this past year, Amanda Twiller, the local Methodist preacher's wife, was slaughtered and then dumped in front of the church parsonage. My name is Bo Handel, and as it turned out, this was to be one of my most trying cases in almost thirty years as sheriff of Caddo County, Texas.

I was enjoying a third cup of coffee and trying to dig my way through the *Houston Chronicle* when I heard a loud knock at my front door. I padded up the hall barefoot and in my bathrobe to find my chief deputy, Toby Parsons, standing on the porch. Toby is a midthirties African-American ex–Special Forces sergeant with a keen mind and a calm, even temperament. But he looked anything but calm and even that morning.

I motioned him inside. "From your expression I conclude that either the courthouse has gone missing or we have a body on our hands. Which is it?"

"A body."

"Any idea whose?"

He nodded. "Afraid so, Bo. It's Reverend Twiller's wife."

I grimaced. "This would be a murder, I assume?"

"Unless she found some way to shoot herself three times in

the back. Her husband found her in their front yard just a little while ago, but it looks like she was killed somewhere else because there's hardly any blood at the scene."

"It's inside the city limits. Doesn't the police department want primary jurisdiction?"

"No. Chief Ogilvie and his wife are on vacation up in Virginia. With him out of town, the city PD doesn't have anybody with homicide experience except Clyde Morgan, and he's filling in as acting chief. He requested that you take over the investigation since he's busy with administrative duties."

"Of course he would," I said, shaking my head with mild exasperation. "Clyde's too damn lazy to cast a shadow." I led the way back to the kitchen and motioned to the percolator. "Go ahead and have a cup of coffee while I get dressed."

I went upstairs to the bedroom I had shared with my wife until she died of cancer five years earlier. I pulled out a fresh pair of dark Wrangler dress jeans and a starched white Western shirt and climbed into them. Once I got my Tony Lama boots situated on my feet and my cream-colored Western summer hat mounted on my head, I went down the stairs. I didn't bother to take a look in the hall mirror before leaving the house, the way I always did in my younger years. By now I was reconciled to what I'd see looking back at me—a weathered, sun-darkened face that would never make women swoon. But neither would it make little kids run screeching for their mothers, so I was pretty sure I could live with it one more day, just as I'd been doing for the past sixty-two years.

A half dozen cops, including two of my deputies, milled around in the front yard of the Twiller house, and an ambulance from the hospital in nearby Nacogdoches was already on site. Much to my relief, only a few of the more curious neighbors had gathered. I also spotted two eager-looking young fellows in summer-weight suits and sunglasses who'd no doubt come in the white Ford sedan that screamed federal government. I had no idea what they wanted, but their presence told me this was destined to be something more than a simple murder case.

We ducked under the crime scene tape and walked over to where the body lay sprawled on the greenbelt between the sidewalk and the street.

"You didn't sound surprised when I told you she was dead," Toby said softly.

"I wasn't. The woman has been out of control for months."

"What's the story on her?"

A good question. What was the story? I knew that she was the wife of the Reverend Bobby Joe Twiller, pastor of Sequoya's First United Methodist Church, and that they'd been in town about three years. The morning he preached his first sermon, Twiller stressed that he hoped to become a refuge and safe harbor to anyone in spiritual need. How successful he was in this endeavor is for others besides myself to decide, but it is a matter of public record that after ten years of marriage, his wife had found his gentle presence in her life so burdensome that she'd begun an affair with the owner of a local liquor store, and then run off to Houston with the man a few weeks later.

Initially, the Twillers' arrival in town had generated quite a splash with the congregation. As time wore on, they had come to be well liked in the community, and with Reverend Twiller at the helm the membership of the old, almost moribund church quadrupled. Along the way a full-time educational director had been hired, and a large and popular Sunday school class for adult singles was added. Then at the beginning of the summer, Twiller announced the creation of a youth ministry that featured a week's encampment on Sam Rayburn Reservoir.

Back in the spring a friend of mine, a sweet, vaguely frayed female social worker for the Texas child welfare department, insisted that I accompany her and her husband to church to hear this paragon expound his doctrines from the pulpit. And hear them I did. Indeed, Reverend Twiller droned on for over half an hour, virtually burying us under an avalanche of pious nonsense, no single sentence of which seemed to bear any logical relation to the others. It was as though he had written the thing by pouring a box of modern Protestant catchphrases into the top of a word processor and then pushing the print button. As I left the church that day, I could only reflect that God's taste in servants had changed dramatically since the days of Jeremiah.

Yet his accomplishments must have seemed meaningless to him that Sunday morning back in late July when his conscience compelled him to reveal his wife's adultery to his congregation, something he saw as rooted in his own failures as a husband. The clear-eyed businessmen on his board of stewards were aware of one fact that was lost on their pastor: Amanda Twiller was a nervous, erratic individual who had been a very poor choice as a minister's wife. They refused to accept his resignation and asked him to stay on. He did, though only as a shadow of his former self. But if the church hadn't given up on Reverend Twiller, then neither had he given up on his wife. At least not until that grim morning when he found her body.

"She was a misfit, Toby," I said under my breath. "And I've heard she had a problem with prescription drugs. You know the pattern. Complaints of chronic pain, doctor hopping . . . About two months ago she left her husband and son and took up with Emmet Zorn, that guy who owns the Pak-a-Sak."

"Ahhh, I got it."

I quickly determined that adequate crime scene photos had been taken, that the area around the body had been fine-combed, and that the only physical evidence that might have been related to the murder was a beer can in the gutter a few feet from the body.

"It needs to go to the Department of Public Safety lab down in Houston," I told the young city cop who had bagged it. "I want it checked for both prints and DNA. And where are Reverend Twiller and his son? I'll need to talk to them."

"Twiller went to pieces and they took him to the hospital," Toby said. "Is he a suspect?"

I shook my head. "Not hardly. If Bobby Joe Twiller was getting mugged, he'd try to convene a seminar on anger management. But I'll need to have a few words with him anyway. How about the boy?"

"Somebody from the church came and got him."

"Good enough."

I turned to the two government boys and gave them a bland smile. "What can you do for me?" I asked.

"Muldoon and Hotchkiss, FBI," the larger of the two said, holding out his hand. "I'm Muldoon, and isn't it customary for an officeholder to ask, 'What can I do for you?'"

"I'm the one that needs help. And I'm a little curious about why you're here this morning. I don't quite see the Federal connection."

Muldoon answered, "This woman has been involved with a man we've had our eye on for some time."

"You must mean Emmet Zorn. What's your interest in him?"

Muldoon's voice fell to a near whisper. "Sheriff, that's something we ought to talk about someplace where it's a little more private."

One of the city policemen came over and handed me Amanda Twiller's purse, a large shoulder bag of quilted suede that was found beside her body. I peeked in the top and saw a jumbo-size prescription bottle. "Look at this," I said.

"What?" Muldoon asked.

"Vicodin, the big, two-hundred-milligram tablets." I squinted for a moment at the label. "The prescription calls for sixty of these damn things, and it's only two days old. One every six hours . . ."

I took my pen and jiggled the bottle around sideways so I could see inside it. "Only about a half dozen left. Looks like the lady got way ahead of herself on her medication." I peered closely at the label. "It was filled at a Houston pharmacy, and the doctor's name is Kane. Wilton Kane. Either of you ever heard of him?"

Both men nodded. "Yeah," Muldoon said. "Kane is real popular with high-strung rich ladies. Specializes in tranquilizers and painkillers. He's been skirting on the edge of losing his narcotics permit for the last couple of years."

A new Chevy pickup glided up to the curb, and Meg McCorkle, Precinct One justice of the peace vaulted out and hurried toward us. In Texas counties that are too small in population to warrant a full-time coroner, the local JP handles this function. It would be Meg who would have to sign the order for an autopsy and authorize the removal of the body from the scene. She was a tall, midthirtyish woman with a merry face and a pair of long, well-tanned legs that came out of her dark green Bermuda shorts and seemed to go on forever.

"I'm sorry it took me so long to get here," she said. "Jeff is out of town, and I had to get the kids off to school."

"Don't fret about it," I said. I turned and introduced her to the two Bureau men.

"Autopsy in Houston?" she asked.

I shook my head. "No, I want it done over in Nacogdoches."

"You sure? The Harris County medical examiner's office is a lot cheaper."

"That takes too long, and I want one of the bullets out of the corpse this afternoon so these young Federal friends of ours can run it through the national computer." I looked at them and smiled. "Right?"

"Sure," Muldoon said.

"The county commissioners aren't going to like it," Meg said.

I smiled at her. "Now, Meg, do you think I really care about that?"

"Okay, just so I can lay the blame on you. I'm hoping to get a raise out of them."

I knew she was as likely to get a raise out of that quartet of penny-pinching jackasses as it was to rain in the next ten minutes, but I didn't say so. Instead I said, "Be my guest. Just please move things along and get the body out of this heat."

"They can go ahead and load it now," she said. "I'll get the particulars from your deputies."

I turned to Toby. "Linda Willis was scheduled to be on duty today. Get on the radio or call her on her cell phone or something, and tell her to meet this ambulance over in Nacogdoches. She's got an autopsy to watch. She knows what questions to ask, but tell her to make sure they do a vaginal swab, and have her get those bullets back up here as quick as you can. Have them take samples of anything they find under the victim's fingernails. I also want blood tests done for every drug they can think of. And send this bag on down to Houston for a complete examination. Fingerprints, the works."

I motioned to the two Bureau men. "You gentlemen come on and follow me and I'll buy you some breakfast. I've got to get something to eat pretty quick or I'll play out before noon."

They headed for their car while I stood for a moment surveying the scene. I shuddered a little as I watched the attendants slide the body-laden stretcher into the back of the ambulance. We were in the second week of a mercilessly hot September, and East Texas had been more than two months without rain. The heat and drought were taking their toll. Violent crime was up all across the eastern part of the state, and cops were facing the weekends with dread. When the sun set, the bars and clubs came alive with fights and brawls. The past week had seen two stabbings in my own county, and in Nacogdoches a well-liked fertilizer plant foreman shot his wife four times and then turned the gun on himself. Their sixteen-year-old daughter said they had been arguing over the electric bill.

I'm not superstitious by nature, but there is one piece of local folklore I have come to accept completely in the years since I first heard it as a child from the old people in my family, who'd gotten it from their ancestors, who in turn had learned it from the Indians. It was something that had lain heavy on my mind the last few days, especially when darkness fell. The air was laden with dust and the moon was beginning its second quarter. Each night it rose crimson on the eastern horizon, and even at its highest point in the middle of the night it was still a reddish orange. Back in frontier times when a summer drought lingered on toward the fall equinox, the Cherokees called it the Season of the Blood Moon, and feared it as a time of madness and death.

CHAPTER TWO

The best restaurant in Sequoya is the Caravan, a cozy, rustic joint with a menu that features fresh Gulf seafood in season and good country cooking anytime. The dining room was almost full that morning, but we managed to get a booth. After the waitress brought our coffee and departed with our orders, I gave the two young agents a bland smile and said, "I'm a firm believer in interagency cooperation, boys. So let's cooperate. What's the story here?"

"How much do you know about Emmet Zorn?" Muldoon asked.

"He's not a local boy, but he seems to be a decent enough guy. He owns half interest in a middling successful liquor store, and claims he used to be a rodeo promoter."

"Have you had trouble with him?"

"Not really. My department has written him up for a couple of minor liquor violations, but that happens with other stores too. I don't have any grievance against the man, if that's what you mean."

"What would your reaction be if I told you he's close to a guy named Lester Sipes down in Houston?" Muldoon asked.

"I don't know that I'd have any particular reaction. Like I said, I don't know that much about Zorn because I've never had any reason to find out. What's their connection?"

"They're old friends from the rodeo circuit," Muldoon said. "How much do you know about Sipes?"

I quickly ran down for them what I remembered about the man. He was a banker, real estate developer, and reputed hood whose vulgarity of lifestyle surpassed even that of the early oil barons. A few years earlier his name had been front-page fodder all over the state, and before that he was a champion bull rider with a nationwide reputation. Tough and durable like most men who practice that sport, he'd come out of the rodeo circuit with a few hundred thousand dollars in prize money and a ruthless determination to get big rich. Within a decade he'd parlayed his stake up to a net worth of several million that included controlling interest in two small coastal banks, one in Crystal City, the other in Kemah. Then he became associated with an outfit that newspapers came to call the "Cowboy Mob" when the story of its marijuana importing scheme hit the headlines. In reality, this so-called syndicate had been nothing more than a crew of rodeo has-beens who'd managed to smuggle over four hundred tons of Colombian Red into the country in the short span of two years using a fleet of commercial fishing boats that had been outfitted with oversize fuel tanks so they could make the trip to South America by way of Yucatán. Investigation showed that these boats had been leased to a nonexistent customer of Sipes's Kemah bank, and the lease had been paid with a "loan" from the bank itself.

The Feds came at him with the RICO statute. The ensuing trial was moved from Houston to Fillmore up in Northeast Texas on a change of venue, and it turned out to be a long, garish affair that generated masses of publicity and lurid stories of late-night parties at Sipes's Crystal Beach marina, where prominent South American politicians cavorted with half-naked call girls. . . .

Muldoon nodded. "That's him."

"I saw him one time," I said.

"Really?"

The waitress came by to refill our cups, and I waited until she was gone. "I was at a restaurant up there in Fillmore when he was on trial. As it happened, we finished lunch about the same time, and I followed him out into the parking lot. He was driving a candy apple red Cadillac Fleetwood and had a pair of body-guards with him who looked like the Marlboro Twins. All three were decked out in fancy Western clothes, boots, hats, the works. And I don't mean just hats, my friends. These guys were wearing the damnedest hats I ever saw. Hats that bore the same relation to the kind of hat I wear that a ski jump bears to your front door-step."

Hotchkiss smiled. "We know those hats. Sipes and all his goons wear them. They're his trademark."

"*One* of his trademarks," Muldoon said.

"Right," Hotchkiss said. "No more red Cadillacs for Lester. Now it's a black Mercury Marquis, and that's all he'll drive. He also bought one for each of his banks to use as courier cars."

"How come?" I asked.

"When we prosecuted him before, he thought he was going to prison for sure. Hell, *we* thought he was going to prison. The reason he didn't was a brilliant old lawyer from El Paso named Durwood Keane. For some reason, Keane drove him to the courthouse the day of the verdict in his own car, which was a black Marquis. People who know Sipes say he's very superstitious, and somehow he got it into his head that Keane's car had something to do with his acquittal. Ever since then he won't drive anything else."

"For real?" I asked.

They both nodded.

I shook my head in bemusement. "My years on this job have taught me that you will never cease to be surprised by the things people do. I even surprise myself sometimes. So why are you still interested in Sipes?"

"We're really not at liberty to discuss that at the moment," Muldoon said.

"Then it must be either drugs or big-time money laundering or both. I won't press you, but it would be nice if you could give me some notion of where Zorn fits into whatever it is you're investigating. You say he and Sipes are old friends?"

They glanced at each other before either spoke. Then Muldoon nodded and said, "That's another thing Sipes is superstitious about. He believes in loyalty. The story is that Zorn helped him one time when he was down and out, and Sipes has stuck with him ever since."

"So that's all there is to the connection?" I asked.

"We think so," Muldoon said. "Except that Sipes may have bankrolled his liquor store."

"Then why does Zorn deserve so much attention?"

"Sheriff, this is a major investigation. We're following every possible lead. Just because we *think* that's the extent of their involvement doesn't meant that it really is."

The waitress brought our orders, and the three of us dug in and ate for a while in silence. Eventually I looked up from my plate and smiled and said, "You two sure got to the crime scene quick enough this morning. How did that come to pass? You wouldn't happen to have an 'unofficial source' here in town, would you?"

More sideways glances. "We got a call from a friend," Muldoon said. "You see, Zorn and Mrs. Twiller have been in and out of that marina Sipes owns at Crystal Beach a lot in the last month. In fact, they took a trip with Sipes down to Brownsville about three weeks ago. So when we heard that Zorn had come back home to Sequoya, we contacted our guy up here."

Their "guy" had to be a cop of some kind, but I didn't say so. Instead I asked, "What else did he tell you?"

"Only that he'd heard Zorn and the Twiller woman have been spending a lot of time in the evenings at the Sawmill Club down in Nacogdoches. Do you know the place?"

"Sure," I said. "It's a big country-and-western dance joint. Have you been there yet?"

"No," Hotchkiss said. "This business has been a hit-or-miss thing for us. We've got other cases, and we've just been gathering information for a team of agents down in Houston that's working Sipes full-time."

"I need to talk to Reverend Twiller," I said. "They've taken him to the Nacogdoches hospital, so I'll just plan on stopping by the Sawmill Club too."

"Good," Muldoon said.

"Hey, Sheriff," Hotchkiss said. "Before we go, I want to ask you about your sidearm. We've heard a lot about it."

"If you've heard about it, then it's doing its job," I said.

He seemed a bit baffled. "I don't understand. . . ."

I smiled at him. "Image, my friends. I have to get elected, so image is important to me. My predecessor was a fellow named John Nightwalker, and besides being a crackerjack cop, he was a very shrewd politician. After he came down with cancer, he got me appointed to fill out his term. Along with a lot of other sound advice, he told me that a sheriff in this part of the country needs something for his constituents to be able to brag about. You know, something to set him apart from the herd, something they can be proud of.

"Now, John was six foot five and weighed two hundred and eighty pounds. He carried a Colt .44 hog-leg with an eight-inch barrel and drove a Ford 427 interceptor. That was his image. Of course, I doubt that he pulled the gun out of its holster in the last ten years he lived, and he drove that damn car so slow the plugs stayed fouled all the time. But nobody noticed any of that because all they saw was their giant sheriff with his big gun and fast car. Well, I only stretch to five eleven on a good day and don't weigh but about one seventy. Since fast cars really aren't my cup of tea, what I did was get me a brand-new Colt .45 automatic and send it to Ferlach, Austria, where a master engraver gussied it up with about a thousand dollars' worth of that fine scroll engraving they do over there. When I got it back home I fitted it out with a fancy pair of ivory grips with eagles' heads carved in them, and started practicing out at my farm just about every day until I got real good with the thing. I mean uncommonly good. I've always had a natural talent with a handgun, and I pushed it right out to the limit. Then I started showing up at the Caddo County Gun Club and shooting circles around most everybody out there. Thus was born the legend of Sheriff Beauregard Handel and his Mighty Forty-Five. It's good politics, my friends, and it's good psychology with the criminal element too."

"Have you ever shot anybody with it?" Hotchkiss asked.

I held up two fingers. "I wish I'd been spared that, but I don't think two is so bad for almost thirty years in office. One of the benefits of having a reputation as a first-class pistolero is that it sometimes forestalls armed conflict, and that's fine with me. I'll take diplomacy over gunplay any day of the week."

"Did either of the guys you shot offer any comments on the experience?" Hotchkiss asked.

"The one that lived claimed it hurt a right smart. . . ."

After they went on their way, I decided to have one final cup of coffee and try to collect my thoughts. But before I could get started on such a probably futile project, a slim, pretty woman in her early thirties with shoulder-length auburn hair and pale blue eyes sat down in the other side of the booth. My niece, Sheila Warbeck, star reporter for the *Nacogdoches Daily Sentinel* and occasional freelancer for several slick, wide-circulation magazines, including *Texas Monthly*. Four years earlier she'd enjoyed a budding career with the *Dallas Morning News,* including two years on the police beat. Then her marriage failed, and after the divorce she abandoned urban life and brought her daughter, Mindy, back home and moved in with her mother, a calm, unobtrusive woman a couple of years my junior. It was hardly the life she had envisioned for herself when she graduated with honors from the University of Texas School of Journalism.

"I just heard about Amanda Twiller," she said. "I also heard you drew the case."

I nodded.

"It's so awful. Who would want to kill that poor woman?"

"Right now I don't have any idea. How about you? You go to the Methodist Church, so you must have known her."

"Bo, I don't think anybody really *knew* her."

"I bet her husband feels like he knew her less than anybody right now. By the way, do you happen to know who's her doctor?"

"Her doctor?" she asked, her eyes wide. "Why are you interested in her doctor?"

"Because it looks like the lady had a prescription drug problem."

"Oh my . . ."

"Her doctor's name?" I urged.

"Dotty Fletcher, down on the square. Almost everybody at the church goes to Dr. Dotty because she's our pianist."

"You're sure about that?"

"Oh, absolutely. I've seen her in the waiting room a couple of times."

"So what did you hear about her?" I asked. "Did you know anything about her private life?"

"Just that she started keeping company with that asshole Emmet Zorn."

Sheila rarely used rough language, and only with the most extreme provocation. I stared at her pointedly for a few seconds. "What's the problem?"

"Nothing, really. Forget about it."

"Has he been coming on to you?"

"Only every time he sees me. I think he's singled me out as his next conquest."

"I'll put a stop to it for you."

"No, Bo—" she began, shaking her head.

"Hush. It's done."

She gave me a shy smile. "Okay, if you insist. My knight in shining armor."

I snorted. "Wranglers and cotton dress shirts, please."

"But mounted on a gray charger and carrying a Rebel flag. Are you still a member of the Sons of Confederate Veterans?"

"Damn right I am."

We grinned at each other across the table. "So, General Beauregard, when will you have something for me on the Twiller murder?"

"Come by the house about seven this evening and I'll fill you in. Of course, a lot of what I have to tell you I can't let you use yet. If something comes up and I can't meet you there, I'll call you on your cell phone."

"Okay. How about giving me a quote now that I can put in my story today?"

"Just say that Sheriff Handel has several promising leads, and that he will leave no stone unturned in his efforts to apprehend the perpetrators of this senseless and savage crime. Does that sound pompous enough for you?"

"It sounds grand," she said, scribbling quickly in her note-book. "Do you? Have several good leads, I mean?"

I shook my head. "No. All I've got is half a lead and a semi-suspect."

"Then I'll see you tonight," she said.

CHAPTER THREE

S equoya lies about forty miles from the Louisiana border in central East Texas, a land of languid, slow-moving rivers and red clay hills covered in dense pine and hardwood forests. It's a county seat, a place big enough that I need a dozen full-time deputies, but still small enough that people who move here soon feel like they know everybody in town. Like the rest of Texas, Caddo County was originally part of Mexico, settled by colonists who wandered up El Camino Real during the long, fading twilight of the Spanish empire. They named it La Ciudad Nueva, which meant the New City, but under Spanish rule it never amounted to anything more than a dismal collection of huts clustered around its plaza, an irregular pentagon which housed the communal well that was always the social center of a Latin village.

The Spanish are long gone now, but the well is still there, curbed and lined with native fieldstone and securely locked against the "depredations of children, idiots and drunkards," as the city council's 1896 ordinance reads. In the early years of the nineteenth century, Anglo-Celtic settlers began to trickle in from the Old South, and by the time Sam Houston and his ragtag army won Texas from Mexico at the Battle of San Jacinto in 1836, the town had become thoroughly American.

The timber boom of the late nineteenth century brought prosperity, which inspired the city fathers of that era to cover ten blocks of South Main with paving bricks of a deep maroon color. That same year the county found the money to build a new courthouse on the old Spanish plaza, a three-story Renaissance Revival structure of dull red brick and white marble trim that rises sedately from a grove of ancient oaks and magnolias. Its copper dome is visible for miles around, and the statue of Lady Justice standing atop its crown is still the highest point in the county.

My first destination that morning was more prosaic—the Pak-a-Sak liquor store over on the north side of town, an ugly modernist pile built back in the 1950s of red brick with a glass and aluminum front. I parked my cruiser and pushed the store's door open to see Emmet Zorn where he stood in front of the counter talking to a skinny young clerk.

Zorn was in his early forties, tall and slim with a handlebar mustache and a full head of heavily sprayed, ash-blond hair that swept up and backward so dramatically that it looked like the work of a moderately skilled taxidermist. The lower end of this amazing apparition was firmly encased in well-shined cowboy boots of full quill ostrich hide that ran about a thousand dollars a pair. In between he wore western-cut pants of tan twill and a heavily-starched white western shirt with mother of pearl buttons. A black bolo tie with a large turquoise clasp and a pair of aviator sunglasses completed his getup.

When I came in the door, he reached up and took off his shades. "Can I help you?" he asked.

"We need to talk outside."

He hesitated a moment before answering, and then gave me a laconic, "Okay."

I went through the doorway and he followed me out into the parking lot. "So what's on your mind?" he asked.

"I thought you might like to know that Amanda Twiller is dead."

"Yeah, I heard," he said. "Terrible."

"When did you see her last?"

"About ten last night."

"Where?" I asked.

"A bar over in Nacogdoches."

"That would be the Sawmill Club, I suppose."

This threw him a little. "How did you know that?"

"Never mind," I said. "Did the two of you go there together?"

He gave me an offhand shrug. "Yeah, we went with another couple that left early. About an hour later I left with some friends, and I don't know what she did after that."

"Did you have an argument?" I asked.

"Nah. Just one of those things, you know."

"No, I don't know. What kind of things?"

Before he spoke he rolled his toothpick over to the other side of his mouth with the tip of his tongue, then he said, "We split up."

"Why?"

"Hey, man, that's personal."

"I can make one phone call to the DA and have you in front of the grand jury when it convenes next week. So why not tell me now and avoid that embarrassment?"

He sighed a deep, long-suffering sigh—the sigh of a man of affairs forced to waste valuable time on a hick lawman who probably wasn't too smart anyway.

"What's it going to be?" I asked. "My way or the grand jury?"

"Okay, I may as well since you've probably heard anyway. The woman was a doper. She abused prescription drugs, painkillers and stuff. She was starting to hook up with some street-level sources and people like that. I didn't want any part of it."

"I'm still going to want you to come in," I said. "I'll need a statement from you since you were involved with the lady."

"Should I bring my lawyer?"

"I don't know. Should you? All I asked about was a statement for the record, and here you start in on lawyers."

He licked his lips and tried to hold my gaze and couldn't. He dropped his eyes and muttered, "No, of course not."

"There's one more thing we need to talk about," I said.

"Yeah? What?"

"Sheila Warbeck."

"Who?" he asked, then repeated himself, "Who?"

"Who-who? What are you, an owl? You know who I'm talking about. The reporter."

"Oh, her. That little redhead. What about her?"

I stepped closer to him so my weather-worn old face was only about a foot from his. "You quit hitting on her, that's what."

"There's no law against—"

"Yes, actually there is," I said. "These days Texas has sexual harassment laws. But since she's my niece, I won't stop to fool around with anything that damn tedious if you bother her again. Now you leave the girl alone. You hear me?"

He caved in quickly. "Your niece? I'm sorry, man. I didn't mean any disrespect. Just guy stuff, you know? She's a pretty girl and all. And I'll be happy to come in whenever you want and make that statement."

"I'll let you know when," I said, turned away, and walked to my car.

The truth is that my hometown is little more than a bedroom community for Nacogdoches, a small city of some thirty thousand inhabitants twenty-two miles to the south that is itself highly dependent on its large state university for its economic health. And if the collection of university pennants and memorabilia on the walls of the Sawmill Club was any indicator, its owner recognized the need to keep the college crowd happy.

There were only two customers in the joint, and much to my relief the jukebox was silent. I walked over to the bar. The bartender was a tall, skinny, middle-aged blonde with a beehive hairdo and a face that reminded me of stale beer. She wore a pair of turquoise jeans that were too tight even for her meager frame and a beaded and fringed top that wiggled and squiggled like it had a life of its own. But when she removed the cigarette that dangled from one corner of her mouth and spoke, her voice was low and sultry and made her seem to look a whole lot better than she really did.

"Well, hello, handsome," she said. "What'll you have?"

I had to laugh a little. "If you really think I'm handsome you are either blind or certifiably insane."

"Weeeellll," she drawled and gave me a careful head-to-heel examination. "You're not exactly handsome, but you do have a kind of rough, country-boy appeal to you. Besides, can't a girl get away with a little artful exaggeration?"

"She might if she was willing to tell me how many grandchildren she has."

She held up three fingers and said, "And one on the way. How about you?"

"Two. My only son is a surgeon over in Dallas. He and his wife have two little boys, and they are hellions."

"Well, if we've both got grandkids, then I reckon we're too damn old to be flirting," she said. "We ought to know better."

"Actually, I thought we were doing a pretty good job of it. But I need some information. I'm the sheriff up in Caddo County."

She leaned over the bar and peered at my badge for a few seconds, then picked up her cigarette and took a drag and let it back out with a sigh. "Lawmen," she said and shook her head. "Here I am hoping to get the gun, and all you laws ever want are the facts."

That broke me up. I was beginning to like this woman. "I need to ask you a few questions, so let's get back to business before we embarrass ourselves," I said. "My name's Bo Handel."

She stuck out her hand and said, "Parker Raynes."

"Pleased to meet you, Parker."

"The pleasure is mine, and you go ahead and ask away. Maybe one of your questions will sweep me off my feet."

"Okay. Do you know Emmet Zorn, by any chance? I hear he's a regular customer."

"Yeah, I do, and that question ain't gonna do it."

"How well do you know him?"

"Well, I sure as hell don't know him in the biblical sense, if that's what you mean."

"Why's that?" I asked, grinning in spite of myself.

"He's all meringue and no pie. And that's a fact."

"Was he in here last night?"

She nodded. "That's why I really wasn't too surprised to see somebody wearing a badge walk through the door. He came in with that Methodist minister's wife that was killed."

This got my attention. "How did you know who she was?"

"The news about the murder was on the radio a little while ago. And as for knowing who she was, neither one of them made any secret of it."

I sat down on a barstool. "I'll take a Coke if you have one," I said.

"Sure. Ice?"

"Please. Did she leave with Zorn?"

She shook her head and laughed. "Hell no. She left with my no-good nephew, Doyle Raynes."

This was a new and unexpected wrinkle. "Your nephew?"

She nodded.

"Do you mind if I ask you a few questions about this boy?"

"No, I don't mind a bit. He's just my nephew by marriage, anyhow. His dad was my husband's brother, and they're both dead. I sorta inherited Doyle and all his problems."

"So you're a widow?" I asked.

"Yeah, and I'm available. Are you looking?"

I laughed again. "No, ma'am, I'm not."

"Didn't figure you were," she said with a sigh. "The good ones never are. Anyhow, Doyle is a doper and he's got no backbone at all. He never really does anything. Too passive. He's one of those guys that life just happens to. You know the kind I mean?"

"Sure I do. The prisons are full of them."

"You ought to know him. He grew up here in town, but he's lived up in Sequoya for a couple of years."

"If I remember right, my deputies have handled him a time or two for public intoxication. I've never heard his name in connection with drugs, but I'm not surprised. He's got that look about him, and my chief deputy told me a while back that he'd gotten real thick with Scott Kimball before that little toad took off for Houston."

"You know Scott Kimball?" she asked. "He used to come in here a lot."

"I know Scott a whole lot better than I want to," I said.

"Didn't somebody try to shoot him or something?"

"Yeah. It was when his brother Hamilton was a senior here at the university. Scott burned some half-wit druggies up in Fillmore, and they came over here gunning for him. But since the two boys looked so much alike, they killed Hamilton instead."

"Now I remember. It was in the papers."

Before I could reply, the door opened and two middle-aged men came in. They were dressed in T-shirts and baggy denim work pants and had the hangdog expressions of the chronic failures of this world. Parker went over and set a Budweiser longneck in front of each of them and collected her money. When she came back down to my end of the bar, she said quietly, "That's what a gal like me gets to pick from. It's either tinhorn Casanovas like Emmet Zorn or guys like those two. They're good ole boys, but life has leeched all the sap out of 'em."

With that, she slapped her towel down on the bar with a loud splat that got everybody's attention and announced loudly to the world, "And I need a man with some sap in him, damn it!" Then she looked at me and whispered, "You sure you're not looking?"

"No, ma'am, I'm not."

"You married?

"Not anymore," I said. We were straying far afield from Amanda Twiller, but I'm a patient fellow, and it is a fact of life that in my part of the world you can often get more information by having a conversation than you can by conducting an interrogation. "My wife died five years ago. We were childhood sweethearts."

"Awwww, gee. That's so sweet," she said and reached over and patted my hand. "Damn! Why does somebody else always get the good ones?"

"Ma'am, I couldn't begin to answer a question like that. Let's get back to Doyle Raynes and Amanda Twiller. Were they alone or was there somebody with them?"

"As far as I know, they were alone, but I guess maybe they could have hooked up with somebody else after they went out in the parking lot. Doyle borrowed twenty dollars from me. He said he wanted to stop and get some whisky because they were going back to his place. He claimed Zorn needed to get back to Sequoya because his business partner was coming into town late that night."

"What time was this?"

"About ten."

"What time did Zorn leave?"

"About the same time they did."

"Was he sober?"

"Very. I don't think he drank but one beer the whole night."

"What kind of car does Doyle drive?" I asked.

"A piece of junk."

I laughed again at her blunt, deadpan way of talking. "I figured that," I said. "But it must have a brand name. Ford, Chevy, what?"

"It sure as hell ain't no Ferrari, so you can scratch that one off your list!"

"Think, now," I urged.

"Well, it's bunged up and tan all over except for one front fender that's gray with that primer shit. Say! You ever notice how many of them old dopers got one gray fender on their cars? Maybe it's some kind of lodge deal, like the Masons."

That had me with my head down on the bar trying to get my breath.

"I remember now! It's one of them Oldsmobile Cutlasses. A girlfriend of mine called 'em Cut-asses on account of how much her and her boyfriend canoodled in the backseat of the damn thing."

I managed to get one of my cards out. "Here," I said. "My cell number and office number are both on there. Please call me if you remember anything else."

When I rose to leave, she said, "What's your hurry?"

I turned back to her, still laughing. "I want to get out of here before the guilt sets in for laughing this much during a murder investigation."

"You must be Presbyterian," she said sympathetically. "My folks were Baptists and my daddy always did say Presbyterians are awful tight-assed. I mean, when a Baptist says something like that about you, then you know you're really in a fix!"

Reverend Bobby Joe Twiller was a graduate of Perkins School of Theology in Dallas who frequently wore brown shoes with blue suits and ended each sentence with the rising inflection of an unspoken question mark. The one time I'd visited with him at length was when the sign out in front of his church had been vandalized. I'd found him wandering around his own office with the distracted intensity of some recent arrival who was determined to get the lay of the land before he committed himself. The problem was that he had been in town almost a year when the incident happened.

But there was nothing vague or indefinite about him this morning in the hospital. He was in the pit of misery, and it was written on his face. After I offered my condolences, I gently asked him to tell me what had happened that morning.

"I just went out to get the paper, and there she was. I don't really read the paper anymore, but I bring them in and put them in the trash to keep them from collecting on the lawn."

"I see," I said. "And you didn't hear anything earlier, did you? A car peeling out or anything like that? Any unusual noises?"

He shook his head. "I couldn't sleep at all the first week she was gone, but Dr. Fletcher gave me some pills that knocked me out. I never wake up until the alarm rings at five in the morning."

"What about your son?"

"Tommy? I doubt he heard anything. He was still asleep."

"Okay, what did you do after you found the body? Did you touch it?"

"Of course I did. She was my wife, for heaven's sake. I lifted her head up and held it in my arms, and just sat there for a few minutes. Then I came inside and called nine-one-one. Then I called Miss Boscombe to come over and get Tommy. After that I just caved in. She was the one who called the ambulance to come get me."

"You must mean Mary Beth Boscombe." I knew she was the church organist. She and Dotty Fletcher had been handling the music program at the Methodist Church for years.

He nodded. "Yes. She's coming down this afternoon to get me and take me home."

"That's real fine," I said. The lady in question was thirty-five and still single, though she wasn't at all bad-looking. All her suitors eventually fled in terror because nobody wants to be married to a Wermacht panzer division. "Excessively organized and relentless" is the way a psychologist friend of mine described her.

"You let her take care of you," I said. "She's a very capable young lady. Let some of the other ladies in the church help you too. And take one of your stewards with you when you go to make the arrangements."

"Arrangements?"

I could tell he hadn't thought very far ahead. "The funeral. And you might think about taking Tommy along and letting him have some say in matters. She's the only mother he'll ever have, and this could be a good way for the two of you to start putting your lives back together."

"Putting our lives . . . ?" he began. "You're saying I should be with Tommy, aren't you?"

"That's exactly what I'm saying. You've got to get a grip on yourself because that boy needs you now more than he ever has before."

He closed his eyes and shook his head. "I guess you don't think I'm much of a man, do you, Sheriff? To just collapse like this, I mean."

"I think you're a fine man. If I'd been through what you've been through I'd probably be in worse shape than you are. But right now you've got to suck it up and do your duty."

"You're right," he said, his voice a little more assertive.

"I'm not going to question you at length right now, but I am going to have to search your wife's things, though. I'd prefer to do it with your permission rather than get a warrant."

He nodded. "Of course. You don't need a warrant, Sheriff. Before she left, Amanda had been using the guest bedroom at the end of the hall."

I didn't ask him to enlarge on the implications of that statement. Instead I said, "How about your wife's prescription drug problem? Did you know about that?"

He sighed deeply. "I'm afraid so."

"How bad was it?"

"She was going to at least four doctors that I know of. It was eating us up financially."

"What kind of drugs was she getting?"

"Painkillers, mostly. Some tranquilizers."

"One last question. I hate to pry into your marital affairs, but I have to ask it. Do you have any idea why a respectable preacher's wife like her would just pick up and run off with a man like Emmet Zorn?"

"I think—" he began, then broke off and let his eyes wander around the room, his face hopelessly sad. "I'm convinced that her various doctors were cutting her off, and he could provide her with drugs," he said at last. "I'm sure he could get them. Men like him can always get anything they want, can't they?"

"Sometimes they get more than they bargained for."

CHAPTER FOUR

Just inside the city limits of Sequoya I found myself behind Sheila's little Datsun. Then, out of the blue, I got one of my bright ideas. I sometimes use ordinary citizens to get information of the sort that a lawman has trouble getting. I don't see these folks as actual informants. Instead, I view them more as concerned members of the community who are willing to donate a little time and effort in the interests of law enforcement. I think of them as "helpers," but Sheila, who has been conscripted into such service several times, refers to herself and her fellow victims as my "serfs." I guess it depends on your perspective. But that afternoon it occurred to me that I needed her help as soon as I saw her car.

I blinked my lights several times and honked my horn, all to no avail. With no other options left, I switched on the flashers and gave her a blast on the siren. When she had pulled over and saw it was me, she launched out of her car with fire in her eyes. "Bo, you asshole!" she yelled. "You scared me half to death."

"Now you settle down and quit cussing," I said with a laugh as I exited from my big Ford Crown Victoria. "That's the second time you've used that word today."

"I may take up cussing full-time. What on earth do you want?"

"I need you to help me with something."

"Now? I'm on my way to the library to file my story. My Internet is out at home for some reason."

"You got it on disc?"

"Yeah . . ."

"I'll file it for you. I want you to go over to Mary Beth Boscombe's house and talk to the Twiller boy for me. Find out if he heard or saw anything last night."

"Mary Beth's?" she asked.

"Right. That's where he's staying until his dad gets out of the hospital this afternoon. In fact, Mary Beth is the one who's going to pick Reverend Twiller up and bring him home."

She stared up at my face for a moment, then gave me a sly smile. "Ahhh . . . I get it. But why do you want me to talk to Tommy?"

"I think it would be a whole lot better for a woman to do it than some man wearing a badge. Especially a woman that he knows. You are acquainted with the kid, aren't you?"

"Oh, sure. I taught his Sunday school class last year."

"Then you're perfect," I said. "And a brilliant young journalist like you will certainly know what to ask and how to ask it."

"Flattery will get you everywhere," she said dryly. "Let me get my disc out of the car and jot down the email address. But just promise me you'll do it first thing when you get to the office. Please?"

"Darlin', if A-rab terrorists have firebombed the place, I'll duck in under the flames and get this story filed for you. My word of honor."

When I got to my office in the basement of the courthouse, I went into the bathroom and splashed cold water on my face. It was shaping up to be another hot day, with the air full of dust. The city had imposed water rationing a month earlier, and lawns all over town were suffering.

I'd just finished sending Sheila's story to the *Sentinel* when my secretary, Maylene Chambers, stuck her head in the door. "Some waitress from the Sawmill Club called for you. You been over there to that Sawmill Club, Bo?"

Maylene was a Baptist who viewed my occasional duty-born forays into the area's nightclubs with considerable disdain, as she did the bottle of whiskey I kept in my bottom desk drawer in violation of the idiotic ordinance that forbade the imbibing of "spirituous beverages" on county property. Nevertheless, she'd been with me from the beginning, and barring death or dismemberment, we both expected her to be with me to the end.

"Yes, ma'am, I have," I said. "I went to that den of iniquity this very morning in pursuance of my duties as sheriff of this county. As I have told you before, a lawman can't get much useful information at the church house. Did she leave her name?"

She looked down at the card in her hand. "Patty French. She said she needed to talk to you bad, and that it had something to do with the Amanda Twiller murder."

"Hey! That sounds hopeful. Did you get her number?"

She shook her head. "She was on her way to see Dr. Fletcher, and said that she'd come by about noon, right after her appointment. She also mentioned that Parker Raynes told her to call you. Do you know Parker Raynes?"

I nodded sagely. "She's the bartender at the Sawmill. In fact, I been sparkin' her right heavy here lately, and I'm getting ready to pop the question any day now."

"I know that's a load of bull, but you could do worse. She's not the bartender, though. She owns the place, and it's a money-maker."

"How come you know so much about the lady, Maylene?"

"She goes to my church."

"Say what?" I asked in disbelief.

"Well, it's a legal occupation, Bo. Besides, they don't serve anything but beer, anyhow. Heck, I've been known to drink a little beer myself." She pointed an accusing finger at my desk. "It's the hard stuff like you keep in that drawer there that's the devil's spawn." With that definitive statement, she wheeled around and left my office.

"Imagine that," I muttered to myself. "Baptists drinking beer." Just when you think you have it all figured out, you get buried under your own ignorance.

I leaned back and stared at my phone for at least a couple of minutes. Muldoon and Hotchkiss weren't aware of it, but their boss, Mack Reynolds, was an old and valued friend of mine. Mack was the special agent in charge of the Bureau's Houston office, and I knew he would tell me what I wanted to know. We'd helped each other numerous times in the past, but the question was, did I need to know why the Bureau was keeping tabs on Emmet Zorn badly enough to call on him again? I wanted to find Amanda Twiller's killer, or killers, as the case might be, but I didn't want to let the investigation snowball beyond that. In the end I decided to postpone phoning him.

I was just about to get back on the computer and start working my fall budget when County Commissioner Charlie Morton strolled in like he owned the place and pushed the door shut behind him. A couple of years shy of forty, Charlie was big and beefy and red-faced and full of hustle and bustle and alpha male aggressiveness. He was also one of the main wheelhorses in the local chamber of commerce and a successful real estate broker who'd acquired a number of rental houses and a small motel. I was glad he'd dropped by because I had a little something on my mind I'd been meaning to talk over with him, anyway. I leaned back in my chair and got comfortable in order to savor the moment.

"What brings you here, Charlie?" I asked.

"Money."

"Goody! How much you got for me?"

"Why do you always have to be such a smart-ass, Bo?"

"I reckon it's in my genes." We stared at each other for a few seconds, then I said, "Spit it out, Charlie. What's on your mind?"

"That autopsy you ordered this morning on Amanda Twiller."

"What about it?"

"Do you realize that it costs this county thirteen hundred dollars more to have an autopsy done locally than it does to do it down in Houston?"

"No, I didn't realize that. Does your wife realize that you've been screwing that cute little Mexican waitress at Poncho's Cantina in Nacogdoches for the last couple of months?"

Ever see a man break out in a cold sweat on a hot day? It can be very gratifying.

"Bo . . ." He looked sick.

"Thought you were being real careful, didn't you?"

"How on earth . . ."

"I had one of my deputies keeping you under surveillance."

"That's misuse of public resources."

I nodded. "That contention could certainly be made. So you just bring the matter before the commissioners court at the next meeting if you want to make it. I will counter with the argument that every intelligence service in the world has known for centuries that the sexual habits of an elected official have considerable bearing on his ability to do his job, especially when he's entrusted with public funds like you are. Governments have fallen because of such hanky-panky. Ever hear of John Profumo and the Christine Keeler scandal in England back in the sixties?"

The name Profumo didn't seem to ring any bells with Charlie. I don't think he had much interest in Christine Keeler, either. He just stared straight ahead like he was looking down a long, dark tunnel that had no end.

"Bo, my wife and I are already on thin ice, and if—"

"I know where you're going with this, Charlie," I said. "You're gonna tell me that if you wind up in divorce court Judge Mac-Gregor will recuse himself because he's close to both of you. Then the case will go to Judge Wilson down in Lufkin, a lady who is known to be an ardent feminist and is suspected by some of being a man-hating lesbian, as well. And when it comes time to divide the property, she will, just as she always does in cases of philandering husbands, ram it up your ass so hard it splinters, and then break it off well below the surface."

"Bo, please . . ."

"She raped ole Bobby Wells, may he rest in peace. You remember Bobby, I'm sure. With him it was that cute little blond desk clerk at the Fredonia hotel. I was there in court the day it happened, and Judge Wilson barely left him with the clothes he was wearing. He'd gone in there that morning right prosperous too. You remember what happened to him after that, don't you?

"Bo . . ."

"Bobby never got it back together. The little blond wasn't interested in a poor boy, so she dropped him and took up with some hotshot young salesman who came through. The judge had frozen all his assets six months before the divorce, and he had to max out his credit cards to live on. That ruined his credit rating, which meant he didn't have any latitude to get his business going again. So about a year later he took that old Winchester pump duck gun of his, stuck the muzzle in his mouth, and—"

He raised his head and looked at me like he'd never seen me before. "Bo, surely you wouldn't . . ."

I just treated him to a happy smile and we sat and said nothing while he mopped his face with his handkerchief. Finally he gave me a tiny nod. "What do I have to do?"

"I need an advocate on the commissioners court. That's all. I haven't had one since Billy Cochran died. I've never asked for anything I didn't really need to do my job, and I'm damned tired of getting turned down. For one thing, you people are way behind on giving my deputies a raise. And while you're at it, Maylene could use a little more money too. This county never has paid her what she's worth. I think the JPs could stand a boost as well."

"Is that all?"

I shook my head. "No. There'll be more in the future. When I said I needed an advocate I was thinking in terms of a nice long partnership. Now get on out of here. I've got work to do."

He rose to his feet and nodded. "Okay, Bo. I'll give it my best."

"I know you will, Charlie, because I'll be at every one of the meetings to make sure you do. And I'll never ask you to do anything illegal. Rest easy on that score."

He nodded and stopped at the door and turned back. Nothing unusual about that. Everybody stops at my door and turns back. It's like some kind of lodge ritual and I'm the only nonmember in town. "Something else, Charlie?" I asked.

"You know, I never expected anything like this to happen to me," he said, his voice tinged with wonder. "I just thought—"

"That you'd get a little nooky on the side, and nobody would be the wiser. It probably would have worked if you hadn't been in public office. Look at it as penance, Charlie. And if you're smart, you'll break it off with that waitress and patch things up with your wife. She's a good woman."

He nodded his head sadly, then he left and I leaned back and put my feet up on my desk. I laughed and wondered how agents Muldoon and Hotchkiss would have reacted to that little exchange. They probably thought political hardball was confined to the big cities.

CHAPTER FIVE

For lunch I had a glass of milk and a couple of slices of rat cheese and a few saltine crackers out of the break room pantry on the second floor. A little after noon, Maylene knocked on the door and ushered Patty French into my office. She was a pretty girl in her late twenties with blue eyes, blond hair, and a very red nose. I stood and got her seated.

"Summer cold?" I asked.

"You better believe it," she said with a nod.

"Would you like some coffee or something? We've got hot water, and my secretary has some tea bags."

"Gosh, no. Hot stuff just makes your nose run worse. Don't you know that?"

It was one of those bumbling moments men often have when they've demonstrated some deep and profound ignorance in front of a female. "My mistake," I said. "Could I offer you anything else?"

She shook her head. "No, I just want to tell you what I have to say and go home and get in bed."

"Then I'm going to record this, and if we need to have you sign a statement, we can cobble it up from what's on the tape and I'll have a deputy bring it by your house later. That way you won't have to wait around."

"Sure."

I quickly set up the recorder and read the day and time and our names onto the tape. "Go ahead," I said.

"Well, when I called in sick today Parker told me about you coming by. See, me and a couple of the other girls got to talking and clowning around and having fun after we closed last night, and I didn't leave until a little after two."

"When you say leave, you mean you didn't start home until then?"

"That's right."

"Where do you live?"

"Here in Sequoya. My address is three-oh-three State Street over on the north side of town."

"You left by yourself or did someone go with you?"

"Just me."

"And you drove straight home?"

"Yes," she said and nodded and blew her nose on what seemed to be her last, disintegrating tissue. I got up and rooted around in my desk drawer until I found a box of Kleenex and set them in front of her. "Thank you," she said and scrabbled a few out of the box.

"Go ahead with your story," I said.

"Anyway, when I came by the Pak-a-Sak the light was on inside. Doyle's car was parked out front and so was Emmet Zorn's."

"Doyle who, ma'am? You need to be specific about that for the record."

"Doyle Raynes. And that preacher's wife was standing beside it looking for something in her purse."

"You mean Amanda Twiller?"

"Yes, she's the one. I forgot her name for a second there."

"Are you sure it was her?"

She nodded. "Oh yes. She's been in and out of the Sawmill for a week or so, and Emmet Zorn told everybody who she was."

"Go on."

"Well, I stopped at the red light there by the store and just happened to see that Doyle and Emmet Zorn were coming out. Doyle had a bottle in his hand."

"And?"

"Zorn locked the door to the store and took off in his Lexus. As I passed by, Doyle and Mrs. Twiller were getting in his car."

"And this was what time?"

"Close to two-thirty."

"Did they go in different directions, or did they follow Zorn?"

"He went on up Main toward the north side of town, and they left going west."

"Anything else?"

She shook her head. "I got home about two-forty and crawled right in bed. Then I woke up about four hours later with this cold."

"Are you certain of the identity of these three people? And I mean absolutely certain?"

"There's not a doubt in my mind, Sheriff. I know all three of them well."

Just then the door opened and Maylene stuck her head in and said, "Sheila is out here, and she says she needs to see you now. Claims it can't wait."

I excused myself and went through the outer office and steered Sheila out into the hallway. "You're not going to believe this, Bo," she said excitedly.

"Lay it on me."

"Tommy Twiller saw the car. Or at least I think it's the car. The kid had to get up to go to the bathroom. He said he knew it was right before sunup because it was beginning to get light outside. He heard some kind of commotion, and looked out the window and saw an old car right in front of the house. And then it took off."

"Did he see his mother's body?"

"Bo, this is the awful part. He said he thought he saw someone lying on the grass, but he just went back to bed and went to sleep. I think he saw her and knew who it was and just couldn't deal with it."

I grimaced. I've always held the opinion that the term "in denial" is psychobabble that doesn't mean much, but I was beginning to have a whole new respect for the concept.

"Did he give you any description of the car?" I asked.

"Only that it was old-looking, and that one front fender was a different color from the rest of the body."

CHAPTER SIX

Thirty minutes later I had an arrest warrant for Doyle Raynes along with a search warrant for his home and car. Before I went upstairs to see Judge MacGregor, I'd told Maylene to have the dispatcher call Toby and tell him to come to the office. I also had her call two experienced deputies in from patrol—Billy Don Smith and Otis Tremmel—both steady men with several years on the force. Toby arrived first.

"What about my autopsy report?" I asked him.

"Linda said they're going to fax it over as soon as it's official, but he put the time of death at sometime between three and six this morning."

"Well, hell," I said in exasperation. "I could have told him that. She was seen alive at two-thirty and found dead at about six. How about the bullets?"

"Already filed in the evidence locker."

"Good. We'll get those two Bureau boys on that tomorrow. What we've got on our plate right now is more important."

Soon Smith and Tremmel arrived, and I got everybody clustered around my desk. "Toby and I are going to take the front," I said. "I want you two guys to take the unmarked car and make sure the kid is at home. He might have flown the coop or just be out or something, and there's no point in mounting an assault on an empty house. If his car is there, then there's every reason to think he will be too."

"What kind of car is it?" Billy Don asked.

"An Olds Cutlass, maybe ten or fifteen years old. Tan with a gray front fender. If it's there, go ahead and get your flak jackets on and park down the street a few yards from his drive where he can't spot you. When you see us pull up behind you, drive around to the rear and get up behind that garage. Now does anybody know the layout of this place?"

"I do," Tremmel said. "It has a long flight of stairs on the side that go up to the apartment. There's no way to get to the landing without passing the windows."

That description rang a bell with me. "Does this happen to be Matt Jones's old place, by any chance?" I asked.

"Yeah," Smith said. "I think it is."

"Then nobody, and I mean *nobody*, is going up those damn stairs. About twenty years ago the DPS narcotics people were pulling a bust on that very same apartment, and a young officer got a belly full of squirrel shot on that stairway. The boy wound up with a colostomy bag, and he still isn't healthy. So we'll either use the bullhorn or I'll call him on the phone. If that doesn't work, we'll try tear gas. Hell, I'll burn him out before I'll let one of my people go up that stairway. Now is that clear to everybody?"

They nodded. I motioned to Smith and Tremmel. "You two get rolling."

Ten minutes later Billy Don Smith called on his cell phone with the information that Raynes's car was in the drive right in front of the apartment. Maylene checked the phone book and found a number listed under the kid's name at the right address. I jotted it down, and then had Toby get a tear gas gun and three canisters out of the armory. We both grabbed Remington 870 riot guns and loaded them with number-four buckshot. Then we were on our way without a hitch. Or so I thought until I got out in the hall and saw Sheila.

"Bo," she said.

"Sheila, don't ask."

"That's not fair, Bo. After all, I'm the one who talked to Tommy."

I sighed deeply. She was right about that. And she had always given me help in the past when I'd asked for it and asked little in return. Which brought to mind that verse in the Bible about not binding the mouths of the oxen that tread the grain. "Will you do exactly what I tell you to do?" I asked.

"Of course."

I made a snap decision that the commissioners wouldn't have approved of. Not that I cared. "Come on, then."

The garage apartment was behind a frame bungalow in a part of town that had been developed in the 1920s. Originally a solidly middle class neighborhood, now it was a little seedy and weather-worn and occupied mostly by young, low-end blue-collar families and marginal retirees.

We'd taken the department's big black Chevy Suburban. When Smith and Tremmel saw us turn onto the street they drove around the block toward the rear. Toby and I got out of the truck and donned our flak gear. I parked Sheila across the street with an admonition to stay put until I called her. A couple of minutes later my cell phone buzzed. It was Billy Don Smith telling me they were coming up the lane behind the garage. Toby and I climbed back into the Suburban and wheeled into the driveway. He stopped well back from the garage and cut the engine, and we piled out and got behind our vehicle.

The air was fiercely hot around us, and the world seemed silent as the afternoon sun beat down relentlessly. I felt a fine dew of sweat on my forehead, and it wasn't just from the heat. I'd seen situations like this go bad and end up with people dead because of nothing more than a misspoken word.

I took out the card on which I'd scribbled the boy's phone number. I punched the number into my cell phone, and he answered on the third ring. "Doyle Raynes?" I asked.

"Yeah?" he answered.

"This is Sheriff Bo Handel, and I need you to come downstairs and talk to me."

"What for?"

"I've got a warrant here for your arrest."

"I didn't kill anybody," he said.

I rolled my eyes and silently called on the good Lord for help. It was clear to me that this boy was never going to be admitted to MIT. But it was also clear that he was just dumb enough with just enough fear in his voice that he might decide to fight it out if he was armed. Time for diplomacy.

"We didn't say you did, son," I said, my voice as pleasant as I could make it. "Besides, this whole thing is a long way from the courtroom. What we need to do is just talk things over and see if we can't take care of business."

For several seconds he said nothing, and I could tell he was weighing the options he didn't have. He appeared at the window for a moment, the phone at his ear, then vanished once again back inside.

"You still there?" I asked.

"Yeah, sure."

"Then don't do anything silly. We're armed to the teeth down here, and you haven't got a chance if you get cute. You come on down and we'll treat you decent. No rough stuff. I give you my word."

"But I didn't do anything."

"It's just a warrant, Doyle. That's all. You'll get a free lawyer if you need one and plenty of time to prove you're innocent if you are. And son, the new jail is air conditioned and the food's pretty good. They tell me it beats the hospital. I know for a fact that it beats being in the graveyard."

There was another long pause during which I barely breathed. "What do you want me to do?" he asked at last.

"Just come out on the landing with your hands on the top of your head. Then walk slowly down the stairs. Don't make any quick moves."

"Okay, just let me get my shoes on."

I didn't like that business about giving him time to get his shoes, but I didn't have any choice in the matter. I turned to Toby. "If he comes out shooting, or even with a gun in his hand, aim low and get his legs. If that doesn't take the fight out of him, cash his check."

"Okay, boss."

But such precautions proved unnecessary. Doyle Raynes appeared on the landing, skinny and shirtless, his hands above his head, and made his way slowly down the rickety stairs. Up close he didn't look like much—watery brown eyes and a wisp of a goatee and stringy hair that had been cut in a pageboy. As soon as he was cuffed I read him his Miranda warning and then served the search warrants.

"You're going to search my car and my apartment too?" he asked.

"That's right."

"Can I be here when you do the apartment? I don't like people going through my stuff."

"No," I said. "But we'll be careful and not damage anything."

I turned and saw Sheila standing at the end of the driveway and motioned her to come on back. She pulled a digital camera out of her purse and started snapping away. I was just about to say something to her when Toby called me over to Raynes's car.

"Look inside," he said. "And take a sniff too."

I peeked into the interior of the Cutlass, then examined the outside once again. The car's body was dusty and covered in road film, but the interior had been vacuumed and washed and was as neat as a pin. Or at least it was as neat as an old junker belonging to a dopehead could ever be.

"What do you smell?" Toby asked.

"Lysol," I said.

"Right. Somebody went to some real trouble to clean up the interior of this thing."

I stood back and looked at the car for a minute, thinking. Then I said, "Toby, get in there and pull that backseat out of its socket and see what you find behind it."

A few seconds later the seat had been wrestled a few inches forward and Toby was shining his penlight into the crevice behind it. Then he stuck his hand in and said, "Blood. And some of it's still tacky, even in this heat. How did you know?"

"The Twiller kid said he heard a commotion, so that means there must have been at least two of them. It just made sense to me they would have hauled the body in the backseat. Call the Department of Public Safety. We're going to need a whole forensics team on this. We'll hold up on the search until they get here. I want them to help with the apartment too."

I turned to Raynes. "Are you going to talk this afternoon, or are you going to lawyer up on me?" I asked.

"I think I better get one, Sheriff. Don't you?"

"I can't answer that question for you, but you need to realize it may be tomorrow before the judge can appoint somebody. I'm guessing you want a court-provided attorney. Do you have any money for one on your own?"

"No, I'm pretty broke."

"I thought so." I pecked my knuckles on the primer-painted fender of the old car and shook my head. "You know, son, this car probably wouldn't bring fifteen hundred dollars on a good day. If you'd taken it out in the country and torched it you might have skated on this thing."

"I couldn't do that, Sheriff. It's my *baby*. I'm restoring it."

A friend of mine says the most important thing about a person is not how much money he has, or what he owns, or how he looks, or even what he's accomplished, but what he wants out of life and hasn't gotten yet. I looked at Doyle Raynes's old heap with its sagging springs and wheezy engine and torn upholstery, and I saw him getting that front fender in a wrecking yard somewhere. I saw him lovingly bolting it in place and dreaming of the day his baby would sport a fancy new paint job. When I saw all that, I felt a stab of sick pity deep in my heart and shook my head sadly.

"Take him on to the jailhouse, Billy Don," I said, turning away. "He's got a killing to answer for."

CHAPTER SEVEN

Toby and Sheila and I went back to the courthouse while Billy Don hauled Doyle Raynes out to the jail for booking. Otis Tremmel had more forensics training than anybody else on the force, myself included. I had him stay on the scene to meet the DPS team.

Caddo County had built a new jail the year before on the north side of town, but we hadn't finished moving our whole operation into our new offices. When Amanda Twiller was murdered, the sheriff's department itself was still housed in the basement of the courthouse, just as it had been for decades. Until the previous May, the jail had also been in the basement, but it had long ago become inadequate.

There had been an advantage to having the jail close to the courthouse because the sheriff is responsible for delivering prisoners to the court for arraignments and trials. Since there was no suitable place downtown to build a new "detention facility," as they are now called, the county located it on the edge of town and bought a van to transport prisoners. Before the end of the year, my office was scheduled to be moved to the new building, but even this was not the best of all possible arrangements. I was expected to provide security for the court. In view of the number of court-house shootings in the last few years, this was not an unreason-able requirement. The problem was that I didn't have enough deputies to station two at the courthouse during office hours and still have the manpower I needed to do everything else I was ex-pected to do.

The air was hot and oppressive when we got out of the Subur-ban, and the whole square looked like it needed a bath. Most of the cars parked around the square held a fine layer of dust, and the windows of the stores across the street were greasy and dull.

"I'm going to the library to write and file my story about the arrest," Sheila said. "Do you still want me to come by tonight, or have I worn out my welcome?"

"Yeah, but I may be a little late. Still got your key?"

"Sure."

"Good. If I'm not there, you just go on in and make yourself at home. Fix yourself a sandwich or something, and have a drink."

I washed my hands and face and went upstairs and got more cheese and crackers and a Coke. Somewhere along the way I was going to need to get something more substantial to eat, but that could wait. I'd had plenty of practice missing meals in almost thirty years on this job. As I came through the outer office I mo-tioned Toby into my inner sanctum and shut the door. I took a long pull of my Coke and kicked my boots off my tired feet and flopped down in my big desk chair. Sighing, I looked up long-ingly at my Browning Superposed hanging in the gun rack and remembered that I'd rolled out of bed that morning planning to go out to the gun club for a couple rounds of sporting clays this afternoon.

"What now?" Toby asked.

"Call Billy Don and tell him that when he gets done at the jail I want the two of you to go get Emmet Zorn and bring him down here. I want to know what he was doing with that Raynes kid last night."

"Okay," he said with a grin. "That sounds like fun."

Mercifully, after Toby left I managed to get in some time on the computer working on my budget and other paperwork. I was interrupted when he knocked on the door to announce that he and Billy Don had their quarry outside.

Zorn came through the door and I motioned for him to take a seat across from my desk. I noticed that he had a new toothpick installed in his mouth, this one red. He'd also changed his tie. The current one was dark gray with a clasp of faux gold with a big piece of green plastic that was meant to pass for jade but didn't. He was also a bit more subdued than he had been that morning. A sheriff's office can have that effect on a man.

"Then I guess you want me to make that statement we talked about earlier," he said.

I shook my head. "Not right now. At the moment I need a couple of answers."

"What?"

"A little while ago we arrested a boy named Doyle Raynes for Amanda Twiller's murder."

That seemed to surprise him. "That's a shame," he said. "I always thought Doyle was a good kid. Do you really think he did it?"

"At this point it sure looks like it. And you and I have a problem."

"Yeah? What?"

"I have a reliable witness who saw you and Doyle with Mrs. Twiller at the Pak-a-Sak about two-thirty last night."

"Maybe I shouldn't say anything about that without a lawyer."

"That's certainly your right, but if you were to tell me what the three of you did after you left the store we might be able to clear this up without involving any attorneys."

He thought it over for a few seconds. "Okay. I pulled something stupid. I may have committed a liquor violation. It was after legal hours, and Doyle wanted to buy a bottle of whisky. So I went in the store and got it for him, but I wouldn't let him pay me. I just gave it to him. Is that a violation?"

"I don't know, and I don't care," I said. "It would have been if you sold it, but it really makes no difference since I'm more interested in the Twiller murder than hanging some chickenshit misdemeanor on you. How did you get to the store? I thought you told me earlier you left the Sawmill with some other people."

"I did," he said. "They dropped me off at home. My car was there."

"I don't guess you'd mind giving me their names, then?"

"It was a buddy of mine named Wayne Pierce and his girlfriend. He lives in Henderson."

"The girlfriend's name?"

"Chelsea something or other. I don't remember. Wayne runs a landscaping company up there. You can find him without any trouble."

"Okay," I said. "We've got you at home by eleven or so. How did you come to be back at the Pak-a-Sak at two-thirty?"

"Doyle called about two and wanted a bottle. He said he'd come by and pick me up. Instead I told him I'd meet him at the store."

"So you claim you got out of bed or whatever and came down here to break the law in the early hours of the morning to accommodate a screwup like Doyle Raynes? I'm not sure that makes much sense to me."

"Like I told you, I thought he was a good kid. He helps me out around the store some, and I kinda took an interest in him. Besides, I was still up, anyway."

"There's one little problem with that. Doyle's aunt told me that he borrowed twenty bucks from her right before he left at ten. He said he wanted it to buy some whisky with, but you claim he didn't call you until two. What were they doing all that time?"

"Man, I don't have any idea. Maybe over to somebody's house or something. I wasn't with them."

"Okay, do you know where they went when they left?"

"Beats me," he said. "Some place to fuck, probably."

I felt my face harden. I don't like the word, and I certainly didn't like to hear it used in reference to a woman who had just been murdered. "Oh? What makes you say that?"

"Doyle had some pills, and she'd do anybody for a few pills. She'd gotten that bad."

I'd had enough of him for the moment. "You can go," I said.

"I need somebody to take me home."

"In a minute. Just wait in the outer office."

Toby pushed the door shut behind him. "Now what do you make of that?" he asked.

"I don't know," I said. "What's your take on him?"

He shook his head. "I haven't got one yet. What do you want to do with the man?"

I rose and put my hat on my head. "Take him on home. We've got nothing to hold him on. And send somebody up to Henderson in the morning and ask this Wayne Pierce guy about Zorn's story. You might run Pierce through the DPS computer too. And have somebody check him out with the cops up there in Rusk County."

"Tonight?" Toby asked. "We're shorthanded this evening."

"Just leave a note on Maylene's desk and tell her to have somebody do it in the morning."

"Anything else?"

I shook my head. "Now I got to go eat or drop."

CHAPTER EIGHT

My father died of a heart attack in the middle of my senior year in college, leaving me with an invalid mother suffering from multiple sclerosis to support. I came back home and took over the family timber business and then got married soon afterward. Although commerce wasn't my first choice as an occupation, I had a knack for it, and at one time I owned two sawmills and a lumberyard. A little more than a decade later, Caddo County's longtime sheriff, John Nightwalker, a giant man of one quarter Cherokee blood, came down with the cancer that killed him a couple of years later. He resigned a few weeks after he got the diagnosis, and for reasons known only to him he talked the commissioners court into appointing me to fill out the two remaining years of his unexpired term. I liked the job and ran for the office in the next election. I've been running ever since, the last two times without an opponent.

Besides patience, my years as sheriff have taught me just how comforting the old rituals and patterns of small-town life really are, and I know that one reason I've thrived in law enforcement was that it lets me feel more involved with my people than I did peddling two-by-fours and plywood slabs across a sales counter. I also liked walking that fine line between force and diplomacy that a country sheriff has to walk, and I've often found myself in the amusing position of having to arrest some of my strongest supporters and do it in such a way that I could still expect to get their votes when the next election rolled around.

I live in the house where I was raised, a Queen Anne Victorian on South Main Street five blocks down from the courthouse that was built by my great-grandfather in the closing years of the Gilded Age. It's two stories, with four bedrooms upstairs and five rooms plus a huge kitchen downstairs, along with a three-bay carriage house in the rear that I use as a garage.

Sheila's Datsun was parked out front. I wheeled into the carriage house, walked up the flagstone pathway I'd laid down years before, crossed the screened-in porch and unlocked the kitchen door. As soon as I stepped inside I heard piano music coming hesitantly from the front room. I tossed my hat on a peg and took the time to wash my hands and face in the kitchen sink.

She'd left a bottle of V.O. on the cabinet. I threw a few ice cubes into a glass and poured myself about three ounces of whiskey. Then I pulled off my boots and socks, relishing the cool feel of the kitchen tiles beneath my tired, hot feet. I quickly drank about half my drink, refilled the glass, and then made my way up the hall toward the living room to find her sitting at my Baldwin baby grand pecking out "Chopsticks." She turned and smiled at me and said, "I'm not much good, am I?"

"I'm not either anymore."

"You sound a whole lot better than I do." She looked around. "This is such a beautiful room. I remember Grandma always called it the parlor."

I laughed, but it was a laugh that sounded sad and without conviction in my own ears. "Now it's Beauregard Handel's Museum of Faded Dreams. I think you know something about faded dreams too, don't you?"

She gave me a wry smile and nodded. "I grew up knowing you

were majoring in music before you had to quit and come home to take care of Grandma," she said. "I've always wondered if you've regretted it."

"Sometimes I do. But like Dad always said, what might have been won't pay the rent or put a dime's worth of groceries on the table. I did what I had to do."

She smiled at me again. "Play something for me, Bo."

"You know I only like to play when I've had enough to drink that I don't care how bad I sound."

"Come on . . . do it for me."

"Move over then," I said and sat down beside her on the piano bench. I put my drink on a coaster and flexed my hands a few seconds to limber them up, then began to play.

"I know that one," Sheila said after a couple of minutes. "It's 'Clair de Lune.'"

"Right you are," I said. "The Ferrante and Teicher arrangement. Try this."

"I haven't got a clue," she said after a few bars. "But it's pretty."

"'The Waltz You Saved for Me.' That was your grandmother's mother's favorite song." I played on for a while, then closed the lid on the keyboard and took her hand. "Let's go back to the kitchen. I've got to have something to eat, and I want to fill you in on the pieces you're missing from this odyssey. Are you hungry?"

"No, I went home after I got my story off to the paper and had supper with Mom and Mindy."

"How is Mindy?" I asked.

"Fine. She's been wanting to know if you're going to take us riding again once the weather cools off."

"Of course I am. I've got my eye on a real gentle little Welsh gelding I'm going to buy for her and board out at my place. I'm going to get her a nice saddle to go with it too."

"Bo, no . . ."

"Yes."

"I can't let you do that," she said.

"I don't see any way you can stop me. Now will you quit all this senseless commotion and let me get something to eat?"

A little later we were sitting at the big round oak table in my kitchen. As I made my way through a corned beef sandwich and sipped on my second drink, I brought her up to date on the case, including what I'd learned from Muldoon and Hotchkiss that morning.

"Did you talk to Zorn?" she asked.

"Yeah. He won't be bothering you anymore."

"That's not what I meant. Did you learn anything that might tie him to the killing?"

"Not really."

"Maybe her demands had become intolerably irritating," she said.

I gave her a sage nod. "Yes, I'll admit that many a woman has been killed for getting on some old boy's last nerve. But when that happens, it's almost always a passion murder, and I'm convinced there was no passion involved in this killing."

"What makes you say that?"

"For one thing, she was shot in the back. Passion murders usually happen in the heat of an argument, and the victim oftentimes gets it right in the face. And secondly, if it had been a passion killing, I think the perpetrator would have tried to hide the body instead of dumping it in her front yard. Somebody was trying to send a message with that move."

"Well, you don't really have to have a motive to prove guilt. Even I know that much about the law."

"That's true," I admitted.

"So kudos to Uncle Bo. You solved this one in record time."

"I ain't solved nothing yet, girl. I'm just getting started."

"But you've got Doyle Raynes locked up and charged with the crime."

"Oh, I'm sure he knows who did it because there's no doubt the body was hauled in his car. He may have even been present, but as far as pulling the trigger goes?" I shook my head. "That clown no more killed that poor woman than you did."

CHAPTER NINE

O n the way to the office the next morning, I dropped in on Dotty Fletcher. Dotty had been the town's leading doctor for almost sixty years. Now in her early eighties and slowing down a bit, she still scurried around with the energy of a gerbil. Her clinic was in back of her father's hundred-plus-year-old drugstore on the square right across from the courthouse. The place looked its age with an uneven, hilly floor, an ancient soda fountain of marble and mahogany, and the better part of a century's worth of patent medicine advertisements decorating its walls. The clinic in the rear was another matter—shiny and modern, a narrow hall lined on both sides with examining rooms.

It took me a few minutes to get to see her. The receptionist led me back to her personal office, a cozy room with an old-fashioned examining table and knotty pine paneling like my own sanctuary in the courthouse. It wasn't long before she hurried in, blood pressure cuff in hand, and sat down with hardly a word and began rolling up my sleeve.

"My blood pressure is fine," I said.

"It was elevated a couple of years ago."

"Yes, but I lost twenty pounds like you told me to, and it settled down just where it should be. You said so yourself."

"Hush. I'm going to check it anyway. I suppose you're here to pick my brain about Amanda Twiller."

"What makes you think that?"

Instead of answering, she pumped up the blood pressure cuff until my arm felt like it was going to explode. Eventually she began to bleed the air off.

"Well?" I asked.

"It's good. How's your heart?"

"It must be working okay or I wouldn't be here."

"I mean have you had any irregular heartbeats or anything like that? Any sudden, unexplained nausea?"

"Nope."

"How about dizzy spells?"

"Not since the last time I drank a half gallon of Thunderbird."

She laughed. "You're a scoundrel, Bo Handel. I don't know why I keep voting for you."

"It's because I do a good job, which is what I'm trying to do this morning, but you keep bringing up my blood pressure."

She looked down my throat and in my ears and poked and prodded some more until she finally gave up on finding any major disasters and admitted defeat. "Okay, you seem healthy enough," she said. "What do you need to know?"

"Anything you can tell me that won't violate doctor-patient confidentiality. Mostly I just want to get your take on her as a woman. What motivated her. Why did she throw over a decent husband and do what she did? Please remember that we're off the record here. Also remember that I'm in her corner and not some reporter trying to dig up embarrassing dirt about her. If I can catch her killer I'll be the last person who can ever do her a service, and I'd sure like to do it."

"I think I can answer your questions without violating anything. In the first place, she'd had two vertebrae fused six years ago in Dallas on account of a ruptured disc. I can tell you that because she told everybody who would listen about the surgery. Secondly, many people who have successful back surgeries still suffer severe back pain for years. Nobody really knows why, but it's a medical fact. Thirdly, every doctor is in a difficult position with chronic pain sufferers. You want your patients to get the relief they need, yet at the same time you don't want to contribute to their becoming addicts, or abet their behavior if they already have. And lastly, I was no longer treating Amanda when she died."

"So she was just a natural-born addict?"

"I think the drugs were just a symptom, Bo. I think what was bothering her was something a lot deeper."

"What?"

"She reminded me of a book called *Madame Bovary* I read back in college for some literature course or other. It was about a French woman who was married to a small-town doctor. Things went along fine until her husband cured a minor nobleman of some ailment. Out of gratitude, this nobleman invited them to dinner and a ball at his chateau. It was really a pretty dull affair, but to her eyes it was the height of glamour. The experience made her unsatisfied with her life as it was. She began to daydream about an endless round of parties and soirees. She had affairs. She ran up huge bills with their creditors until she brought financial disaster down on herself. Then she committed suicide by taking arsenic. She wanted life to be something that it couldn't be, and that was Amanda. She wanted excitement, romance, brilliant friends, adventure in faraway places, exotic tropical nights. What she got was the First United Methodist Church of Sequoya, Texas."

"And the Reverend Bobby Joe Twiller," I said. "Let's not forget him. I guess living with that poor guy could make even a drugstore cowboy like Emmet Zorn seem dashing."

She laughed and reached over and whacked me on the arm. "Get out of here, you rascal. I've got patients to see."

As usual when I arrived at the office I found too many things that demanded my attention and too little time to deal with them in. The sheet said that the department had answered three domestic disturbance calls during the night, none resulting in an arrest. There had also been two shootings in the county the evening before, one an accident and the other a semi-accident. In the first one, a man had simply blown off two of his toes with his own shotgun.

"He'd just bought himself a new bird gun," Maylene said. "He was sitting there on the sofa with his feet propped up on the coffee table admiring it when he decided to check the trigger pull by aiming at his foot. He thought it was unloaded."

What complicated the matter was that the man had been taken to the hospital in Nacogdoches County, while the incident itself had occurred in Caddo County. More paperwork. "Write it up and send it in to the Darwin Awards," I told her.

The semi-accident was one of those East Texas things. A woman had been aiming for her husband, but missed and put a .22 bullet through her daddy's arm. It all started when the family sat down for supper. As soon as the blessing had been pronounced, her husband made a disparaging remark about the gravy, and gunfire erupted soon afterward.

"The husband doesn't want to press charges," Maylene said, "and neither does the father."

"Good. Call the jail and have them turn her loose right now. Her kids need her. And maybe her aim will improve next time."

"Bo!"

"That man is an ill-tempered troll, Maylene. I've suspected him of abusing that woman for a couple of years. This ought to put the fear of God into him."

"Maybe so. But I doubt it. Those guys never learn."

I looked at her thoughtfully for a few moments over the tops of my reading glasses. "You know, here lately I've been wondering if anybody ever really learns anything. It seems to me that we all make the same mistakes over and over again."

"Well, I learned the Texas two-step," she said pertly. "It took me might near a month, but I learned it."

I was rendered speechless. I know that we live in a time of rapid change, and I've been able to accommodate myself to most of it. Women's lib was hardly a blip on my radar screen, and I can live with the idea that all the gays are coming out of the closet. But the notion of a Baptist woman Maylene's age dancing was too much to absorb. I just pretended I never heard her and went on about my business.

The bullets from Amanda Twiller's body had been delivered to the Feds, and the search of Raynes's apartment had turned up a half ounce of marijuana and, as Zorn had claimed, some unscripted Valium and about a dozen Tylenol Number Four capsules, also unscripted. But no gun. Or anything else of importance. The blood type from the car matched Amanda Twiller's, but DNA analysis would have to wait.

My deputies had canvassed the Twillers' neighborhood, and no one had seen or heard anything that morning. The fingerprints on the beer can we found at the scene didn't match Doyle Raynes or anybody else on record. The tentative conclusion was that the can had nothing to do with the crime, and had probably been thrown out by some unrelated late-night revelers.

The pathologist had faxed the autopsy report over, but it didn't tell me much that I didn't know except that the vaginal swab was negative for both semen and spermicide. It was impossible to determine if a mature woman her age had recently indulged in intercourse. The blood tests had revealed evidence of both opiates and cocaine in her system. The cocaine surprised me a little. I'd pegged the lady strictly as a downer fan.

"Where's Linda?" I asked Maylene's retreating back.

"Domestic disturbance call, Bo. She's on her way back to the office."

"I want to talk to her when she gets here."

I was about fifteen minutes into my computer work when my other female deputy, Carla Wallace, came by and stuck her head around the door. Carla was ex-army, a couple of years past forty, tall, slim, and shapely with short, dark hair and a no-nonsense attitude. Because she had never been married and only rarely dated, most of the male deputies assumed she was a lesbian. I knew better, but since people are generally happier with illusions they've cobbled together on their own than they are with the truth, I didn't bother to straighten them out.

"Come on in," I said. "Sit down and take the load off your feet."

"My feet are fine," she said with a smile. "And I've got desk duty at the jail today so I need to get on back there."

"Then what's up? And why aren't you there?"

"Billy Don is filling in for me so I could come to see you. In return, I'm saving him a trip up to Henderson."

"I don't get it."

"You wanted to know about Wayne Pierce, and I'm your girl. His sister is married to my baby brother. I know him well. So what do you need to know about ole Wayne?"

I quickly told her about Zorn leaving the Sawmill Club and later meeting Doyle Raynes and Amanda Twiller. "I guess I want to know if you think he'd lie to alibi somebody out on a deal like this."

"Absolutely not."

"What makes you say that?"

"He'd have too much to lose. Wayne has his degree in landscape architecture from Cornell and a growing business. He's straight-up, honest, and has never given his family any trouble. That is, if you take into account that he's thirty-five years old and still a child about his social life."

"And Mom and Dad want him to settle down and produce grandchildren," I said.

"Precisely."

"How about his girlfriend?"

"What's her name? He has a pretty fast turnover."

"Chelsea something or other."

"That would be Chelsea Wicks. Hmm . . . maybe he's getting serious. He's been with her since last spring. She's a portrait photographer, and a damn good one. Got a studio in Henderson."

"Okay, I'll take your word for it on Wayne and company. Zorn claims they left the Sawmill together the night Amanda Twiller was killed. He said they dropped him off at his house. Would you call and check that out for me?"

"Sure."

"I can't help but wonder why a guy like him is hanging around with Zorn."

"Wayne likes the clubs, likes people, and from what I hear Zorn is pretty good company. Supposed to be a heck of a piano player. Gets invited to a lot of parties."

"Well, well," I said. "I've never seen that side of him."

"Just face it, Bo. Not everybody is as dull and antisocial as you and I are."

I laughed, then said, "Speaking of sociable, you need to come over to the house for supper one night this week."

"Call me and say when," she said and blew me a kiss as she slipped through the doorway.

Two minutes later the door opened again and Linda Willis stepped into my office. Linda was about thirty and recently divorced for the second time. A little plump, a little cheeky, and more than a little aggressive, she had a pretty face, a pug nose, and mop of short hair that seemed to change color every time the wind shifted direction. What I appreciated most about her was that she was tough-minded and smart and willing to charge hell with a bucket of water.

"What's up, boss?" she asked.

"We have verbal permission from Reverend Twiller to search his wife's room. I want you to do it, and I want you to be thorough."

"What am I looking for?"

"I don't know. Anything to tie her to anybody who might be a suspect. Whatever else that looks interesting."

"That's pretty vague, Bo."

"I know it is, but you're a smart girl, and this is a good chance to exercise your creativity. We know she's been running around with Emmet Zorn and whooping it up with prescription pain-killers. Use your judgment, but tag and bag and date anything you take out of the house."

"Who do you want me to take with me? Otis is outside."

I shook my head. "Nobody. I'm not comfortable with any of my male deputies rooting through this poor woman's underwear."

"You're positively Victorian, Bo."

I laughed. "Maybe so, but I am the boss."

"You be da boss man, all right," she agreed.

"Report directly back to me on this. Don't pass go, don't collect two hundred dollars, and don't—"

"Tell anybody about anything I might find, right?"

"You got it. Now get rolling."

CHAPTER TEN

I finished my paperwork on Raynes and went upstairs to have a talk with District Attorney Tom Waller. Tom was in his first term and getting his feet on the ground as chief prosecutor. He'd had three years of prior experience as assistant DA, and before that two years in private practice with a big Houston firm. But like many of us, he'd hearkened when his hometown sang its siren song, and he was settled in, probably for the rest of his life, in the county where he'd been born and bred. From my standpoint he was easy to work with because he remembered me as sheriff from back when he'd been a kid, which gave me a definite advantage.

"So this is it on the Twiller murder?" he asked.

"Not by a long shot."

"Why not?" he asked in surprise.

"That boy had no reason to kill her, and he didn't have the balls to do it even if he'd had a reason. There's more to this mess, and you can bet on that. When is the arraignment? This afternoon?"

He shook his head. "Tomorrow morning. Meg McCorkle was reluctant to set the bonds on anything this heavy. She just passed the buck on upstairs to Judge MacGregor, and he had to be out of town until late this evening."

"Who's Raynes's attorney?"

"The judge appointed Walter Durbin by phone."

I wasn't surprised. Durbin was one of the two best trial lawyers in town, a six-foot two-inch cattleman, real estate investor, and attorney with a general practice. He was reasonable, and he would give the boy good representation without holding out false hopes.

"Tom, where this kid is concerned I'm going to need some wiggle room. I'm convinced he didn't kill that poor woman, but I'm equally convinced that he knows who did. What can we offer him if he talks?"

"You really don't think he did it?"

"No, I don't," I said.

"Why not?"

"My instincts. Remember that I started this job when you were about ten years old."

"And you'll never let me forget it, will you?" he said, shaking his head ruefully.

"Nope."

He played around with his pen for a moment, then said, "I don't think there's any doubt that he helped transport the body."

"Neither do I."

"If he wasn't involved in the planning or execution, I could go as low as ten years for accessory after the fact."

"I'll see what I can do."

I was on my way across the street to Walter Durbin's office on the third floor of the old Sequoya National Bank Building when Carla called on my cell phone to tell me that Zorn's story checked out. I went on upstairs and told Walter's office manager, Nelda Parsons, that I needed to see him. Nelda was about forty and the same shade of café au lait as Toby, which was natural since she was his older sister by a few years. Their family went all the way back to slavery days in Caddo County, and their father pastored the largest black church in town. She was about five two and petite with short hair and velvet-like skin and liquid brown eyes a man could get lost in. Besides her physical attributes, which were considerable, she was brilliant and said to have a photographic memory. I was convinced that she and Walter had been lovers for several years, but he was divorced and she was a widow, so it was nobody's business, mine included. "You can go on in," she said. "I think he's feeding the snake."

It was common knowledge around town that Walter kept a six-foot python that belonged to his daughter in a big aquarium in his storage closet. "What's he feeding it?" I asked.

"Things," she said, staring me right in the eyes and not smiling. "There's always something around this office that needs to disappear."

"If you run short, let me know," I said. "I've got a few 'things' I'd like to get rid of, myself."

When I entered the inner sanctum, he was just closing the door to the storage closet. I didn't ask him to reopen it. In his early fifties, he was big and broad-shouldered and bald with well-tanned skin and pale blue eyes. A former national guard colonel, he'd been in Desert Storm and won the Combat Infantry Badge and a Bronze Star. He'd also resigned his commission not long after that fracas ended. After we shook hands, I sat down and outlined my problem for him.

"Have you talked to Raynes?" I asked.

"This morning."

"Walter, let me get right to the point. I don't think the boy killed Amanda Twiller, but I'm just as sure that he knows who did."

He leaned back in his big chair and put his booted feet up on his desk and gave me a sad smile. "I believe you're right on both counts. The kid just doesn't have it in him."

"That's exactly what my gut told me as soon as I got a good look at him yesterday."

"So where do we go with it?" he asked. "Since we're obviously talking off the record here."

"I don't really want to see him go down for murder one. But it is shaping up as a slam dunk."

"It looks bad. I'll admit that."

"So tell me, is he clamming up because he's scared or because he's protecting somebody?"

He held up his hands in supplication. "I can't get a fix on the kid, Bo. It's like trying to push toothpaste back into the tube. He won't look me in the eye, and he gives evasive answers to every question I ask him."

"Will you let me question him? With you present, of course?"

"I'm willing, but he says he won't talk to you, so . . ."

I laid out the deal the DA would go along with. "Put it on the table and see what he says," I said. "Ten years is a hell of a lot better than life."

I rose to leave and I was almost to the door when he said, "You know, Bo, if I had to guess, I'd say that poor boy is both scared *and* protecting somebody. He's scared of going down for life, and he's shielding somebody too. Or maybe we're just imagining things."

"I don't think so, Walter. When you add it up, together we've got over five decades of experience dealing with these old criminals. That has to be worth something."

"Maybe so, but it hasn't made me rich. Has it made you rich, Bo?"

"In friends and experiences, sure. But I've always been thankful I haven't had to depend on my salary to get by. In fact, my deputies need a raise right now."

"County commissioners," he said, disdain heavy in his voice. "They want to spend all the money out in their precincts fixing potholes and installing driveway culverts for their constituents."

"Things are looking up on that front. Charlie Morton has come around to my point of view on just about everything."

"Ha!" he said. "You must have caught him with some bimbo."

"Now, you know I can't talk out of class."

"Right. The shame of it is that Charlie is the most intelligent and able fellow on the court."

"That's why he'll make the most effective advocate now that he's born again."

He laughed. "I bet his conversion experience was something worth seeing."

"It was spiritually moving, Walter. It truly was."

I'd been back at the office for about an hour when Linda popped back in. "Did you find anything?" I asked.

"Yep," she said. "The woman was a neat freak. There were about a hundred empty prescription bottles lined up in rows like little soldiers on the top shelf of her closet."

"Anything else?"

She nodded and tossed a letter across the desk to me. "I don't know what it means, but it was hidden way at the back of one of her dresser drawers."

I opened the letter and quickly read the two pages of neat, almost prim handwriting it contained.

"Who is this Nobel Dennard character?" Linda asked. "Do you know him?"

"Yeah, I do."

"That letter is a threat, isn't it?"

"Legally, no. It is skirting a fine line, though. The man is a lawyer and he knows better than to make outright threats."

I sighed and put the letter back in its envelope and reached for the phone. "Go get the Suburban," I said. "Wait for me around at the courthouse front entrance."

"Okay. Where are we going?"

"Over to Center. But first I'm going to call this gentleman and tell him he damn sure better be there when I get there."

CHAPTER ELEVEN

Center is the county seat of Shelby County, which lies due southeast of Sequoya bordering Louisiana. On the way we passed through the small village of Timpson. Like dozens of other East Texas towns, it had once been a thriving cotton market, but it was now paused in a timeless autumnal moment over the precipice of its ultimate oblivion. Half the businesses in the old part of town were boarded up, and the rest were struggling. Empty windows stared like sightless eyes out onto the passing years. As we drove down a side street I pointed to the long-defunct Fox Theater. "I saw my first movie there," I said.

"Really? How come?"

"This is where my mother was born and raised. One Saturday when we were visiting her sister Emma, she and Aunt Emma decided to take me and my cousin to see *High Noon* with Gary Cooper. I was about five at the time."

"Good flick."

"Turn left at the next street," I said.

"That's not the way to Center, Bo."

"I know, but I want to see my aunt's old place."

It was a few blocks north of the main highway, down near the end of the street—a big, shady, sprawling white clapboard affair with deep verandas and a world of memories. I pointed it out to Linda.

"Nice," she said. "I could hunker down in a house like that for the rest of my life. Is your aunt dead?"

"She and Uncle Homer were killed in a car wreck back in 1980."

I directed her to take a left. After a couple of blocks we passed a huge white-columned house that looked like something out of *Gone with the Wind*.

"Wow, that place is beautiful," she said. "I wonder what the story on it is."

"Rat Turd Blair. That's the story."

"What?!"

"His name was R. T. Blair. The kids all called him Rat Turd. He was a prosperous merchant here many years ago. See that screened-in porch on the side? Mr. Blair dropped dead of a heart attack one cold day between his car and the steps. He'd been fishing, and the authorities took his coat off to examine the body. They hung it on that porch, but his wife could never bring herself to move it. It hung there until it rotted."

"Bo, you know so many interesting stories."

I laughed. "And I don't even tell the good ones. I think there's a prizewinning novel in every country graveyard in this state if you could just get at it."

Back on the main road and a dozen miles farther on we came to Center. In the middle of the square loomed the massive Irish castle–style courthouse, the last one remaining in the country, now renovated as a community center and museum. Nobel Dennard kept his office on the second floor of a fine old building he owned on the south side of the square opposite the courthouse. I knew the man, but I didn't know him well. Though his practice was mostly confined to civil matters, over the years he'd had a few minor criminal cases in Caddo County that had brought us

in contact with each other, and for a while we'd both been dele-
gates to the East Texas Council of Governments. He was tall and
slim, with wavy, prematurely silver hair, a matinee idol's face, and
ruddy skin.

His office was suitably lawyerly with its eighteenth-century-
style walnut paneling and English hunting prints and brass-studded
wing chairs of burgundy-colored leather. I quickly introduced him
to Linda, and he motioned for us to sit and then took his place
behind about a half acre of mahogany desk that looked like it
might have come from Versailles and gazed at me blandly. "What's
the problem, Bo? You sounded mad as hell on the phone."

"I've got a dead body on my hands, Nobel."

"Whose?"

"Amanda Twiller."

"Gosh, I hate to hear that. What happened?"

I ignored his question. "So you admit knowing her?" I asked.

"Sure, but what—"

"Somebody shot her three times."

He seemed authentically surprised. "You don't meant it! But
why?"

"I thought you might be able to help me out on that, Nobel."

"Me? Why me?"

"You didn't know she was dead? It's been all over the news
for two days."

He shook his head. "I've been down at my deer lease trying to
get things ready for November."

"I suppose you can substantiate that?"

He shrugged. "Yeah. Two of my buddies were there with me
the whole time. We share the lease."

"Give me their names and phone numbers," I said.

"Sure." He quickly scribbled on a notepad, tore off the sheet,
and handed it to me. "What I don't understand is why you came
to me."

I tossed the letter across the desk.

He read it quickly and tossed it back. "So? I don't even have to talk to you about this, you know."

"That's true," I said amiably.

"So I don't think I will."

I gave him a cold smile. "Okay, in that case, I'll just have to go back home and call a press conference and tell them the investigation is zeroing in on a prominent Shelby County attorney Mrs. Twiller had been romantically involved with. A lot of people might not be able to put it together. But I bet some would. Your wife, for example. Some of your more prosperous clients."

His face held a sour frown. "I've always heard you were mean as hell, Bo."

"Nah, just playful and fun-loving. Now what's it going to be? The easy way or the hard way?"

"What do you want to know?"

"For starters, you admit that the two of you had an affair?"

He laughed an insincere little laugh and gave a futile shrug. "Sure. What's the point in lying when you could dig into the area's motel registers and whatnot and prove it?"

"How did you meet her?"

"I was a delegate from my church to a regional ecumenical convention in Houston. She and her husband were there."

"You seduced a woman you met at a religious conference?" Linda asked, a hint of disgust in her voice.

"I suppose that must seem a little ironic to you," he said. "But I promise you that other people have done it long before me."

"Let's have the whole story, Nobel," I said.

"It's not much of a story. We met, she gave signals that she might be available, and I responded. The first time we got together in Nacogdoches when her husband was in Dallas. There were a lot of other times too. Here and there. You know how it goes."

"No, actually I don't," I said. "How long did it last?"

"About three months."

"What ended it?"

"I did."

"Why?"

He squirmed around a little in his chair. "I hate to talk about a dead woman, Bo. I know that at heart she was a good person. We had a lot of fun together."

"That letter indicates otherwise, Mr. Dennard," Linda said.

"I felt like I had to be a little blunt with her. I regretted having to do it."

"Why did you end it?" I asked again.

"I became aware that she was misusing prescription drugs, and I could see a disaster looming in her near future. I didn't want to be part of it."

"I've always heard that painkillers reduce people's sex drive," Linda said.

"They seemed to have the opposite effect on Amanda," Dennard said.

I tapped the letter with my fingertip. "Exactly what did you mean when you said she stood to suffer more than you did if the affair was revealed?"

"I was referring to something she and I had talked about earlier. I was pointing out that if she exposed our romance, which she was threatening to do, a lawyer like me with a financially dependent spouse was in a better position to weather such a storm than a minister's wife. That's all. I had no intention of doing anything to harm her."

"So you claim," I said.

He shrugged. "If you know the two men on that piece of paper, then you know that neither of them are the sort who would lie in a situation like this. Just check them out."

"I know Johnny Higgins, and what you say about him is true.

But that doesn't clear you completely. This has all the earmarks of a murder for hire."

"Really?" he asked. "But who do you think would . . ." He broke off and gave me a twisted smile. "A former lover might have, right?"

"On the money, Nobel," I said.

"If it comes down to it, I'll give you access to my finances. Now, if you'll excuse me, I really need to see an important client in about five minutes."

We rose to leave and he stuck out his hand. After a moment's hesitation I took it.

"I'm sorry about blowing up and threatening not to cooperate," he said. "Alpha male syndrome. But you probably know a little about that."

"No," I said with a firm shake of my head. "I'm an omega male myself."

"Huh?"

"Last letter in the Greek alphabet. You alphas start things and I finish 'em."

We were a mile or so out of town when Linda finally asked, "So what do you think?"

"About what I expected."

"He did offer us access to his finances, Bo."

I gave her a dismissive snort. "Anybody as smart as Nobel has a cash stash somewhere."

"Do you think he did it?"

"My gut tells me no."

She grinned. "Does it tell you anything else?"

"Yeah. It says we need to stop and get a cup of coffee and a piece of coconut cream pie at that café in Timpson. My treat."

"I'm trying to take off a few pounds."

"Then you can sit and suffer in silence while I indulge."

"Is the pie really good there?"

I turned and looked at her with mock amazement. "Have you ever heard of bad coconut cream pie?"

"Point taken, as you always say."

"Then get a move on. All this talk has got me hungry."

CHAPTER TWELVE

I went home early that afternoon and had a quick drink, then dozed off on the sofa in the den. I awoke with a start when the phone rang right beside my ear. It was Toby. I looked at my watch and discovered that it was a little past six-thirty. "Why in thunder are you still at work?" I asked him. "You should have gone off shift this afternoon."

"Billy Don and Otis called me, and now I'm calling you."

"It's that bad, huh?" I asked.

"Maybe it's that good. You need to come on down and see for yourself."

Ten minutes later I entered the basement hallway to hear yelling coming out of my office. "I want a lawyer! You people deaf? I want my phone call and a lawyer!"

I stepped through my doorway and saw Toby perched on the corner of my desk with Otis and Billy Don leaning against the opposite wall. In the place of honor in front of the desk sprawled a slim young black man who couldn't have been more than thirty. He had a shaved head, a gold earring, and enough gold chains around his neck to have ransomed a fair–looking princess back in the olden days. The rest of him was loosely encased in slick black and purple nylon gangsta crap that I found deeply annoying.

"What have we got here?" I asked, as I came around my desk and took my chair.

"What we have," Toby said, "is one Mr. Willard Peet of St. Louis, Missouri. Mr. Peet has been careening around town in his eighty-thousand-dollar Beemer, smoking dope and snorting coke and trying to find Emmet Zorn."

That was the most interesting thing I'd heard all day, and I said so. I also said, "I assume he made a bit of a nuisance of himself, which brought him to your attention."

Otis spoke, "That's right. We'd already gotten a couple of complaints on this bird, and so had the city police. When nobody at the Pak-a-Sak would tell him anything about Zorn, he started asking people on the streets, being verbally abusive in several cases when our good citizens couldn't satisfy him. Then we saw him run a stop sign. We pulled him over and smelled weed when he rolled down the window. Probable cause for a search, etc., etc., bang-bang-bang. The domino effect. And here he is, and there on your desk is his bag of marijuana and a little glass vial that no doubt contains nose candy."

"I want a lawyer!" Peet yelled once again. "What's wrong with you people? Can't you understand what a man's saying?"

"Bo, all this talk about lawyers and stuff is getting on my nerves," Toby said.

"Who do you think you are, niggah?" Peet asked, looking up at Toby. "You think you're some kind of top-shit mutha because these peckerwoods let you wear a badge and carry a gun? Sheet, I bet it ain't even got no bullets in it. I want a lawyer! I know my rights."

Toby leaned down where their faces were about a foot apart and braced his arms on Peet's chair, and said softly, "Who do I think I am? I'll tell you who I am. I'm ex–Staff Sergeant Tobias Parsons, formerly of the U.S. Army Special Forces. First wave into Iraq. Ever shot it out with somebody who's shooting back at you, Willard? I don't mean some gangbang bullshit. I'm talking about real fighting men who've been trained to kill. Ever done that? I have. For several weeks. Then I caught a big chunk of shrapnel in the belly. I'd show you the scar, but I don't want to see you puke all over our nice floor."

"Man, I don't need this jive-ass crap—"

"You're gonna think jive in about fifteen minutes, my friend. What's going to happen is that me and Sheriff Handel are going to go down to the Caravan and have ourselves each a nice medium-rare rib eye for supper. And while we're gone, we're going to leave you to the tender mercies of Billy Don and Otis standing right over yonder. In a special, soundproof room we have here just for that purpose. Then when we come back you're going to tell us what we want to know, and you're going to be happy to have the opportunity to do it."

"You can't get away with this kind of shit no more."

"This is deep East Texas, fool," Toby said. "This is the land of midnight burials in unmarked graves. We can get away with any damn thing we want to down here because nobody will ever care what happened to you. It's not like you're a civil rights worker or anybody worth worrying over. Take a good look at this room. Do you see any federal cops hovering around with the Bill of Rights in their hands? No, what you see is a comfy old pine-paneled office in the basement of an old-timey courthouse. You see mounted deer heads, fine shotguns, Winchester calendars, all that good Southern shit. And you see three good-ole-boy cops, plus one truly badass black dude who does *not* view you as a credit to our race. This is your worst nightmare come true, Willard. Believe it."

Peet gaped around frantically for a few moments, his face greasy with sweat. "Man, this ain't happening."

"Oh, but it is," I said softly.

"Can't we cut some kind of deal?" Peet asked.

"Why should we deal when we're holding all the aces?" I asked.

"No deals, Willard," Toby said. "Maybe a little charity if we're approached right, but no deals. We don't need to deal for what we've already got."

"Say what?"

"Charity," I said. "It's a lot like divine grace. An unmerited favor given to an undeserving individual. You better listen up because here it comes, and you only get one chance to grab the brass ring. You tell us what we need to know, and out of the goodness of our hearts we'll stick this weed and this vial of coke somewhere and forget all about them. Then when we get through, I'll have somebody escort you to the county line and turn your car back over to you and let you get on your way back up to St. Louis."

"How do I know you'll do what you say?"

I started to rise from my chair with a long-suffering sigh. "Toby, I'm hungry. Let's see about those rib eyes."

This galvanized Mr. Peet into action. "Wait! Wait! Okay, I'll go for it. You don't leave a dude no choice."

"Wise move, Willard," Billy Don said, speaking for the first time.

I sat back down. "Then start talking," I said.

"Okay, what do you need first?"

"Once again, why were you looking for Emmet Zorn?"

"I was sent down here to set up a transaction, you know? Like for some merchandise this Zorn dude is supposed to have."

"What kind of merchandise?" Toby asked.

Peet wiggled around in his chair and shrugged off-handedly. "You know, product."

"There's lots of products in this old world," I said. "Cars, trucks, boom boxes, grapefruit . . ."

Peet twittered. "It ain't none of that shit, man. That's for sure."

"You wouldn't be talking about cocaine, now would you?" I asked.

"Yeah, I guess. Blow. Toot. Whatever. I mean, I hate to mention the word outright, if you see what I'm saying. It's like I got one of them inhabitations against it."

"I think you mean inhibitions," Toby said.

"Yeah, I got one of them things."

"How much coke?" I asked.

He shrugged and wiggled and looked down at the floor. "I don't know for sure. People other than me got to grade the stuff and weigh it and all that shit. I'm just the negotiator, but it looks like maybe a million worth."

For one of the few times in my life I felt my mouth fall open. "A million dollars . . . ?"

"That's what my man said." He leaned forward and put his hands about an inch apart and pointed them first in one direction, then in another as he spoke. "See, some dude that my man knows and trusts also knows this Zorn dude, and he says Zorn is the real deal, man. It's like Zorn gets the shit from his man down in Houston, see? Then he holds it here for some other dude from Dallas to come get it. Or maybe he takes it to Dallas, I dunno. But Zorn don't buy the shit and resell it, you understand. He just gets a transfer fee for getting it up to Dallas. Like UPS or whatever. But on this deal, my man is willing to pay more than the dude in Dallas. I mean, you see what I'm saying?"

"You're saying that Zorn is screwing his man in Houston, whoever he is," I said.

"Sounds like it, don't it?"

"So do you know who Zorn's man is?"

"No, dude."

"Come on, Willard," Toby said. "Get cracking with the facts. The sheriff and I can still go have those steaks if we need to."

"Man, I don't got a clue. I mean, this business ain't like Bill Gates and Steve Jobs getting together and doing a big deal with their names all over contracts and pictures in the newspapers and shit like that. It's more like a need-to-know kind of setup, if you see what I'm saying. And I try not to absorb any information I don't really need."

"Yeah, I bet you don't," I said. "Why is your man so desperate for this particular shipment? He has to know it's going to be a onetime deal because Zorn sure as hell isn't going to be able to do it again."

"Like, the Feds pulled a big bust and my man's supplier is out of business. Lots of other dudes hurting too. Big drought on the street, man. I mean, it's like supply and demand, if you know what I'm saying. If my man could get this shit out there in the next couple of weeks or so, then . . ."

"Speaking of your man, who is he?" I asked.

"Aw, no, dude! You can't expect me to answer no question like that! I mean, you're talking about God there when you talk about my man. You ought to know I can't give that up. You trying to get me killed?"

I shook my head and laughed. "Willard, this may come as a shock to you but you can bet the Feds and the St. Louis cops know who you and your man both are. It's just that I don't know. And I want to. So give it up."

"You think they really know?"

"Sure they do. Unless your man started up in the business in the last month or so."

"Naaah," he said, shaking his head firmly. "My man, he ain't none of this Johnny-come-lately shit. He's old school. I mean, the dude been doin' this shit three, fo years at least."

"Then you can be sure they know, so you just give his name up, and then we'll know too."

I gave him time to rationalize his actions, time to recall some slight or insult, either real or imagined, that he'd suffered from his "man" sometime in the past. When people are snitching, they always have to have that rationalization to justify what they are doing. They can never quite admit to themselves that they are betraying their associates for no other reason than to save their own skins.

"Bob Jones," he said.

"Damn, Willard!" Otis said. "I could come up with a better lie than that, and I'm just a dumb old country boy."

"That's the dude's righteous name. I swear. Robert Elwood Jones. He goes by Bob."

"I hope you realize that I'm going to check all this out," I said. "If you've lied about anything, then this coke comes back out of my desk and goes to the DA. A nationwide warrant will be issued, and we know where you live."

"Ain't no lies, dude."

There were more details, but they didn't matter. When we were finished with him I called in one of the night-shift deputies and instructed him to follow Peet to the county line. I didn't bother to tell Peet that it would be very unwise for him ever to come back to Caddo County. Even as dense as he was, he could figure that out.

"There's still one question left unanswered," Otis said. "Where was Zorn and why didn't he meet with Peet?"

"And it's a damned important question too," I said. "Any speculations?"

They all shook their heads.

"What we've learned tonight is certainly a new take on Zorn," Toby said. "I never saw him as into anything this heavy."

"Me either," Billy Don said.

"The kind of money Peet was talking about does strange things to people," I said.

"Looks like he's been involved in trafficking quite a while," Otis said. "Long before he decided to stick his man in Houston."

"It sure does," I said. "And this puts him in a different light in relation to the Twiller murder. Or at least it does to me. It may even give us a little leverage with him."

"You think?" Toby asked with a grin.

"Indeed I do," I said. "There is a lesson in this, my friends. When you're conducting a murder investigation, you've got to be a mole with your eye on the hole and not get sidetracked by any of the peripheral crap that always orbits around. We had a choice tonight of getting some information we needed to help us clear a major case, or of saddling the taxpayers of this state with one more idiot to feed for forty years. We made the right choice. Besides, Peet will either wind up dead or in federal prison before long, anyway."

"I think you and Toby should give up law enforcement," Otis said. "You need to take that two-man act of yours to Broadway."

I laughed. "We did do a number on that fool, didn't we? Sound-proof rooms and midnight burials in unmarked graves . . . Toby, you ought to write crime novels."

CHAPTER THIRTEEN

Before I left the office I gave Toby the contact numbers of Muldoon and Hotchkiss and told him to get Peet's license number and info to them in case they wanted to pull him in for their own purposes. Then when I got to the house I made a call to Mack Reynolds, my old friend who was the FBI SAC in Houston. I found him at home, and we had a heart-to-heart talk. He moved fast. Thirty minutes later Hotchkiss called my cell phone to tell me that he would be happy to buy me breakfast at the Caravan the next day.

When I got to the restaurant that morning I found Hotchkiss waiting for me with a pair of coffee cups and two menus. We made small talk until after the waitress had poured our coffee and taken our orders. Then we got down to business.

"I hope you don't take it wrong," he said, "but we just didn't feel free to give you the whole story the other day. In fact, we thought maybe we'd said too much as it was."

"I understand," I said and gave him a rundown on our session with Willard Peet. "I also know that Sipes has to be the man in Houston that Peet was talking about last night."

"He is. This fits in with some other information we've gotten. Apparently, Sipes has some missing cocaine."

"How in the hell did you find that out?" I asked.

"We're keeping close tabs on the man. And that's all I can say about that. But he has jumped into the cocaine trade with both feet. For a while after that trial in Fillmore, he confined his criminal activities to laundering drug money for other dope dealers through a bank he controls in the Cayman Islands. We've had him under scrutiny for years, but he's managed to avoid any further indictments. He even married a divorced socialite who came from one of the oldest families in Houston. That gave him a little veneer of respectability. But guys like him can't stay straight, and now it's coke. Mack assigned me to the Zorn-Sipes connection full-time. We'll be working together if that's no problem with you."

"Glad to have the help. Where does Zorn fit in the scheme?" I asked.

"He brings the coke up from Houston and holds it here in town for a buyer from Dallas. The people from Dallas check the grade on the stuff, then make a call on their cell phones authorizing a wire transfer to an offshore account. Other people down in Houston get on their computers, and, once the money is in the bank, Zorn releases the coke."

"What's to keep the Dallas people from just smoking Zorn and taking the merchandise?" I asked.

"It just doesn't work that way anymore. At least not with these people. You've got old, established customers buying from old, established suppliers. A lot of this stuff gets cooked up into crack and sent on further north. Too much profit to get greedy. Everybody stays cool, and everybody makes out good."

I sat back and thought for a few moments. "I never made Zorn for anything like this. Wonder what happened?"

"Who knows? I think he's always been a nickel-and-dime

chippie nibbling around the edges of the crust. I guess he decided he wanted some of the pie."

"How much is Sipes paying him?"

"Ten thousand a trip."

"Why haven't you just nailed Zorn holding the stuff and made him roll over on Sipes? Seems simple enough."

Hotchkiss shook his head. "Even with Zorn's testimony we need something else to connect Sipes to the drugs. You see, he never actually touches them himself. You can imagine what a really good lawyer like Bean or Holbrook would do to a guy like Zorn on the stand. Besides, Zorn and the Dallas connection is only one conduit that Sipes has going. There's another guy in San Antonio and another in Little Rock, both doing the same thing."

"How do they handle the logistics of it all?" I asked.

"Zorn gets a call from a prepaid cell that tells him to go to one of several safe deposit boxes in various banks scattered around Houston. Actually, they're safe deposit bins, the kind businesses rent. The coke is waiting in hermetically sealed containers, along with Zorn's fee. The deposit boxes are rented to a seemingly legitimate export company in Peru that has no known connection with either Sipes or his bank."

"So who puts the coke in the bank box?"

"A couple of college boys. Can you believe they're both honor students?"

I shook my head in wonder. "Where in hell do they get it?"

"Right off the boat. And they get paid very handsomely to make the delivery to the bank. Being smart boys, they have sense enough to know not to try to screw Sipes. The truth is that they're just a couple of dipshit rich kids getting some cheap thrills and picking up a thousand apiece for each trip to the bank. We'll eventually get them, but there's no point in busting either them or Zorn right now until we have a positive link to Sipes. The DEA is working the case too. We're on top of the money-laundering angle."

"How's that working out?" I asked. "You guys have gotten your wires crossed with them in the past."

"Not a chance this time. The whole thing's being coordinated by the attorney general's office. Nobody is going to jump without the go-ahead from Washington."

"Where did Lester Sipes come from?" I asked. "I know about the rodeo circuit, but what's his background?"

"He grew up dirt poor in the worst part of Fort Worth. His dad was a well-known hood named Dewey Sipes who hung around those old gambling dives out on the Jacksboro Highway and ran with guys like Tincey Eggleston and Asher Rhone. Hell, he was tough enough to work for Benny Binion in the policy racket back in the 1940s. If you've ever heard any of those names, you've got his number."

"I've heard them all."

"Then you know that Lester was to the manor born, so to speak."

"Anything else you need to tell me?" I asked.

He gave me smile as bland as the one I'd given him the first day we met. "Only that we thought we had Sipes on money laundering a few months ago, but a witness disappeared and the case fell apart. So remember that anybody who gets tangled up with Sipes is dealing with a guy who didn't hesitate to do away with a federal witness. That's pretty heavy in my book. And if that isn't enough, try this. He had another old friend of his who screwed him a couple of years ago, but not nearly as bad as Zorn has."

"Yeah?"

"They fed that guy to the crabs off the South Jetty down at Galveston. A piece at a time. Meat cleavers and bone saws."

CHAPTER FOURTEEN

I caught Judge MacGregor just as he was about to convene court and told him I needed a search warrant on Zorn. "And just what will you be looking for?" he asked.

"Among other things, there's the possibility that we might find a million dollars worth of cocaine."

A small, white-haired leprechaun of a man, MacGregor gazed at me for a moment with eyes of the purest blue, then sighed. "You have never joked at a time like this, so I will assume you aren't now. But I must say it grieves me for things like this to come to our little town. And what is the legal basis for the warrant? An 'unnamed informant'?"

"No. I have solid information I obtained from the FBI. But I don't want to mention the coke on the warrant."

He blinked a time or two. "And why not?"

"My real interest is in finding anything that might connect him to the Twiller killing. Amanda Twiller was carrying on an affair with Zorn."

"So I'd heard," he said. "Very sad."

"Right. But the Bureau doesn't want Zorn blown on the coke right now. They're after a bigger fish, and I need to accommodate them if I can."

"I have also heard that Mrs. Twiller had developed a prescription drug problem. Do you think that's true?"

"I have every reason to believe it is, including her husband's word on the matter."

"I see," he said and nodded. "Then let's list prescription drugs and 'other' controlled substances on the paperwork, but keep it generic. Don't name any drug specifically. That way you can still use it later if you find a big sack full of cocaine or something equally distressing. I think that's reasonable since everybody in town seems to know that the woman had developed a substance abuse problem. Tell my secretary to type it up and bring it into the courtroom for me to sign."

I'd been back in my office about fifteen minutes when Linda Willis came in and laid a piece of paper on my desk.

"What's this?" I asked.

"The ballistics report on the Twiller murder gun. The Bureau's lab wizards claim it came from a CZ nine-millimeter, and it doesn't match up with anything previously used in a crime."

"What in the Sam Hill is a CZ?"

"Designwise, it's a double-action modification of John Browning's Colt 1911 semiauto, like you carry. They're made in the former Czechoslovakia for the former Czech army. I think their cops use them too."

"Are they commercially available here, or are we dealing with something rare and exotic?"

"No, you can get 'em here," she said. "Very sweet pistols, as a matter of fact. I've shot a couple of them. Great trigger pull right out of the box. Actually, they're a lot like the FN-made Browning Hi-Power, which you probably remember was another of old man Browning's designs."

I leaned back in my big chair and peered at her skeptically.

"Linda, it's plain unseemly for a sweet young woman like you to know so much about firearms."

"Gotta be ready for when the commies invade, boss."

"The commies are defunct. Now it's A-rab terrorists. They're the enemy du jour."

"Whatever," she said. She pivoted around, snapped to attention, and started marching out of the room singing the Marine Corps Hymn.

"Whoa!" I yelled.

She executed a perfect about-face and saluted.

"You've got another search to do," I said. "This time take Toby with you."

"Groovy. Who's the subject?"

"Emmet Zorn. And where is Toby, anyway?"

"He took a domestic disturbance call as soon as he came on a little while ago."

"Damn," I said. "That's how many in twenty-four hours? Five?"

"Six."

"What's wrong with people?"

"I think it's the weather. This drought is getting on everybody's nerves. Even my parents'."

"Well, Linda, you should realize that anybody who went through the ordeal of raising you is bound to get a little cranky from time to time."

"Thanks, Bo. What are we looking for at Zorn's place?"

"The warrant lists any documents or physical evidence that might connect him to Amanda Twiller. Drugs are also mentioned."

"Unscripted prescription drugs?"

"That's an interesting question, isn't it?"

"You want me to call Toby?" she asked.

"Yeah, tell him to cut it short or call somebody else to take over. Have him meet you at Zorn's place. If Zorn's not there, which he probably won't be, secure the warrant to the door."

I got a call from one of my informants that caused me to pause and reflect for a few seconds. Then I picked up the receiver and dialed Hotch's cell number. I decided it was time for him to pay me back a little for his mendacity at our first meeting.

"Hotchkiss here," he said.

"Indeed it is, and I already need your help on something. Time for you to start paying for your sins."

He laughed. "Mack told me this would happen. So what do you need?"

"I just talked to one of my snitches on the phone."

"Yes?"

"I'm busting a bookie in a few days and I need a little help with him. My informant gave me some particulars on the guy, and I'd like to be able to apply a little federal pressure on him. He's already had one interstate gambling charge that was probated, so—"

"So if we catch him with the goods he's a shoo-in for about five years' federal time."

"You got it," I said.

"But you're after bigger fish."

"You got that too. I'll tell you about it the next time we talk."

"Okay, but try to give me at least a day's notice on the bust."

"I'll do my best."

We hung up and I spent a dull morning applying myself to more of the paperwork that was becoming a constant plague of my occupation. Then, at about ten-thirty, Walter Durbin appeared in my doorway. "I've been fired," he said.

"As Raynes's lawyer?" I asked. "Did he get somebody else?"

"Yeah. Harvey Holbrook."

"Damn," I said. Holbrook was one of Houston's top criminal

defense lawyers. He was also a truly vicious little queen with no more sense of ethics or common decency than a hog in heat.

"My sentiments exactly," Walter said. "Holbrook showed up in court and told the judge that he'd been retained to represent the boy. He claims he knows you."

"Yeah, I know him too."

"What's he like personally?"

"Queer as a three-legged goat and mean as hell."

"Well, from what I garnered in our short conversation this morning, he doesn't care for you, either. What's the story on that?"

"About six or seven years ago he tried a pretty big case here in town and won. He got a little drunk at the post-trial celebration, and damn near slammed his Jaguar into my cruiser on his way out of town. While I was trying to reason with him, he called me a motherfucker and got physical. So I slapped the fire out of him."

"Did you charge him with drunk driving?"

"Nope," I said. "I nailed him for public intoxication and disorderly conduct. Easier to prove and more humiliating. Plus I threw his ass in the drunk tank overnight."

He laughed. "I hope he got a letter of censure from the state bar."

"He did, and he didn't like that either."

"Well, he's what you're up against now. The judge had no choice but to let him get to the boy, and it didn't take him two minutes. When I tried to tell Holbrook about the deal the DA offered, he suggested I take a hike. Says he's going to fight it out in court."

"Arrogant little prick, isn't he? What about bail? Did Mac-Gregor deny it?"

He nodded. "Yeah, but Holbrook is appealing the ruling. He's going to the appeals court over in Tyler this afternoon."

I stared at him in disbelief, and I'm sure my mouth was gaping wide open for the second time in less than two days. "So you're telling me that one of the most expensive criminal lawyers in this state is not only representing this kid, but that he's tooling over to Tyler to bell the appellate court on behalf of a poor little drug skank who probably couldn't raise a hundred dollars cash if his life depended on it?"

"That's right."

"Walter, what in the hell is going on?"

"I can't begin to imagine, but I would dearly love to know who's fronting Holbrook's fee."

"So would I," he said. "Why don't you come by about five and have a drink with me and Nelda, and we'll do some speculating on that."

"I will if I can, but I don't know where I'll be then. This case has been turning me every which way but loose."

Two hours later I'd finished my budget and cleared all my other paperwork, and I was trying to decide what to do for lunch when Toby and Linda cruised back in, wide-eyed and excited. "You've got to see what we found," Linda said, pulling a small digital camera out of her pocket and nudging my shins with her foot. "Get up and gimmie your chair. I want to download these photos to your computer."

"Don't mind me," I said. "I'm just the boss, and I sure don't want to get in your way."

"Oh, hush, Bo. You're going to love this. It's a real mystery."

She was right.

It was a box, about fifteen inches long, a foot wide and two feet deep, built into Zorn's floor. The hardwood flooring had been carefully sawn out and the box had been framed in between the floor joists. One shot showed the underside of the flooring, revealing how the strips of oak had been tacked to a pair of one-by-half inch pine planks, a setup that allowed the flooring to be replaced as a lid for the box.

"Somebody went to one hell of a lot of trouble here," I said. "How did you find it? I suppose it was under a rug or something."

"The hall runner," Linda said. "I stepped on it and it felt different somehow, so I pulled the runner aside."

"She's got sensitive feet," Toby said. "We put it all back together, and I couldn't feel a thing when I stepped on it."

"I'm guessing it was empty," I said.

They both nodded. "And clean as a pin inside," Toby said. "No dust, no residue, no nothing."

"What do you think it was made for?" Linda asked.

"Guns, gold, money, jewels, or drugs," I said. "Take your pick."

"Drugs," Toby said.

Linda nodded her head in agreement. I sat in thought for a few moments. "Anybody want to hazard a guess why Zorn was out of pocket when Peet came to town?" I asked.

"That's been worrying me too," Toby said. "It doesn't make any sense."

"What I'm about to tell you stays between the three of us for the time being. The Bureau says Zorn has been muleing cocaine for Sipes. Large amounts of cocaine. Peet says he brings the stuff up from Houston and holds it for the buyers in Dallas or wherever. That explains the hidey-hole you found. Now, Peet said he came down here to set up the St. Louis transaction. What if Zorn misunderstood and thought he was supposed to meet Peet for the actual buy? Let's say maybe he opens the cupboard only to find it bare. So with the stuff missing, he must know it wasn't a casual burglary, right? Not some guy who broke in and just happened to find the stuff. Which means somebody else must have known it was there, somebody Zorn trusted but who decided to rip him off. So what does Zorn do when he finds the stuff is gone?"

"He goes ape shit," Linda said. "And he starts frantically looking for the friend and fails to connect with Peet."

"Good theory," Toby said.

"But why would he let somebody else know about the stuff?" Linda asked.

"I don't know. Maybe he had an accomplice or a partner. Did you leave the box like you found it?"

"Yeah," Linda said. "We both thought you'd want us to."

"You did good," I said. "Let's just keep it our little secret for now. Did anything else turn up on the search?"

"No," Toby said. "Except we found out that Zorn is very neat and organized. And he's got about fifty of those string ties and fancy tie clasps hanging in his closet."

"You should see that damn place," Linda said. "It looks like some young bachelor's dream pad out of *Playboy* magazine back about 1970. He's got a round waterbed with satin coverlets and a bunch of airbrushed nudes hanging on the walls. What an asshole."

I sat on the corner of my desk. She was still in my chair, swiveling back and forth a little, her feet barely touching the floor.

"Now, Linda," I said. "I was thinking I might tell ole Emmet that you're available so maybe he'd come sparkin' you some fine fall evening. Probably with a bouquet of roses in one hand and a dainty, heart-shaped box of chocolates in the other."

"Bo, only a damn fool would talk that way to a woman who's wearing a .357 Magnum," she said.

I laughed and stood up. "Young folks, I'm happy as a lark all of a sudden. Whether or not we ever unravel this mess, the image of Emmet Zorn down on his knees peeking into that damned hole in his floor with those little eyes of his has made my day. Lunch is on me, so let's go."

CHAPTER FIFTEEN

Sycamore Ridge Cemetery is a two-acre strip of land that lies on a low bluff a half mile past the western edge of town. It's bordered by an oil-topped county road on one side and the edge of the bluff on the other, with a perimeter marked by a century-old fence of wrought iron that's overgrown with masses of honeysuckle. In the spring the ground is a carpet of wildflowers that ripple gently beneath the spreading branches of tall magnolias and ancient cedars. But now the grass lay in withered strips among a forest of tombstones that ranged from humble, homemade concrete slabs on up to the great granite and marble obelisks erected by the leading citizens of the previous century.

I had two reasons for attending Amanda Twiller's four o'clock service. In the first place, it was the right thing to do since the family was well established in the community. And second, there is a strong belief among lawmen that oftentimes a killer can't stay away from his victim's funeral.

The Methodist bishop had sent a young man fresh from the seminary to function as Twiller's assistant until he recovered from his wife's death. Twiller started to read his wife's favorite poem, but he broke down and the new preacher had to finish it for him. After a short eulogy, we sang "Amazing Grace," and then the young man gave a closing prayer. And that was all. I saw no one that looked suspicious or stood out in the crowd of perhaps two hundred that showed up. Before I left the cemetery I asked the funeral director, an old hunting buddy of mine named Leonard Ott, to photocopy the guest register for me before he turned it over to the family.

I never made it to Walter's office that afternoon. Two more minor shooting scrapes out in the country and a robbery attempt at the north boundary of the county kept the whole department tied up until well after dark. Everybody was grateful for the fall of night. The day had been miserably hot and dusty, and the very world itself seemed wilted under the burning sun.

I went home and took a quick shower and decided to turn in early. As I was brushing my teeth I looked out the bathroom window to see the waxing moon, now a thin, menacing crescent, where it hung red and ominous in the eastern sky. I peered at it and shuddered and said a silent prayer for rain and cool weather. Before it rose again the following night I would have yet another murder on my hands.

CHAPTER SIXTEEN

The next morning I decided to drive down South Main Street to the Burger King at the edge of town to get a couple of sausage biscuits to eat at my desk. On my way back, I passed the Caravan and saw Sheila in front of the building wrestling with a guy twice her size. Muttering imprecations about the needless complexities of life, I wheeled into the parking lot and climbed out of my cruiser after first slipping a fifteen-inch lead-filled slap-jack into the back of my Wranglers.

As I drew closer I could see that her tormentor was about forty or a couple of years younger. He was bulked up like a bodybuilder and had a narrow head on a big body, black hair, and a face that reminded me of a sink full of dirty dishes. Dressed in the same sort of trendy nylon wind suit Peet had sported, his eyes were glazed and pinpoint, and he held Sheila's left forearm in one huge hand with a viselike grip.

"Turn her loose and back off," I ordered.

He looked at me and smirked, but he didn't give up his hold on Sheila's arm. Bad move on his part. He made another unwise decision when he concluded that a little debate was in order. "Who the hell are you, country boy?" he asked.

I decided to show him who I was. There's no point in arguing with somebody stupid enough or hopped-up enough to contest a lawman's point of view in such a situation. At least not in my part of the world. I reached behind me and grabbed the slapjack and brought it around in one smooth motion. His right hand was busy holding Sheila, but his big, thick left arm was available in all its bulging glory, his elbow sticking out in virtual invitation. And that's where I got him.

It must have hurt something fierce. It took him a full second to react, but when he did his eyes bugged out a little and his mouth made a silent O. He let go of Sheila and reached for his elbow, but by that time I'd lost interest in any voluntary cooperation he might have been willing to offer. My second blow was a truly vicious roundhouse backhand that caught him just behind his right ear and brought him to the ground.

"God, Bo!" Sheila said.

"You okay?"

"Yeah, but gee . . . I've never seen you do anything like that before."

I grinned at her. "You had Uncle Bo pegged as the teddy-bear type, huh?"

"Not anymore I don't."

By then muscle boy was on all fours trying to get to his feet. I put my knee into the center of his back and came down with all my weight, driving him down on his belly. He tried to resist when I started pulling his arms around behind him to get the cuffs on, but another middling hard lick with the slapjack took all the fight out of him, and I had him trussed up in a matter of seconds.

"What's this all about?" I asked Sheila once I got to my feet.

"I asked him for an interview," she said. "That's all. But then I noticed that he's high on something, and I tried to back away. When I did, he grabbed me."

I was puzzled. "But why would you want to interview him?"

"That murder-for-hire trial down in Beaumont last year that got so much press. He was the defendant."

"I seem to remember something—"

"That's Big Paul Arno, Bo. His picture was on the front page of every newspaper in the state. He's wired in with the Mafia down in New Orleans."

As I said, needless complexities. I figured Arno matched up with the dark blue Cadillac with Louisiana tags that sat parked beside the Caravan. I called for assistance. After two of my day-shift deputies arrived I instructed them to impound it and give it a thorough search.

We still maintained a pair of holding cells in the basement of the courthouse, and that's where I jugged Arno for the time being. I also insisted that Sheila come down and sign an assault complaint. About the time I finished the paperwork, a phone call told me that the search had turned up a loaded nine-millimeter pistol and a small glass vial of white powder.

"That pistol isn't a CZ by any chance, is it?" I asked.

"Nope, it's a SIG Sauer. One of the fancy ones."

I told them to bring the gun and the vial to the office and log them in as evidence. When they arrived I tasted the contents of the vial, an experiment that left no doubt in my mind that it contained cocaine, but it would have to go to the DPS lab for expert confirmation. I also told them to take Arno out to the new jail and book him on assault and possession.

"Why did you broach that guy in the first place?" I asked Sheila.

"I'm a reporter, Bo. That's what I do. Besides, hoods usually won't manhandle the press like that. It doesn't pay for them in the long run."

I had her sign the complaint, then told her to go on about her business.

"Okay," she said. "But I think you owe me an explanation. Could this guy somehow be connected to the Twiller killing?"

"I don't know," I said. "But come by the house tonight and I'll fill you in on what I find out about him."

"Sure," she said and smiled and scampered off to do Sheila things. I was about to call Muldoon and Hotchkiss when Maylene told me Tom Waller was on the phone.

"Bad news," I heard him say as soon as I lifted the receiver.

"Let's hear it."

"The appeals court overruled Judge MacGregor's denial of bail on Raynes."

"What? Why?"

"They said that bail cannot be denied in noncapital cases unless there is what they called 'compelling evidence' that the defendant is a flight risk. Actually, Judge Fox said that and managed to get the other idiot on the court to agree with him. See, Fox hates MacGregor and loves to reverse him, so . . ."

"If that kid's not a flight risk I don't know who would be," I said.

"He's less of one since he's been promised a job clerking in one of our well-established local businesses. That was one of Holbrook's big selling points."

"Which is Zorn's liquor store, I suppose."

"Correct. How did you ever guess?"

I snorted. "How did Holbrook manage to get a hearing so quick?"

"He knows where all the bodies are buried, Bo."

"He's still got to come up with the money," I said.

"Not so. An outfit named Coastal Bail Bonds signed on for the full amount. The kid will be out by noon."

We hung up, and I called Muldoon and Hotchkiss. Muldoon

didn't answer but Hotchkiss was only five minutes away, and he was familiar with Sheila's assailant.

"So what's the story on this Arno character?" I asked after he got situated in front of my desk with a cup of fresh coffee and a few of Maylene's homemade cookies.

"They call him Big Paul, and he's an authentic bad guy."

"Sheila mentioned the New Orleans mob. Is he part of Scorpino's old outfit?"

"Yes and no. He's not actually a made guy and can't be because he's not Sicilian. His ancestors came from up around Ravenna."

"I thought they'd quit being so particular."

"Not in the Big Easy. Scorpino was old-fashioned, and his heirs stick to the rule out of respect for him. But Arno is the next thing to being made. He freelances and can ignore some of the rules. Plus he doesn't have to kick as much of his income upstairs to the boss."

"Could Sipes have hired him?" I asked.

"It's not very likely since he has his own crew of cowboy thugs that came out of the rodeo circuit with him, and he trusts them more than he would any mob-connected guy. But we know that Arno has done some freelance strong-arm work in the past for Sipes's suppliers down in South America. Urging people to come around to their point of view and so forth. With that deal down in Beaumont he got a little too energetic and the fellow wound up dead."

"I see," I said. "But why do you think they'd be interested in Sequoya?"

He shrugged. "Who knows? Maybe they're concerned about a possible leak in their pipeline."

I pondered for a few seconds, then shook my head. "It sounds more likely that they were fronting the stuff to Sipes and he still owes them for it. I mean, you've assumed he's an independent, but he may just be a cog in the machine."

"I guess that's possible."

"I was going to question Arno and get nowhere," I said. "Maybe you'd like to do the honors instead."

"Hell yes, I would."

"My deputies should be taking him out to the jail right about now. Go on out there and tell him that he's looking at a long stretch of hard time if that vial tests positive. Clue him in on what kind of time East Texas juries are handing out for cocaine possession these days. Then tell him I'll give him a pass if he tells us why he's up here and who he's working for."

"Have you talked to the DA about that?" he asked.

"No, but he'll go along with it."

"Okay, but don't expect Arno to buy it. That code of silence, you know. Plus boundless confidence in the power of lawyers."

"I realize that," I said. "Now back in the old days—"

"Yes?" he said with a grin.

"A man like Arno?" I said and laughed. "John Nightwalker would have put a well bucket on his head and whipped it with a piece of chain until he was ready to cop to being Judas Iscariot."

Maylene came in and laid a note on my desk. I'd asked her to check the town's motels, and she'd discovered that Arno had been registered at the Eight Ball on South Main since noon the day after Amanda Twiller was killed. I pushed the note across to Hotchkiss. He read it and raised his eyebrows. "Do you make him for this?" he asked.

"I don't know. We know her body was transported in Doyle Raynes's car, and I don't see a pro like Arno working with a fool kid like Doyle."

"Maybe he did the hit, and Raynes and somebody else moved the body."

"Could be, I suppose," I said. "Stranger things have happened."

"I'd like to sign his gun out and shoot it so I can run one of its bullets through our computer."

"Sure. There's a firing tube and a bullet trap out at the new jail."

He nodded and just then his cell phone rang. After about thirty seconds of listening and whispering, he put it back in his pocket and laughed.

"What?" I asked.

"Lester Sipes has booked the biggest suite in the Fredonia Hotel in Nacogdoches, and he's supposed to arrive there in the early afternoon."

"Do you think he might be hunting his lost merchandise?"

"I wouldn't be a bit surprised," he said.

"I don't suppose you would have any objections if I paid him a little visit this afternoon at the hotel?"

"Rattle his cage all you want. Just let me know in the unlikely event that you learn something."

"Sure," I said. I sat and ruminated for a while as Hotchkiss sipped the last of his coffee and finished off his cookies. "I don't know that much about big-city mobsters, but I didn't think they molested straight citizens in public like this guy was doing with Sheila. At least not without a real reason. And I thought they generally went peacefully when arrest time rolled around."

"They're just thugs and bullies in spite of all the crap you see on TV and in the movies about respect and honor. But it is true that Arno is more of a loose cannon than most of those guys. For one thing, he's gotten strung out on coke in the last year or so. In the old days that would have been an automatic death sentence, and I think that they probably would have whacked him years ago except that he's so good at what he does."

"Which is murder, I guess."

"Yeah, and he can do it in such a way as to make detection almost impossible."

"One other thing is on my mind," I said. "The day Amanda Twiller was killed, you and Muldoon told me this was a sideline case with the two of you. You seem to be devoting a lot of time to it. What gives?"

"Since your talk with Mack Reynolds the other night I've been assigned to Sipes and what he calls 'related matters' here in Sequoya full-time. Mack says I can profit from your experience and he wants me to work closely with you."

"Well, maybe I can profit from yours too," I said and quickly told him about Harvey Holbrook and Doyle Raynes's bond. "Could you check on this Coastal Bail Bonds outfit and see who's behind it?"

His eyes were hard and bright and his smile cold. "I don't need to check. I know the story on it."

"Which is?"

"It's backed by Sipes's Kemah bank. In fact, my guess is he owns the damn thing."

CHAPTER SEVENTEEN

I never got around to eating my sausage and biscuits that morning, and by eleven-thirty I was ready for something substantial. I left the office with nothing particular in mind and wound up at Seabrook's, a barbecue joint over on the north side of town. The place had been built back when I was a kid by a black Korean War combat vet named Rufus Seabrook, a consummate grump who was never shy about voicing his scorn for the human race. What saved his business from failure was the quality of his barbecue. If better ribs or brisket have ever passed mortal lips, I don't know where such a thing might have happened. Now in its third generation of family ownership, Seabrook's was a local institution.

I made my order and paid for it at the counter, and managed to get my favorite corner booth just as the noon rush began. I was waiting on my ribs and had just gotten my iced tea sweetened to my satisfaction when Charlie Morton walked up and slid into the seat opposite me.

"Need to talk to you, Bo."

"Always willing to talk, but I hope you're not trying to wiggle out of our agreement."

"No, I'm just being a good citizen."

"Charlie, I love those good citizen deals, so you just let her rip."

"I know Emmet Zorn was seeing that Twiller woman who was murdered, so I thought you might like to know he came to me about two weeks ago and wanted to put his house and store on the market."

That was interesting. "Really? Did you take the listings?"

"Sure, and I've already sold the house. I didn't even have to put a sign in the yard. The deal goes through forty-five days from the date when we signed the contract, which was five days ago. As far as the store is concerned, I told him that I handled commercial property, but not businesses per se. Luckily, though, I knew a guy in Dallas who's been looking for a little something to retire to down here in East Texas, and he may buy the store. If he does, I'll buy the property myself and lease it to him."

"How much did the house bring?" I asked.

"Seventy-two thousand. It's nothing special, a nice two-bedroom frame house built just before World War Two. But older cottages like it are popular with young couples just starting out, and his has been well maintained over the years. It has beautiful hardwood floors. Heart maple."

I couldn't help but grin, thinking about the hole in the hallway floor. "How about the store?" I asked. "What's it worth?"

"I've offered him a hundred and seventy-five thousand on the property, and he'll let the business itself go for the retail value of the inventory, less markup. Which averages about twenty-five percent. But my point is that it looks like Zorn is planning to bugaloo out of town, and I thought you might want to know."

"You bet I do. I've heard Zorn has a partner in the store."

"He did at one time. I've seen the abstract on the property and all the paperwork on the business. I wouldn't have called my friend in Dallas otherwise. The partner pulled out about six months ago and signed the whole thing over to Zorn. I assume Zorn bought him out, but no details appear in the records."

"I don't suppose you remember the guy's name?"

"Sure I do. And it's a name you'll probably remember from the newspapers."

"Who?" I asked, already knowing his answer.

"Lester Sipes."

When I got back to the office I found Emmet Zorn waiting to see me.

"Come into my inner sanctum," I said.

He came through the doorway with the search warrant in his hand and wariness in his eyes. I sensed that he was mad but too smart to give vent to his anger. Wise move on his part. I decided to kick things off before he could quiz me. "It's legal," I said.

"I see that, but why?"

I pointed at the chair in front of the desk and he dropped reluctantly into it. "Didn't you read it?" I asked.

"Not completely."

"You should have. A search warrant has to name what is being sought."

"Which was?"

I decided it was time for a creative lie. "Any unscripted drugs or anything else that might have tied you to the Twiller murder. An unnamed source said you'd been procuring her some Vicodin from contacts down in Houston."

"And you believed him?"

"I believe everything; I believe nothing," I said in a phony French accent, mimicking Inspector Clouseau. "But since the door to this office is shut and it's your word against mine, I don't mind telling you that I just used the information as an excuse to see if we could find anything to link you to Amanda's death. Which we didn't, and that means you are less of a suspect than you were this time yesterday. Be happy about that."

"I don't like people going through my things, especially when I'm not there."

"Who would?" I asked. "But notification in person isn't a legal necessity if the owner isn't on the premises at the time of the search. Just so long as the warrant is left in a conspicuous place, the requirements of the law have been met."

"So now you're convinced I wasn't involved?"

"I'm more convinced than I was yesterday. And by the way, Doyle Raynes was granted bail by the appeals court over in Tyler as a result of Harvey Holbrook's efforts. Holbrook doesn't come cheap and he doesn't do charity work, so I can't help but wonder what your part in that was."

"I asked a friend in Houston to help the kid out. That's all."

"This friend must be pretty well heeled."

"He is."

"And charitably inclined?"

"Sheriff, what do you want from me?"

"Nothing more right now. Take a hike. I've got work to do."

CHAPTER EIGHTEEN

That afternoon I hit a few of my informants and learned nothing new. Then I decided to visit Danny Kettle. A few years my junior, Danny was a child of the sixties in one respect and one respect only. He'd never had the long hair, never espoused the leftist politics, never worn the freak clothes, never used the hippie/druggie jargon that eventually got mainstreamed. What he did was discover marijuana during his junior year in college, and he'd been blissfully stoned ever since.

Danny's wealthy grandmother had left him a generous trust fund. His father had been a prosperous realtor, and his parents' deaths had left him even more money and a nice fifties-style, split-level house on the east side of town. His life consisted of banking his trust checks, smoking dope, and jabbering distractedly with his live-in girlfriend, a charming New Age nutcase named Wynette Dobbs who was known locally as Wendy the Wiccan. It was a match made in heaven since Danny was a gentle nihilist who believed nothing, while Wendy was an equally gentle optimist who believed everything that came along, provided it was nonsense. Between the two of them they managed to keep all their bases covered.

I pulled up in front of his house and shook my head with a

smile on my face. The yard was a model of well-groomed suburban respectability, the work of a local lawn maintenance firm Danny contracted with. The house was in excellent repair, its wooden trim freshly painted, and a sedate, late-model gray Buick sedan sat primly in the carport. Sometimes it was hard to believe that the place's owner had been fried on weed for the last four decades.

Danny had his feelers deep into the local drug culture since he socialized with many of the town's young dopers. Early in his career as a cannabis zombie, he'd been reluctant to accommodate me in one of my frequent quests for information. After he watched in horror as I flushed a half pound of high-grade Colombian down the toilet, we reached an understanding: if Danny wanted to stay toked up, he had to pay for the privilege by being forthcoming about what I needed to know.

I rang the bell three times before he finally drifted to the front door. "Oh, hi, Bo," he said. "Come on in."

The house was as orderly inside as out. Danny himself was a plump, bland man of medium height with short gray hair and a pink face that was unlined as a baby's bottom. I took a grotesque modernistic chair that was surprisingly comfortable while Danny flopped down on a bulbous peg-legged sofa that was straight out of *I Love Lucy*.

"Have you ever considered getting some new furniture?" I asked. "This stuff is a bit much."

"I know, but it was my mom's, and I hate to think of getting rid of it. She grew up poor, and this place was her dream house."

"Where's Wendy?"

"She and some other lady have gone crystal farming."

"What in the hell is crystal farming?"

"Beats me, Bo. She told me how it works, but you know I can't keep that kind of shit together in my head. So what can I do for you?"

I gave him a cold smile. "What do you think, Danny? Information."

"Yeah, but about what?"

"The Twiller murder."

"I thought you nailed the Raynes kid for that."

"I did," I said. "But there was somebody else involved."

"I wish it hadn't happened, Bo. I hate violence. I really do."

"I know you do, Danny. That's one reason I've cut you as much slack as I have over the years. That and the tips you've given me. So what do you know about Emmet Zorn?"

He spaced out on me for a few moments. Like most tea heads, he often displayed the annoying quirk of not reacting to a question until long after it was asked, if at all. "Danny, what about Zorn?" I prodded gently.

"Zorn? Oh yeah, Zorn. I'm on it, Bo. Thinking, thinking. Hmummm, let me see. I guess the last time I saw him was at a party Wendy and I gave here about a month ago. He wasn't actually invited, but he and that Twiller woman came with some other people who were. But he won't ever be allowed to come back."

"Why not?"

"You need to understand that I've got certain fixed guidelines for parties. Nothing but food and drink consumed in the house. All smoking, whether it's tobacco or anything else, is done on the patio. And no hard drugs. That's an ironclad rule. Anyway, I caught Zorn and some kid doing lines in the kitchen and asked them to leave. That's when he got real buddy-buddy and told me he knew how we could make some real money. I let him know that I had enough money to suit my modest needs, and then he tried to sell me the stuff."

"What stuff?" I asked.

"Coke. A bunch of it. He claimed to be in tight with some big dealer somewhere and said I could double my money. I told him I wasn't interested because I could get fifty years in prison too. Besides, I'm against hard drugs. You know that."

"Was he trying to impress you or did he really want to sell you the stuff?"

"Who knows? If he was trying to impress me, anybody could have told him it doesn't work."

I had to laugh a little. "You're right on that. You're the most underwhelmed guy I ever met."

"What's the point in getting cranked up about all the important people some guy claims to know? I mean, we're all going to be dead in a few years, anyway."

"So just toke up and watch it all slide by. Right, Danny?"

"Works for me, Bo. Always has."

"How about Doyle Raynes?"

"I can't tell you much about him. Kind of a sad little guy, it seems like to me. He's been to a couple of our parties with some other people. Mostly he just goes on about how he's trying to restore that old junk car of his. I have a hard time believing he killed that woman."

"I know," I said. "But there's no doubt the body was hauled in his vehicle, so he had to be involved somehow. What about Amanda Twiller? Did you know her?"

"Not really. She came with Zorn that night. I think she was all pilled up, but she didn't cause any trouble."

"Did she leave with Zorn?"

"I think so. Some of this stuff is hard to remember."

I rose to my feet. "I want you to get on the phone and call some of your doper buddies and find out anything you can for me, Danny."

He spaced out again. "Phone?" he finally asked.

"The telephone, Danny." I pointed at the side table. "That thing over there."

"Oh, you mean the *phone*. Sure, Bo, I'll do what I can."

He followed me to the door. "I'm really kinda glad you stopped by," he said. "It's been a sad day for me."

"How come?"

"I can't find Little Trixie."

"You mean your black Chihuahua?"

"Yeah."

"Danny, that dog died a couple of years ago."

"Are you sure about that? I could swear she was here just yesterday."

I sighed and gave him a gentle pat on the arm. "Have a couple more joints, Danny. She'll come back."

CHAPTER NINETEEN

Like most successful bull riders, Lester Sipes was a small man. He also had a very big hat. Which he happened to be wearing right there in his own hotel suite, along with a western-cut suit of dove gray silk and a pair of sharp-toed cowboy boots that obviously held lifts. When we entered the room he stood gazing out the window with his back toward us. Then he turned around and we saw the hard, chiseled face of a man in his early fifties who'd no doubt led an active and strenuous life. His skin was sun-darkened and weathered much like my own, and his eyes were hooded and deeply set behind lightly tinted aviator bifocals.

"They tell me your name is Bo Handel, Sheriff," he said. "Is that right?"

"It is indeed," I said.

He looked at Toby. "And you are?"

"Toby Parsons, Caddo County chief deputy."

"Pleased to meet you both," he said without offering to shake hands with either of us. "I've had mixed experiences with law enforcement officers over the years. My father was killed by a Texas Ranger named Bonaparte Foley."

He whirled back around to gaze once more out the window, leaving us to absorb this strange announcement. While he was peering at far-distant horizons, he rocked back and forth on his high-lift boots a few times, then he turned back toward us and motioned for us to sit in the room's two armchairs. He himself took the exact center of the sofa and opened an ornate humidor on the coffee table and removed a long cigar.

"Old man Foley actually did me a favor when he wasted the bastard," he said.

"Really?" Toby said. "That's a strange thing for a son to say."

"I think you'd understand if you'd known my father. I feel sure he saved me the trouble of doing it myself."

He stopped speaking and left us to meditate in silence while he went through that tiresome sniffing and clipping ritual with his cigar you often see in old movies—Lord Huffing-Buffington at his exclusive London club getting ready to tell the grimly amusing story of how the wogs in Rangoon buggered Lady Lifton. Eventually he got the damn thing burning and situated in the side of his mouth to his satisfaction.

"My old man was a piece of trash," he said. "A cheap hoodlum of the lowest sort. He beat me and he beat my mother, and he had no taste whatsoever. You should have seen how he dressed."

I was tempted to comment on the irony of his criticizing anybody's wardrobe, but I didn't. Instead I told him we needed to ask him a few questions. He appeared to ponder this idea momentarily, then he lost interest and turned his head a little to look at Toby. "I can't help noticing that you're black," he said.

We were both startled by such an oddball remark, but Toby recovered quickly and looked at me and said, "What's he saying, boss?"

I nodded sadly. "It's a fact, Toby. We've tried to keep it from you, but . . ."

Sipes gave us a quick stretching of his thin, rubbery lips that was meant to look like a smile and didn't. Then he puffed thoughtfully on his cigar. "I'm telling you all this just to let both of you know I don't hold any grudges against cops. I'm not a racist, either."

"None of that has been worrying us, Mr. Sipes," Toby said. "But we would like to know about you and Emmet Zorn."

"Emmet and I are old friends. He helped me one time when I was broke and at my wits' end."

"How about the Raynes boy?" I asked. "Your bonding company got him out on bail. Even if there was no actual cash outlay, there is substantial risk involved. We're a bit curious about that."

He removed his cigar from his mouth and spread his arms expansively. "Emmet says the poor kid is innocent, a victim of circumstances. And part of the joy of being in my position is that I'm able to help those less fortunate than myself."

"I think it's more than likely the kid has something on you or Zorn," I said. "If Zorn were to go down he might decide to cut a deal and take you with him. So I see a little self-interest working behind the scenes."

"I regret that you take that attitude, Sheriff. Is it so difficult to believe that I can have charitable impulses from time to time?"

"After everything I've heard about you, it's damn near impossible."

"One can hear anything," he said. "For example, you may have heard some silly stories floating around about my choice of automobiles. You may have been led to believe that I drive the kind of car I do because I'm superstitious. But that's not true at all."

"It's not?" Toby asked.

"No," he said and leaned forward and gestured dramatically with his hands like a stage magician trying to pull a rabbit out of a hat. "You see, I don't believe in cause and effect. I believe events are controlled by association. I believe that if a black Mercury comes into my life at the same moment a fortunate event occurs, then by surrounding myself with black Mercurys, I can attract other fortunate events my way. A friend of mine who's far more conversant with the subject than I am tells me that my view is borne out by quantum theory."

He stopped speaking and puffed on his cigar while he regarded us with smug satisfaction as though he'd just solved a problem that had vexed the world's greatest thinkers for a thousand years.

"Nonsense," I said. "Cause and effect rules this universe, and in your case the cause is that a big shipment of your cocaine has gone missing. The effect is that you're up here in my part of the country looking for it, and looking pretty damn desperately, unless I miss my guess."

"I don't know anything about any cocaine."

"Then maybe you can tell me why a guy named Paul Arno showed up in town a couple of days ago."

It was a wild shot in the dark, but it hit the target dead center. Sipes jerked like he'd been struck by a bolt of lightning. He recovered quickly and muttered, "Never heard of him."

"Sure you have," I said.

He sat and sucked on his cigar until the coal looked so hot I thought the whole thing was going to explode.

I decided to turn the screws a little tighter. "My friends at the FBI tell me that Arno is connected to the remnants of the old Scorpino mob down in New Orleans. According to them, the New Orleans outfit's not involved in your cocaine business, and Arno isn't really a made guy. He's freelance. Which makes me think he might be working for your suppliers. What happened? Do you still owe them for the stuff? Or maybe you're just fronting for somebody down in Colombia. Everybody has you figured as a kingpin, but what if you're just a delivery boy in a big hat?"

Sipes shivered a little, then seemed to pull his composure back around him like a shroud. He rose and took his cigar out of his mouth and did his staring-out-the-window routine again. When he turned back to us his face was once again impassive. "When my assistants told me you were here, I thought—"

"Thought what? That maybe I'd be satisfied to sit around and listen to you bullshit about quantum physics and elevator boots? No thanks. I've got a murdered woman who was connected to your friend Zorn, and I've got several pounds of a very dangerous drug loose in my town. I'm not in the mood for chitchat."

He looked right at me, and for just a moment it was like a veil had lifted. I could see in the deep wells of his eyes the burning ambition and iron will that had brought him up out of the slums of Fort Worth. "Then since you don't have a warrant, I believe I'll have to ask you to leave."

We went out past the same pair of bodyguards who had let us into the suite. Like Sipes, they wore western-cut suits and monumental hats. However, this duo stood about a foot taller than their boss and came equipped with handlebar mustaches.

"That guy and his charade got under my skin," I said once we were out in the hall.

"You're right about it being a charade. He may have a few screws loose, but he uses his goofy reputation as a sort of shield. So what now?"

"Let's go off the clock and have a beer," I said. "How does that sound?"

After we had a cold one at a little hole-in-the-wall joint on the edge of Sequoya, I dropped Toby off at the courthouse and went home early. I took a quick shower and stretched out on the sofa in the den to wait for Sheila to stop by. I thought the day was almost over, but the hard part was just about to begin.

CHAPTER TWENTY

Everybody called them Gog and Magog. Those weren't their real names, of course. Their birth certificates said Lon and Don Flanagan. The Flanagan boys were identical twins, now forty years old, six feet eight inches tall, and pushing three hundred pounds apiece, most of which was bone and gristle. They were pulpwood cutters, part of an extensive clan that had eked out a precarious existence for generations by feeding the paper mills of central East Texas.

Gog and Magog lived simple lives that consisted of work, hunting, sex with their rawboned wives, and what they called "frolic," by which they meant the periodic near-destruction of the Roundup Club, a large country-and-western dance hall that sat just past the city limit out on Route 9 South. These annual events constituted a sort of demented fall harvest festival for the pair, and usually began near the end of a weeklong drinking binge. Or as Magog explained to me when I talked to him in the jail after the last such affair, "All we wanted to do was have a few more beers and listen to the music."

Nelda Parsons's father was the one responsible for their unorthodox nicknames. One night a decade and a half earlier, he chanced to be driving past the Roundup just as that year's frolic burst out through the front doors and rolled onto the parking lot. Teeth, hair, and eyeballs were flying every which way, along with unlucky patrons and assorted lawmen, including a pair of rookie city cops who'd been foolish enough to answer the frantic call for assistance that had gone out over the police radio. Sweet and gentle man that he was, Reverend Parsons was so shocked by this unrestrained orgy of redneck violence that he later said that for a few horrifying moments he thought the tribulation had come to town, and that Armageddon was at hand.

This statement got wide currency and inspired some other Bible scholar to reach far back into the maelstrom of Old Testament prophecy and extract from the Book of Ezekiel the names Gog and Magog, those two evil nations destined to plague the righteous in the earth's Latter Days. The twins were flattered and let it be known that they considered the nicknames the highest compliments ever paid them.

So it was not a joyful moment for me when Linda Willis hammered on my door a few minutes after seven that evening and interrupted my visit with Sheila to tell me that the Flanagan boys were firmly ensconced at the Roundup a full month before they were due to mount their annual assault on the public peace of Caddo County.

"Have they caused any trouble yet?"

"No, but everybody's on edge. Otis stopped by there for a beer and said that the place feels like last year when we were under a tornado warning for two whole days."

"By the way," I said, "why are you still on duty?"

"I'm pulling a double. One of the evening guys called in sick, and I need the money."

I didn't like my deputies working double shifts, but with barely enough people on the force to cover all three shifts there was nothing I could do about it. "Let me get my boots on," I said.

"I want to go too," Sheila said. "It sounds interesting."

"Why not," I said, shaking my head in bemusement. "The more the merrier."

"You drive," I told Linda when we got to the Suburban. I opened the rear door for Sheila to climb into the backseat.

"What are you going to do?" Linda asked once we were on our way.

"I'm going to make them go home."

"Can you do that? Legally, I mean?"

"Of course not, but I'm going to do it anyhow."

"I've wondered why they always do what you tell them to do," she said. "I mean, they'll fight us deputies, and they'll fight the city cops and the highway patrol, but they won't give you any crap. Why's that?"

"That's one of those stories that's too rough for your young and tender ears."

"Damn it, Bo! I hate it when you say stuff like that. If I wasn't driving this damn truck I'd kick you in the shins."

"Settle down," I said with a laugh. "When we get there you both just stay well back away from those two. And whatever happens, don't shoot one of them. We don't want to annoy them any more than we have to."

Except for the jukebox wailing out a Garth Brooks song that nobody was paying any attention to, the Roundup was almost silent, and the whole place seemed to breathe a sigh of relief when I came in the door. I spotted the twins sitting at a table on the far side of the room, calm and placid and looking like a pair of well-fed bison in striped carpenter's overalls. I walked right up to their table without hesitation. "A little early this year, aren't you, boys?" I said.

"We ain't looking for no frolic tonight, Sheriff," Magog said.

"That's right," Gog said. "We come to town to see you."

"Me?" I asked in surprise. The Flanagans weren't the sort to take their problems to the law, and other than a few times over the years when I'd sent word that I needed to see them, they had never sought me out.

"That's right," Magog said. "We just thought since we were here in town we might as well have a few beers."

"That's right," Gog said. "We got plenty of time 'cause he ain't going nowhere."

"Who's not going anywhere?" I asked.

"That ole boy we found out by our place. Somebody done shot him full of holes and dumped him in the ditch. We heard you was investigating murders this week, and we figured you might want another one."

The Flanagan family was spread all over central East Texas, but the Caddo County branch lived in a cluster of surprisingly neat trailer houses far out in the woods on the upper edge of the Angelina River floodplain in the western part of the county. In wet weather you need a good pickup with mud-grip tires to get there, and a four-wheel-drive vehicle is an even better bet. But the drought made it a snap in the department's Suburban.

We followed the twins' 4X4 Dodge pickup. The route led off the main highway onto a graded county road, and then after a couple of miles onto a narrow logging road that was really nothing more than a pair of ruts that wound their way between two tall dark walls of forest. About a hundred yards short of the last curve that marked the clearing where the Flanagans lived, the Dodge stopped and both men stepped out.

The body was lying faceup in the ditch with four bullet holes in its chest, and it was already beginning to swell a little with the heat. I called out the DPS forensics people once again. Bob Thornton, the local Texas Ranger who covered three counties, showed up right behind them. I was there half the night. We set up flood-lights and combed the area and found nothing. We interviewed Gog and Magog and their wives and children to determine if anyone had heard or seen anything. No one had. I called one of my day-shift deputies to work early and detailed him to follow the ambulance and observe the autopsy. I knew that when it was over I'd have a handful of bullets, and my instincts told me they would match the ones that had killed Amanda Twiller. Which gave me two murder victims and little else. I felt sure that both killings were somehow linked to Sipes and the cocaine trade, but I had no idea how. Nor did I have any idea who'd actually pulled the trigger. And at that point I wasn't too optimistic about ever finding out. The most recent victim, of course, was Doyle Raynes.

CHAPTER TWENTY-ONE

I arrived late for work that morning already worn out and needing sleep. In the outer office I told Maylene to call out to the jail and find out if anybody had come to pick up Raynes when he'd been released on bond the day before. Then I entered my inner office to find Agent Hotchkiss sitting in the visitor's chair in front of my desk drinking coffee. The previous evening I'd left a message about the murder on his voice mail. I filled my own mug and dropped wearily into my chair. "Another day, another dollar," I said.

"Have you got anything on the Raynes killing?" he asked.

"Not a damn thing yet."

"I talked to Arno yesterday," he said.

"I don't suppose you got anywhere with him, did you?"

"Of course not. Deals like we have to offer aren't even on his radar screen. But you got his attention yesterday. He's not used to having his ass kicked, and I don't think he'll want a second application any time soon."

"That makes me feel good. Did you mention the Twiller killing?"

He nodded. "He claims he has an alibi for that, and a motel

receipt from Lake Charles to back him up. And we know he didn't do Raynes because he was in jail."

"What's his alibi?"

"He says he was in that motel with a woman and that she'll confirm his story."

"Do you have her name?"

"Sure," he said and pulled a notebook from his inner coat pocket. "Here it is. Lavonne Avante."

"Must be a stage name. She sounds like a showgirl turned hooker. How about the motel?"

"It's a place called the South Winds Motor Hotel."

"I better check this out," I said.

"I'll do it. I'll make some phone calls and get back to you."

"I also want to impose on you again for a little ballistics work. We'll have the bullets from Raynes later this morning, and I'd appreciate you running them for us as soon as you can. I have a hunch you'll find that they came from the same gun that killed Amanda Twiller."

"That wouldn't surprise me either. And that business of throwing Mrs. Twiller's body on the parsonage lawn stinks to high heaven. If this was a straight-up killing, the perps would have tried to hide the body rather than dumping it in public that way. Either that or just walked off and left it where it fell. The Bureau's behavioral specialists would say that somebody was trying to send a message."

"I've been aware of that all along," I said.

"But what message was it?"

"If I had to speculate, I'd say contempt for Twiller and everything he stands for. Contempt for this community, and contempt for humanity. But in the end, who really knows why these old criminals do half the stuff they do? Sometimes I wonder if they even know themselves."

I called Otis Tremmel and told him to broach Zorn about his whereabouts the evening before. "And if he has an alibi, check it yourself," I said. "Don't trust what he says."

I was about fifteen minutes into my computer work when Carla Wallace slipped into the room, closed the door, and tripped the lock.

"I couldn't help but notice that you latched that door behind you," I said. "Am I in trouble?"

She gave me a quick smile and shook her head and settled gracefully into one of the two chairs in front of my desk.

"Well, if you ain't here to fuss at me, what *is* on your mind?"

"I could have phoned, but I decided to come talk to you in person when Maylene called out to the jail. I just heard about the Raynes boy when I came on this morning. I know who he left the jail with yesterday."

"Who?"

"A lawyer from Center named Nobel Dennard. You know him, don't you?"

That was interesting. "Yes, I do. But how do you happen to be acquainted with the man?"

"I grew up in Center, remember?"

"That's right," I said. "I must be getting senile. So Dennard picked the kid up, you say?"

She nodded. "I was getting off shift as they were leaving. The Precinct Three constable had brought in a drunk driver to book into the jail and—"

"Tom Cryler himself? Not one of his deputies?"

"No, it was Tom, and I happened to notice that he followed Dennard and Raynes down the road when they drove off. I called him on his cell phone a few minutes ago, and he said he stayed behind them all the way out to the old Antioch community."

"Sounds like they were headed toward the river, doesn't it? And that's where the kid's body was found."

"I know."

"Carla, did you know that Linda and I questioned Dennard day before yesterday on the Twiller killing?"

"God, no!"

I nodded. "I've been playing this one close to my vest."

"What made you suspect him?"

"When Linda did the search of Mrs. Twiller's bedroom she found a letter from Dennard that could have been interpreted as threatening. I say 'could' because the wording was ambiguous."

"Don't tell me," she said. "Nobel had an affair with Amanda Twiller."

"That's right, he did. Apparently he was afraid she would expose him to his wife."

She laughed. "His wife knows, Bo. She has to. Nobody could be that stupid. I mean, he was notorious years ago when I was in high school."

"Aside from his philandering, what's the man like?"

"Well, I know that he helped my family recover some damages against one of the big timber companies back when I was in high school and nobody else would take the case. Really fought hard for us, and he was up against some powerful people too."

I nodded. "I see."

"What are you going to do?" she asked.

"Under the circumstances I don't have much choice. Hell, I've already been to see the guy and he wasn't forthcoming, so I'm going to talk to Tom Waller, and then I'm going to ask the judge for a murder warrant on Dennard for the Raynes killing. The Twiller matter I'm going to leave hanging in the wind for the time being."

She nodded and rose from her chair. "I want to see you clear the case, Bo. But I hope Nobel is innocent. I have to be honest with you about that."

"I understand," I said and came around the desk and gently brushed her hair for a moment with my hand and she melted into my arms. After a long, gentle kiss, we broke the clutch. "I wish we could be together more," I said.

"We shouldn't, though. Not as long as I'm working for you."

"I'm just grateful that you don't resent the time I spend with Sheila and Mindy."

"It doesn't bother me a bit, Bo. They're your family, and Mindy needs a man in her life."

"When the weather cools off you're going to start going horse-back riding with the three of us on Saturdays."

"Bo, I don't think we should—"

"Sheila knows, Carla."

"Oh my God! How?"

"She's smart, and she figured it out. Don't worry. She thinks you're good for me."

"Still . . ."

"No still to it. And when this mess is over you and I are going to slip off down to Galveston for a few days. How about that?"

She tilted her head back and lowered her eyelids and gave me a look that was half amused, half affectionate. "Long moonlit walks along the beach, huh? You're a cream puff, Bo Handel. A marshmallow. And one of these days I'm going to toast you."

I kissed her on the tip of her nose and grinned at her. "You're getting pretty close to toasting me right now, so maybe you ought to get on out of here before things get out of hand. You also need to write me up a statement about what you saw yesterday for the record. Track down Tommy Cryler and have him do the same."

"Will do. Are you going to arrest Nobel yourself?"

"No, I'll send a couple of deputies. I won't talk to him today, either. I want to let him stew awhile first."

"Good luck," she said.

"By the way, I took two really nice prime New York strips out of the freezer this morning. Why don't you drop by about seven this evening?"

"I'll be there," she said, her voice happy. "Do you want me to bring anything?"

"Just your libido."

After she left, I put my feet up on my desk and ruminated for a few minutes. When Toby knocked on my door the morning Amanda Twiller had been found, the last person on my mind had been Nobel Dennard. Now it appeared he was in it up to his eyeballs. Whatever "it" was. I didn't particularly like the man, but I didn't dislike him enough to get any personal satisfaction out of his plight.

Then there was my own plight. Why had I, a year earlier, after twenty-eight years in office and at an age when I should have known better, let myself get involved with one of my own deputies? Why had it happened?

I suspect it happened because she was a damned fine-looking woman and I'm a lecherous old goat. Longings repressed during thirty-five years of unthinking fidelity to my wife. "Live with it, Bo Handel," I muttered to myself and laughed.

Introspection is such a wonderful thing.

CHAPTER TWENTY-TWO

After a light lunch I decided to take a rare afternoon off and get some much-needed sleep. I considered leaving a set of elaborate instructions for my staff, but eventually came to the conclusion that I had good people who could use their own heads. I did tell Maylene to see to it that Hotchkiss got a copy of the Raynes autopsy report and the bullets recovered from the body. Then I went home.

I was sound asleep about two minutes after I fell in bed, and I don't remember a time when I'd needed it more. I woke up a little before six and fired up the charcoal grill. After I threw two big grade-A Idaho potatoes in the oven to bake, I began whipping up a tossed green salad with avocados. At a little before seven Carla knocked on the kitchen door. She gave me a quick peck on the cheek and got the bottle of V.O. out of the cabinet and started building us both a drink.

"How goes it all?" I asked.

"Okay, I guess. Billy Don and two deputies from the Shelby County Sheriff's Office arrested Nobel Dennard at his office this afternoon."

"No trouble, I suppose."

"Not a bit," she said. "The man is now securely locked in our jail. And Otis said Zorn is alibied out for all day yesterday. He was at the store until about six and then he went to the Roundup Club here in town. The clerk at the store and the waitresses at the club back him up."

I nodded. "Do me a favor while I finish cooking our supper. Call the jail and tell them that I said to keep Nobel in one of the one-man cells on the third floor. I don't want him in the felony tank, where he might have to fight to keep from being abused. Give him some magazines, let him have coffee now and then, and so forth."

"Okay, but why the red carpet treatment?"

"In my judgment this guy will react better to the carrot than to the stick. Besides, he's a substantial citizen and there's no reason not to give him a little consideration."

"Anything else?"

"Yeah, call Agent Don Hotchkiss and ask him to see if the Bureau has anything on Dennard. The number is on a card stuck to the refrigerator."

"Will he cooperate?" she asked. "I've never had much luck with getting those guys to give up info."

"Use your feminine wiles," I said. "Say 'pretty please.'"

"In your dreams, Bo."

"Just call him. Hotch is a different breed."

An hour later we found ourselves in the den, both as full as feed-lot hogs.

Carla stretched out on the sofa with a long moan and said, "My libido is buried under all that food. I seem to have reached the age when I can't feast and canoodle on the same night. No doubt senility looms just over the horizon."

"To tell the truth, I'm more interested in getting your opinion about this murder case." I laid out the whole story, the letter,

Nobel Dennard, the arrest, Willard Peet and the cocaine. Everything I knew and could think of.

"And?" she asked when I'd finished.

"Tell me if I'm focusing too intently on Dennard."

"Well, he was obviously one of the last people to see the Raynes boy alive. Do you have any other suspects?"

I shrugged. "Maybe Zorn."

She blinked. "That's a new wrinkle."

"It's weak, I know. Can you think of any possible motive Zorn could have had for wanting Amanda Twiller dead?"

"You said he was in the process of dumping her, right?"

"So he claimed."

"So maybe she had something on him and was threatening to expose him. After all, that's what she did with Dennard. Or she might have actually loved Zorn. Did you ever think about that?"

"Not really. I figured it was more a union of convenience since her husband said her various doctors were cutting her off."

"There's nothing in this world more vindictive than a woman who's just been dumped by a man she really cares about."

I couldn't help but smile. "I'll take your word for it."

"How about Arno?" she asked.

"He has an alibi. Or at least he seems to, and there is absolutely nothing to connect him to the crime. That woman who owns the Sawmill Club said Doyle Raynes had gotten pretty tight with Scott Kimball before Scott left town. I'm going to need to follow up on that, but I don't really expect it to go anywhere since Scott hasn't been seen around town in months. He's just about burned his bridges here in Sequoya."

"You know his mother pretty well, don't you?"

"Willa? Sure. She goes to my church, and I've been around her all my adult life."

"What's her story?"

"Not much to it. Her mother died when she was about three, and her daddy wound up raising her by himself. He had some help from an old colored woman named Eula Kemp who kept house for him. The Kemps had lived out there on the Hathaway place forever. They were descended from family slaves."

"Isn't one of the Kemps still alive?" she said.

"Jesse Kemp. He's a Vietnam vet who lives in a shack on top of that big hill about a quarter mile behind Willa's house. He owns that land up there. Willa's great-grandfather left the Kemps a hundred acres in his will."

"Why? That's a pretty big chunk of real estate."

"He did it because Jesse's father was his son."

"Really? Who was his mother?"

"A young black widow who lived out there on the place. Hathaway's wife was dead, and nature took its course."

"So that means that Jesse is Willa's uncle, right?"

"Her great-uncle. Everybody knows about it, but it's just one of those things that people don't talk about. Her daddy wanted her to go to college, but she and Bob Kimball got married not long after high school. They had those two boys in three years. A few years later Bob got killed, and then her older son was murdered. So here she is—waiting tables at the Caravan and having the life worried out of her by a psychopathic brat who's her only living relative. Except for Jesse, of course."

"What's Jesse like?"

"A chronic alcoholic. He gets a veteran's disability from the government because he was shot up pretty bad in Vietnam. The first of every month Willa gets his check and cashes it and makes him buy about half of it up in canned goods and salt pork and dried beans and other nonperishables because he doesn't have electricity. Then she takes him to the liquor store, where he spends the rest on cheap gin and vodka. The booze lasts him about ten days or two weeks. After it's gone he has the DTs for a few days, then he just settles down to wait for the next check. That's his life, and that's the way he wants it."

"You don't sound too sympathetic."

"I have more respect for him than sympathy," I said. "He's the toughest man I've ever met. The way he lives would kill a mule, but it's by his choice, and he won't take any help from anybody, not even Willa."

"Willa always uses her maiden name as a middle name," she said. "I've wondered why."

"I think it's because her people were original settlers here in Caddo County, just like mine. At one time the Hathaways owned about a thousand acres of land and a big mercantile store. It's all gone now, but the name still means something, and that's important to Willa. She's a proud woman despite the mess her life has been."

"I know that," she said. "That's why I hated seeing her with a man like Emmet Zorn."

"What?"

"They were an item before he took up with Amanda Twiller. Didn't you know that?"

"No. Are you sure?"

"As sure as death and taxes," she said. "But it didn't last."

I shook my head in disbelief. "I would have expected Willa to set her sights a little higher than that."

She gave me one of those looks—half exasperation, half pity—that men get from women when we've said something truly stupid. "She set her sights on what was available to a woman who's in her forties and terribly lonely."

I nodded, but wisely I didn't respond since the same thing could be said of another attractive woman near the same age who was hooked up with an old geezer of a sheriff.

"Bo, Sheila came by the office this afternoon to see you. She's worried about that complaint she signed against Paul Arno."

"I'll go ahead and tell her to drop it if she wants to. We don't need it since we've got him on the cocaine."

"Thanks," she said with visible relief. "That's what she was hoping you'd say. So was I."

"I doubt that she has to be concerned about him. I expect he's gone on back down to New Orleans by now."

"Maybe you're right."

I wasn't. Paul Arno was still in Sequoya and would be for a long, long time because nobody would ever come forward to claim his body.

CHAPTER TWENTY-THREE

Early the next morning I dropped by the Caravan to see Willa only to learn that it was her day off. I decided to drive out to where she lived on her family's old farm about six miles northwest of town. A couple of miles past the city limit, my cell phone rang. It was Hotchkiss telling me the FBI had nothing on Dennard—no past suspicions, no pending investigations, no nothing. His name had never even been a temporary blip on their radar screens. "As far as we're concerned he's clean as a hound's tooth," he said.

Willa's house was a sprawling one-story white frame structure built back in the closing days of the nineteenth century. I parked under one of the ancient magnolias in the yard and made my way up the front steps and across the deep porch that surrounded the place on three sides. I knocked on the door, and a few seconds later it opened to reveal Willa wearing a pair of shorts and a cotton shirt.

If it hadn't been for her coal black hair, she would have made a perfect Valkyrie—about five-eight with long, fine-boned arms and legs and a sculptured face with high cheekbones and eyes of deep blue. Even in her forties as she was now, it was easy to see how Bob Kimball had fallen under her spell.

"Hi, Willa," I said.

"Hello, Bo. Is this a social call?"

"Maybe," I said as gently as I could. "I don't really think it's anything bad. I'm just tying up a loose end."

"Then come on in and have a cup of coffee, and we'll make it a social call."

She led the way back into the kitchen and motioned for me to sit at the breakfast table. Then she poured us both a big mug from the percolator on the cabinet and sat down across from me. "It's fresh," she said. "I just made it. And I guess you came to ask about Scott."

I nodded and sipped at my coffee.

"I haven't seen or heard from him in three months," she said. "For a while before that he was back and forth between here and Houston, then he just disappeared."

"What was he doing down there?" I asked. "Do you have any idea?"

She sighed deeply. "The usual Scott crap, I guess. Has it ever been anything different? He said he had some gambling debts and needed money. And like a fool, I wound up giving it to him. That boy sure knows how to push my buttons. He wheedled and played on Bob's death until he got two thousand dollars out of me. How can somebody be so stupid?"

"He's your son, Willa. That's what parents do. It's awful hard to give up on your kids."

"I guess you're right. But why are you asking about Scott this time?"

"You know about Amanda Twiller, of course. I have some solid information that before he left for Houston, Scott had been running around with Doyle Raynes, that boy I arrested for killing her. Raynes was murdered day before yesterday."

"I read about that in the paper," she said. "Do you think Scott could have had anything to do with that? God, I hope not . . ."

"I have no reason to think so at this point. It's just that I need to follow all the leads in a situation like this, no matter how weak they are."

"As far as I know, he hasn't been here in three months. He sure hasn't come to see me if he has. And I never heard him mention that Raynes kid."

"Willa, will you let me know if he comes back into town? I really would like to talk to him."

"Of course I will, Bo. I won't lie for him, and you know it. I might borrow the money to hire a lawyer if he was in really bad trouble, but I won't lie for him, and I won't hide him, either."

"Thank you. It's not something I looked forward to asking you to do."

She set her cup down on the table and stared at me with tears in her eyes. "Thinking about Scott always makes me realize that my life hasn't amounted to much."

"That's not true, Willa. You're kindhearted, and you have a world of friends. There's nobody in this county I'd trust more than you."

She wiped away her tears and gave me a wan smile. "I appreciate you saying that, Bo. I really do. But all the good friends and fine reputation in the world don't seem to matter when I consider that I have no education and no career, and that my husband and one son are both dead and the other son is crazy . . . I've wondered sometimes if Scott isn't my punishment."

"Willa, don't—"

"Bob reenlisted in the Guard when his first hitch was up. We needed the money, and he joked about staying in for twenty years to get retirement. But I didn't want him to, and I was mad about it. Mad and lonely. I would have preferred to go to work, but he wouldn't have it. Then he got called up for two months of active duty and—"

"Hush," I said firmly. "I might have done the same thing in your place."

She smiled wanly. "Good old Bo. You're always on my side, aren't you?"

"Why wouldn't I be?"

She took a deep breath and shook her head. "Scott was a strange child from the beginning. He seemed indifferent to me and to Bob both. Worshiped my dad, though. Even when he was just a baby, Daddy could get him to sleep when he was fussy and nobody else could. He was nine when Daddy died, and that's when the trouble started. I always thought if Dad had lived until he was grown, then maybe . . ."

She stopped speaking and looked down at her cup. I said nothing because there was nothing I could say. We finished our coffee in silence, and then I rose to leave. On the way out she stopped to show me two portrait-sized photos of her boys that hung in the hallway. The shots had been taken just before Hamilton was killed. Except for their golden brown hair, they looked like their mother, with angular Nordic faces that were so fine-boned they were almost feminine. Both boys had been breathtakingly beautiful as children, and they hadn't lost their good looks as they grew older. But there was more to them than their physical appearance. They had some ineffable quality that drew people to them like moths are drawn to a bright light. Although they looked enough alike to be twins, there were differences. Hamilton, the older of the pair, had been open and puppyish—a kid who'd worn his goodwill for his fellow man written on his face. Scott, who was perhaps the more handsome of the two, if such a distinction could be made, had eyes that were coldly distant, and the hint of a smirk hovered around his mouth.

I was glad to take my leave because I hadn't really wanted to come. I walked slowly out to my car and stopped and stood for a few moments looking around. Behind the house lay a large pasture that rose gently upward and crested in a ridge of low wooded hills about a quarter of a mile away. On the ridge's top I could see the tiny cabin where Jesse Kemp lived. By now he would have drunk up his veteran's check, and he would be lying inside, inert and catlike, living on dried beans and salt pork and waiting for the first of the month when he could start his strange cycle once again. I shuddered a little and climbed in my cruiser and drove away.

CHAPTER TWENTY-FOUR

On the way into town I called the jail and told them to bring
Nobel Dennard down to one of the interrogation rooms.
A few seconds later my cell phone buzzed. It was Danny Kettle.
"What you got for me?" I asked.

"Well, Bo, it's pretty interesting, but I can't identify my source
because he'd kick my ass if he found out that I told you who he
is. I hope you can live with that."

"Sure."

"Okay. You were asking about Zorn, and this guy I know happened to come by to make a little delivery not long after you left. He
says Scott Kimball stole that cocaine Zorn was trying to sell me."

"Go on," I said.

"Well, he said Zorn has been frantic ever since it happened."

"I'd think he would be if the story is true," I said. "But how in
hell does this guy claim he found out about something like that?"

"He claims Zorn halfway hit him up about strong-arming the
kid a little for him. See, the story is that Scott is trying to ransom
the stuff or something. Apparently, he doesn't have the contacts or
resources to move it himself, but he wants Zorn to cut him in on
the deal. He says they're trying to hammer out a compromise."

"Danny, I have a hard time believing Zorn was careless enough to let Scott know he had the stuff in the first place. And secondly, nobody has seen Scott around town in months. I just talked to his mother, and she hasn't seen him either."

"Well, I do know that Zorn likes to put on the dog about what a player he is. I mean, hell, he told me he had some of the stuff weeks ago, so? Besides, there aren't any secrets anymore, Bo. It's all out there if you can see the patterns. People talk, somebody else puts two and two together, and then, bingo! There it is. I mean, if they can haul the president in and make him explain his blow jobs on national TV, what chance have the rest of us got?"

I shook my head in amusement. "Your logic is infallible, Danny. Did your informant happen to give you any idea where Scott could be found?"

"No, and this isn't the kind of guy I can ask something like that. Actually, I didn't really ask about Zorn. His name just came up in conversation, and my guy was laughing about it. He thinks Zorn's a jerk."

"Danny, how reliable is this source of yours?"

"Gee, Bo. You're asking me to make judgments in what ought to be your area of expertise. I mean, I just lay the shit out there and you're supposed to evaluate it."

"Come on, Danny. Give me some idea."

"Well, he does like to have people think he has all the secret, inside info denied us lesser mortals. I might not bet any heavy money on the story, but I still think he's solid enough that you ought to look into it a little. I mean, don't hold it against me if it's all crap. I'm just the conduit."

"I won't, Danny. And keep on it for me, will you?"

"Do I have any choice in the matter?"

"No," I said with a laugh. "But I phrased it politely because good manners never killed anybody."

"Talk to you later, Bo."

I called Toby and told him quietly to ask the other deputies and the city cops if anybody had seen Scott Kimball in town in the last few weeks.

"Do you want me to check things out with my informants?" he asked.

"Let's not ring their bells at this point. I have my doubts about the story, so just be casual about it."

I found Nobel Dennard drinking a cup of coffee under the watchful eye of one of the jailers. I'd let him keep his street clothes, minus his belt, and he looked a little rumpled and showed a day's growth of stubble.

"Did you get your phone call?" I asked.

"They let me phone my wife before we left Center."

I nodded. "You'll need some clean clothes unless you want some jail-issue orange coveralls. I'll tell them to let you make a couple of calls a day. I'm not holding you to strict jailhouse rules."

"I appreciate that."

"Have you had breakfast?"

"Yeah, and it was pretty good. I'm not a gourmet, so I doubt that I'll have any complaints about the chow."

"And I know you have heard the Miranda warning and understood it."

"Right."

"Do you have a lawyer?"

"For the time being I'm representing myself."

I gave him a rueful grin. "You know what they say about a lawyer who defends himself, don't you?"

"Sure. That he has a fool for a client."

"Call if you decide to get somebody else. And let your wife know that she can bring you some clean clothes and some books. Everything will be searched pretty good, so tell her not to bring anything that might embarrass either of you."

He nodded. "And once again, I appreciate it."

"Now, Nobel, we got to talk a little about the case. Three reliable witnesses saw you leave the jail with Doyle Raynes in your car. One of the precinct constables followed the two of you all the way out to the old Antioch community. Doyle was found murdered that same night down near the river about a mile off that very same road."

"Your point being?"

"You can see that this looks bad for you."

"Maybe it does, and maybe it doesn't. But I have nothing to say about it."

"Have you ever heard of a man named Lester Sipes?"

"Sure. With all the publicity he got a few years ago, everybody has heard of him."

"Have you ever met him?" I asked.

He sighed and shook his head. "Bo, I will admit to nothing beyond what is common knowledge or public record. I have heard of Sipes and that is all I will say on the subject."

"How about Emmet Zorn?"

He shook his head once again. "I have nothing more to say."

We locked eyes and stared at each other for the longest time, neither looking away. Then I said, "You know, Nobel, I got some real doubts that you had anything to do with this mess, no matter how bad it looks for you. That means I would be easy to convince if you would just say something in your own defense."

"Sorry, Bo. I can't do it."

"Can't or won't?"

He laughed a little. "Is there really a difference?"

Back at the office I received two calls in rapid succession. The first was from Tom Waller. He had the particulars of Arno's release, and I didn't like them one bit. "What do you mean we have to give him his gun back?" I asked in disbelief.

"He's got a Louisiana concealed carry permit, and Texas has a reciprocal arrangement with those folks over there."

"But how in the hell did a guy like him ever get a permit in the first place?"

"He qualifies, Bo. He's never been convicted of a felony. We can have it suspended until there is a disposition on the charges, but it will take a couple of weeks to run it through the bureaucracy. Meanwhile, by law he's entitled to his weapon."

I hung up the phone just as Maylene came in and laid a half dozen outgoing letters on my desk for me to sign. "What?" she asked, no doubt reading my face.

"Oh, nothing much. There's just a Mafia hit man running around town with a legal pistol in his pocket, and at the same time it looks like we've also got a million dollars' worth of high-grade cocaine loose somewhere."

"Well, Bo, nobody ever promised you a rose garden."

"Thanks, Maylene. It does my heart good to know I work with such sympathetic folks."

The second call was from Hotchkiss telling me that the bullets from Doyle Raynes's body came from the same weapon that killed Amanda Twiller.

"And you were right about Lavonne Avante," he said. "She's a call girl. Actually, she manages the Lake Charles branch of a fancy escort service out of New Orleans. She only works very special clients herself, and she doesn't come cheap. And there's more. The South Winds Motor Hotel is an interesting place. It was built about thirty years ago by an old guy named Rousas Shima as an investment for his retirement. Elderly Albanian immigrant, works hard, retires and converts all his assets into a nice little business that's meant to see him through his golden years. Sounds like a heart-warming story until you find out that Rousas was a good friend and occasional business partner of Angelo Scorpino, the late and unlamented mob boss of South Louisiana."

"Who runs the place now?" I asked.

"Rousas's grandson, a punk named Thomas Shima. He goes by Toodles, and he's got a couple of larceny convictions."

"Toodles? Where in the world do these people come up with these damned names?"

"Beats me," he said with a laugh.

"I assume Toodles is a known associate of all the right folks."

"Of course. He's mobbed up to his eyeballs."

"I need to look into this, but my badge doesn't pull much weight outside Texas. That federal ID of yours would be a big help."

"When do you want to leave?"

"It's a two-and-a-half-hour drive, so let's get moving."

"Give me thirty minutes to make a few phone calls. I think I can grease the skids a little."

The time was well spent. It turned out that Toodles Shima was on federal probation for credit card fraud. Better still, he was on thin ice with his probation. Hotchkiss had spoken with his supervising officer, and she was willing to go with us to question him.

CHAPTER TWENTY-FIVE

Lake Charles is a refinery and port city of some seventy thousand inhabitants on the Calcasieu River about thirty miles inland from the Gulf of Mexico and the same distance from the Texas border. Back in the 1920s, it was opened to oceangoing ships when a deep water channel was dredged up from the Gulf. Hurricane Rita had done the place a considerable amount of damage, but signs of rebuilding were everywhere. The town's lone skyscraper, the twenty-one-story Capital One Tower, could be seen for miles across the flat coastal plain of South Louisiana.

On the way over, Hotchkiss asked me about the bookie I'd told him about earlier. "When are we taking him?"

"A couple of days."

"What's the story on the guy?"

"His name is Lloyd Quinn, and he came out of Houston originally. The man was a pretty successful poker player until a couple of heavies caught him using a holdout table and beat the ever-loving hell out of him. Really broke him up. See, he was managing a bowling alley and running his poker game in a back room. One of the guys he's been cheating used a bowling pin on him, and the experience more or less broke his spirit. Since then he's been nickel-and-diming and writing a little book. My information is that he's

working for an old character over at Fillmore named Sam Weyland, who is the guy I'm really after. Twice before I've busted his
people, but they wouldn't roll over on him."

"Mack said you didn't fool with gambling much."

I sighed. "I don't mess with the nighttime craps games that go
on in deserted buildings out in the country. Nor do I get upset
about some guy running a little poker out of his den on weekends.
I don't like it, but I have too much to do to chase after that kind
of penny-ante crap. But gambling with bookies in this part of the
country is done mostly by phone, and that means it's really gambling on credit. Which means people sometimes get in over their
heads, and you know what that leads to."

"Right. Strong-arm collections."

"You got it. And I won't tolerate that kind of thing in my
county."

"Why do you think this guy is booking for Weyland?"

"That's what my informants say. He hasn't got two nickels to
rub together, so he has to have somebody bankrolling him."

When the agent spoke there was bitterness in his voice. "I'm
ready whenever you're ready. My dad gambled away damn near
every dollar he ever made, so I have no patience with the practice. You give the word and we'll bring the full weight of the
federal government down on this Mr. Quinn's testicles."

I'd been to Lake Charles several times before and had no trouble
finding the café a couple of blocks off Interstate 10 where we were
to meet Shima's probation officer.

She turned out to be a white Creole named Camille DeMour.
Tall, slim, and about fifty, she had short silver hair and an elegant
face with high cheekbones and warm brown eyes. We introduced
ourselves and I asked if she could give us enough time to have a
piece of pie since neither of us had eaten breakfast.

"Sure, but if you want something more substantial this place always has seafood gumbo ready to serve, and it's very good."

Hotchkiss and I each ordered a bowl of gumbo, and while we waited for our food I filled her in on Arno and the background of the two killings. "I know he didn't do the Raynes boy," I said. "He was in jail when it happened. Supposedly he has an alibi for the Twiller shooting, but considering that his alibi witness is a hooker, and the receipt comes from a motel owned by a man known to be connected to organized crime, you can see why I needed to check this out."

"Indeed I do, and Toodles Shima will cooperate or I'll have him up before a revocation hearing. I'm just looking for an excuse, anyway."

"Ma'am, that's pretty strong," I said. "I didn't come down here to cause you any trouble."

"You won't. It's my prerogative. Toodles is scum, and his father and grandfather were scum before him. I hate these people. My dad and my grandfather were both captains in the Louisiana State Police. The syndicate was a nickel-and-dime affair until Huey Long's day. He gave them free rein in South Louisiana in return for their support. Granddad knew him well, and said he was the most ambitious man to infest this planet since Napoléon. He wanted to be president, you know."

"Do you know anything about this Lavonne Avante?" I asked.

"She's a whore. What else is there to know? Her real name is Joan Fulmer, and she's North Louisiana white trash. At one time she was a stripper, but she wanted better things. I suppose she serviced the right people enough times, and as a consequence wound up running this fancy escort business here in town. I've heard that she invests wisely, and they say she's a millionaire several times over."

"That's rare for a hooker," I said. "Most of them wind up broke and living in ratty trailer houses somewhere."

She gave me a cold smile. "She's not your average whore. You'll see what I mean."

Our gumbo came. Hotchkiss and I were both starving, and we bolted it down. When we finished, I lingered inside to pay the check, then joined my companions outside.

The South Winds turned out to be a sturdily built, woodsy place of dark brick and weathered cedar. Besides about fifty rooms in two wings that curved around a large pool, it consisted of a central building that housed the offices, a restaurant, and a night-club. It was only a block off I-10 on the edge of an upscale sub-urb, but occupancy seemed low.

"It doesn't look like they're very busy," I said.

"They've been hurting since gambling became legal," Ms. De-Mour said as we stepped from the Suburban. "This town has too many hotels because of the casino industry. Several of the casinos have their own hotels, and they rent their rooms very cheaply as a draw and make their money on the gambling. Toodles would love to get a gaming license, but his felony conviction prevents it. This place is not his only means of support, and the land alone is worth more than the replacement cost of the buildings. I expect it to burn down some night."

Camille DeMour seemed to know her way around the South Winds. She led us right on past the protesting desk clerk and down a short corridor. At its end stood an imposing walnut door with fancy brass hardware. She didn't hesitate and she didn't knock. Instead, she reached down and turned the knob and walked right in with us behind her. The office held two men and a young woman, and they were all laughing like George Carlin was there giving them a personal performance.

One of the men was thickset and prosperous-looking and about sixty. The other man sat behind the desk in a tall leather execu-tive's chair. He was slim with dark hair and sharp, ratty eyes that no doubt were in the habit of seeing things they weren't meant to see. He wore a peppermint-striped cotton dress shirt, a red tie, and a pair of fancy red suspenders.

The girl looked like a cocktail waitress. She was in her twenties, with short blond hair, a short skirt, a short frilly apron, and probably a severe shortage of brains. She kept giggling several seconds after her companions stopped, then she turned around and saw us, and her mouth fell open.

"Who the hell are you people?" the thickset man asked.

Hotchkiss stuck his ID about six inches from the guy's nose and said, "I'm Special Agent Don Hotchkiss of the Federal Bureau of Investigation, and that's all you need to know. Unless, of course, you'd like for me to start poking around in your business. Or maybe you'd prefer to leave?"

The man didn't answer. He just flashed a quick smile, sprang to his feet, and after treating Toodles to a two-finger salute, he strode briskly out of the room. The girl rose gracefully and slid her hand across the desk toward Shima. "Tonight after work?" she asked.

He closed his eyes and seemed to wish he were somewhere else. Then he gave her a faint nod without touching her hand.

As she left, she glanced at each of us in turn with a smug little smile on her face that was meant to let us know that she had something going with the big boss. As if that weren't already obvious.

"To what do I owe this visit?" Shima asked Camille. "I was trying to have a business conference here, you know."

"I'm the man you need to talk to," Hotchkiss said.

"Huh?"

Hotchkiss pointed at DeMour. "She writes you up for violating the terms of your probation, which specifically forbid you from consorting with known organized crime figures. I arrest you right here and now, and within the hour your ass is firmly lodged in the Calcasieu Parrish Jail. Tomorrow morning bright and early we haul you down to the federal courthouse where we ask for an expedited revocation hearing, which we will get and which you will lose. By tomorrow afternoon you are on your way to federal prison. Now, how does that sound to you?"

"What organized crime figures?"

"Big Paul Arno," I said.

He seemed confused. "Paul Arno? . . . Just who in the hell are you?"

"I'm Sheriff Handel from over in Caddo County, Texas, and I'm here working a murder case."

"I don't understand," Shima said. "I've never been there."

"No, but Arno has," I said. "I beat the crap out of him and threw him in jail a few days ago."

This seemed to impress him. "You beat the crap out of Paul Arno?"

"So you admit knowing him?" Ms. DeMour asked.

"I know who he is. I try to stay away from him as much as possible. He's nuts and he's dangerous."

"Your father didn't find him too nuts to make use of his services on at least one occasion," she said.

"I don't believe that," he said without much conviction. "And I resent it."

They stared at each other for a few seconds. "Why have you got it in for me?" he asked. "Look, I admit to a little credit card fraud. Hell, I pled out so there's no way I can deny it. Minor stuff, and that's all it's ever been with me. I'm just a little guy trying to get by in a tough old world, and a few times in the past I've trimmed the edges a little. You know, cut a few corners. But I don't run with people like Paul Arno. Besides, I'm trying to do all the right things now."

"Sure you are," Camille said. "And I just got elected to the College of Cardinals."

He threw up his hands in exasperation. "Maybe if you tell me what this is all about . . ."

Hotchkiss laid a photocopy of the hotel receipt on Shima's desk. "A woman named Amanda Twiller was killed up in Sequoya a few nights ago," he said. "Two days later, Sheriff Handel arrested Arno for assaulting a female reporter in front of a local restaurant. So we have a possible murder for hire, and we have a known hit man in town at approximately the same time. The only problem is that Arno claims that he was here at your motel with a hooker named Lavonne Avante when the killing took place, and he has this receipt to back him up."

"Let me see that," Shima said and reached across the desk. "Hmm . . . Are we off the record here?"

"What do you mean?" Hotchkiss asked.

"Is Arno ever going to know I helped you?"

"We'll never tell him," I said. "He may put two and two together, but he won't hear it from us."

"And that's the best deal you're going to get," Ms. DeMour said.

"Okay," Shima said. "Just please don't rat me out. Arno hasn't been here in a couple of months."

"How would you know?" Hotchkiss asked.

"My people always tell me when he comes by because he's a pain in the ass. Besides, he never fails to drop by the office so I can see how important he is."

"What does he do?" I asked. "Rent a room to meet some woman?"

"Rent? You gotta be kidding me. Big Paul doesn't rent things. He takes them. He never pays a nickel, always runs up a big bar bill, eats like a hog in the restaurant. But no, he usually doesn't fool around with girls while he's here. He just checks in when he needs a place to stay while he's in town on business."

"What kind of business?" Hotchkiss asked.

"I don't know. I've heard he's got some street-level scams going here in Lake Charles."

"How about this receipt?" I asked, pushing the paper across the desk toward him.

He examined it carefully. "The desk clerk who was on duty at this time and date is a straight-up girl. She wouldn't fake a record of any kind even if I asked her to do it. My guess would be that he got Willie Day to cut this thing before he even left for your town."

"Who's Willie Day?" I asked.

"The guy who handles all of our computer stuff. He's a weird little geek. Skinny, jumpy, wears all that 1960s Beatles stuff. Turtlenecks, bandy-legged pants, that kind of crap."

"Is he your employee?"

He shook his head. "Private contractor. He's got a bunch of other clients."

"Could he make the computer print a bogus date on the thing?" I asked.

"This kid could change the dates on coins coming out of the Denver mint. You can't believe what he can do with a computer. He's the best there is, but he'd pimp his own mother down to Rio if there was fifty bucks in it for him."

"We need to talk to him," Hotchkiss said.

Shima shrugged. "Until he gets back from vacation, you can't. Not unless you want to fly to Bermuda. We got a letter two days ago saying he was leaving and giving the name and number of the guy who would be handling his accounts while he's gone."

Just then Camille DeMour's cell phone beeped. After listening for a few seconds, she said, "We're having a party. You just come right on back. Toodles will be very happy to see you."

Shima held up his hands in supplication. "What now? I was trying to get some work done here, you know."

"An old friend of yours has come calling," she said.

The door opened and a man who appeared to be in his midforties in a rumpled seersucker suit stepped into the room. He was of medium height with a bit of a potbelly, a hard, homely face, and happy eyes.

"Meet my cousin, Roland DeMour," she said. "Roland is a lieutenant with the state police. Works organized crime. He and Toodles go way back."

Roland DeMour gave Shima a little wave. "Hi, Toodles baby. Been missing seeing you around."

"Ahhh, God . . ." Shima groaned. "What did I do to deserve this?"

"What about Lavonne Avante?" Hotchkiss asked.

"I don't think she's been by here in months," Shima said. "That cherry red Mercedes of hers is hard to miss. It's the only one in town."

"Does she meet some of her tricks here?" I asked.

"Oh, hell no," he said. "Our walls aren't thick enough to stifle the screams."

I looked around, puzzled. "Screams?"

"Lavonne is a dominatrix," Camille DeMour said. "Whips and leather and high-heeled boots. She no longer takes straight calls. Instead she specializes in high-priced floggings for the carriage trade. You know, lifestyles of the rich and needlessly angst ridden."

"I don't think we have to worry much about that up in Sequoya," I said.

"It's a right-wing thing, dearie," she said. "On the other side of the spectrum, you have the guilt-obsessed rich liberals who've inherited fortunes that came from screwing the public and polluting the environment. They throw themselves into every trendy cause that comes along, no matter how idiotic. The rich righties hire whores like Lavonne to give them a good thrashing so they can purge their guilt and then go right on screwing the public and polluting the environment."

Even Shima laughed.

"If you want, I'll go with you to see Lavonne," Roland DeMour said. "That's why Camille called me."

"Sure," I said. "We'd be obliged to you."

As we rose to leave, Shima said, "Just don't rat me out to Arno."

"That will be our little secret," Hotchkiss said. "At least it will be as long as you keep giving me information when I need it."

"Awww, shit," Shima groaned. "I thought this was one of them quid pro quo deals."

"Nope," Hotchkiss said. "It's one of those permanent deals."

CHAPTER TWENTY-SIX

Expedited hearing?" Camille DeMour said to Hotchkiss once we were out in the hall. "That's a new one on me. I didn't know that federal revocation procedures allowed such a thing."

He shrugged. "I'm learning some really creative law enforcement techniques from Sheriff Handel."

We drove her back to the café to get her car. She took her leave of us, and took our professions of profound gratitude along with her. It was Roland DeMour's day off and he had come in his personal vehicle. He left it at the South Winds and rode with us, first to the café to drop Camille off, then he directed us across town to a shady, upscale suburb where the houses would have averaged a quarter million dollars or more.

"This escort deal has a small office downtown," he said. "Lavonne has a couple of girls covering it, but mostly she works out of her house."

"You know her pretty well?" I asked.

"Sure. Hookers are some of the best snitches a lawman can have. But I'm sure you know that as well as I do."

"Only in theory. We've had very few cases of prostitution in my county over the years, and they've all been outsiders just passing through."

"What's Avante like?" Hotchkiss asked.

"Thirty-five years old and looks ten years younger. Smart, classy, fluent in both French and Spanish, has all the social graces. And she's learned it all on her own. Her old man was a drunken plumber. He beat her mother to death when she was about fifteen, and she's been peddling her ass in one way or another ever since. That part I could kinda admire if that was as far as it went. I mean, we all do what we have to, and it's to her credit that she didn't let the world beat her down. But at one time she was a blackmailer, and I know of a couple of guys she ruined just because it amused her to destroy their lives."

"That's a good way to get killed," I said.

"Yeah, but she's quit all that business. Me and her have come to an understanding."

"Yes?" I asked.

DeMour laughed a tight little laugh. "Yeah. For some reason I can do things for her that nobody else can do. I think it's because I know what makes her tick."

Lavonne Avante's house was constructed of dark brick and weathered wood much like the South Winds, with a front door of seasoned oak that looked like it belonged in a medieval castle. DeMour ignored the bell and pounded on the door. A few seconds later it opened to reveal a black maid in a black uniform and a white apron. She obviously recognized DeMour because she smiled and stepped back to admit us.

Inside, the place reeked of money—sophisticated, carefully spent money. The floors were mottled white marble in fifteen inch squares with simple Oriental rugs in greens and golds. The walls were a soothing dark green. A bit of carefully chosen modern art here, an exquisite Chinese vase on a Louis Quinze table there, evidence of good taste everywhere. It was hard to believe that the home was owned by a nouveau riche prostitute who laced herself up in a leather corset and whipped men for pay.

DeMour led us into a library whose walls held row after row of books. Much to my surprise, most of them showed signs of actually having been read. At the far side of the room a woman sat behind a French Empire desk, talking on the telephone. Off to her right, double doors of lightly tinted glass opened onto a landscaped garden.

The woman herself was small and petite, with short, dark hair, ivory skin, and dark eyes. She wore a white silk blouse and a pair of black lounging slacks. Her only jewelry was an antique garnet ring on the third finger of her left hand. When she put down the phone and turned to look at us, I saw a face that belonged on an eighteenth-century cameo. Her background might have been plebeian, but her appearance was pure aristocrat.

"Hello, Lavonne," DeMour said.

"Hello, Fat Rolly," she said. "So you've come to see me again."

"Can't stay away."

"What's the matter, Fat Rolly? You bored? And by the way, you've gone and dribbled spaghetti sauce on your shirt. Poor Rolly. He's such a slob."

He gave her a serene smile, his eyes sleepy, a calm, knowing smile on his face. "You know what happens when you talk to me that way, don't you?"

"Is that what lights your fire, Fat Rolly?"

"It's not a matter of what lights my fire, dearie. It's your fire that we're talking about." He pointed at me. "This is Sheriff Handel from Texas. And this other gentleman is Agent Hotchkiss of the FBI. You're going to tell them what they want to know or I'm going to drag you in that special room of yours and use some of your own toys on you. How would you like that, my little Bumblebee? So you better be a good girl and mind your manners."

She motioned for us to sit. Hotchkiss and I took a pair of French Empire chairs that sat beside the desk while Roland DeMour perched on the corner of the desk itself.

"We need to know about Paul Arno," I said.

"What about him?" she asked.

"When did you see him last?" I asked.

"I haven't seen him in a couple of months, but I talked to him last week. He called me."

"What was the nature of that call?" Hotchkiss asked.

Avante stared at the young agent for a moment, then mocked in a high falsetto, "'*What was the nature of that call?*' Damn, but you sound like that idiot who does the Crime Stoppers segment on TV. Is there some kind of special school where a guy like you can learn to talk like he's got a broom handle up his ass?"

DeMour reached over and rapped his knuckles on the desk right in front of her. "I told my friends how sweet and cooperative you were going to be," he said. "And here you go embarrassing me. You keep on, and it's going to be a hot time on the old town tonight. And you know what I mean by that, don't you, Bumblebee?"

"I think Fat Rolly's getting all excited," she said.

I didn't. Roland DeMour was as calm as an icicle, but Lavonne Avante's face had an expectant look like I used to see on the faces of country girls seeing the Texas State Fair midway for the first time.

"And I think you need to cut the crap and get with the program," DeMour said.

"Why not?" she said with a dismissive shrug. "Arno's nothing to me, anyhow. He told me that if anybody called or came by asking, I should say that I spent the night with him at the South Winds last Monday night."

"But you didn't, did you?" I asked.

"Hell no," she snapped. "I've never slept with that bastard."

"Then exactly what is the nature of your relationship with Arno, Miss Avante?" Hotchkiss asked.

She gaped at him once again, then asked, "Please tell me where you learned to talk that way."

"Cut the wiseass and answer his question," DeMour said

She laughed but her expression was eager. "My relationship with Arno is that he's nuts about one of my girls. And that's it. I've known him for years, but he hasn't been a client until the last few months. Actually, he's not really a client because he never pays. I don't think he pays for anything."

"So we've been told," I said. "What's this girl's name?"

"Brandi Springer. She's out of town right now visiting her family in Dallas."

"Do you have their phone number, by any chance?" I asked.

"I run an escort service, not a welfare agency. I don't keep dossiers on my people. Which means I have her number here in town, but not her parents' number."

"I wonder why he didn't get this Brandi to alibi him out instead of you," DeMour said.

Avante laughed. "Probably because she has the brain of a gnat, Rolly. Even a pinhead like Arno would have sense enough to know she couldn't hold it together under questioning from a deputy constable, let alone somebody who knew what they were doing."

"I don't suppose he told you why he wanted you to do this," I said.

"No, and I didn't ask."

"Did you agree to lie for him?"

"Of course I did. I don't need any trouble with a guy like that. Now are you people through? I hope so because that's all I know."

DeMour looked across at me. I nodded, and Hotchkiss and I rose. Lavonne Avante got to her feet and walked with us to the hall door. "You're not leaving too, are you, Roland?" she asked.

"What do you want me to do?"

"Roland, no . . ."

"Want a little session, do you?"

"Roland, please . . ."

"Spell it out for Rolly. Let our friends hear. You know you love that."

"Roland, please don't make me . . ." Then to my utter amazement, Lavonne Avante put her hands over her face and actually started crying.

He pulled a card from his pocket and handed it to me with a shrug. "Call me if I can help any more with this deal."

"You're staying here?" Hotchkiss asked.

"Yeah, she can take me back to get my car later. You two go on ahead."

When we reached the front door the maid appeared out of nowhere. "Good afternoon to you gentlemen," she said sweetly. "You all come back now, you hear?"

As we walked across the drive toward the Suburban, Hotchkiss asked, "Bo, what in hell was going on back there?"

"Hotch, most hookers are flakes in one way or another. Beyond that, that story is too rough for your young and tender ears."

CHAPTER TWENTY-SEVEN

On the way back to Sequoya I called the office and put out a statewide hold and alert bulletin on Paul Arno. I also instructed them to call the Dallas PD and see if they had anything on Arno's girlfriend. We pulled into Nacogdoches in time to eat a late supper at a barbecue joint on the north side of town. I got home a little after nine to find Carla stretched out on the sofa in the den wearing a pair of loose white cotton shorts and a halter top, reading a book.

"I walked over," she said. "I thought you might want me to fix you something to eat."

I shook my head. "I done et, but I could use a drink. How about you?"

"Sure, and if you're too tired from your trip, we can just snuggle. I like that too."

"Let's have that drink and see what happens, okay?"

"That's fine."

In the kitchen I poured us each a healthy dollop of V.O. over ice. Carla downed half of hers with one quick pull.

"Just snuggle, huh?" I asked, sipping at my glass.

"If that's all you're up for, Bo."

"No unreasonable demands, you say?"

She shook her head and grinned. "Never."

"I'm beginning to think you're too perfect. I keep waiting for the other shoe to drop."

"I'm not wearing shoes," she said and drained her glass.

"You don't appear to be wearing much else, either."

Her laughter was like a tinkling silver bell as she set her glass down and drifted toward me, a knowing smile on her face, a smile that was as old as sin itself.

As always, Carla was gone when I woke up the next morning. She slept less than any woman I ever knew and seemed to have an alarm clock inside her head.

The first thing I did when I got to the office was look over the sheet from the night before. To my relief, it had been a quiet evening. No major eruptions at any of the clubs, and only one domestic dispute. But Arno hadn't turned up. A quick check revealed that he was still registered at the Eight Ball Motel on the south side of town, but had not been in his room all night. I was deep into the usual paperwork when Maylene buzzed to tell me that a Sergeant Wolf of the Dallas Police Department Vice Division was on the phone for me.

I picked up the receiver. "Bo Handel here," I said.

"Hello, Sheriff. When I got to work this morning, I found a note telling me to call you. I understand you're inquiring about Brandi Springer."

"Right. It's a murder investigation or I wouldn't have bothered you folks."

"No problem. Just what do you need to know about her?"

"Give me all you got. The whole ball of wax."

"That would take a week. This girl comes from a family of hoodlums. Her dad was an oldtime Dallas gambler named Claude Springer who owned a domino hall down on the east end of Elm

Street and ran a sports book out of the back room. Her mother is a former call girl who pimped Brandi out to some rich perverts when she was about thirteen. Her brother is in federal prison for mail fraud. Her father's brother was a hired goon for Cat Noble back when he was fighting Benny Binion for control of the Dallas gambling rackets. And it goes on and on."

"What's the girl like herself?" I asked.

"Twenty-five years old. Beautiful, sexy, and dumb as a bag of rocks. She just sits there filing her nails and waiting for something to happen. With a body like hers, something always does. I've handled her three times, twice for prostitution and once for misdemeanor larceny. How does she tie in with your murder?"

"The main suspect so far is a New Orleans hit man named Paul Arno. She's supposed to be his girlfriend."

"Never heard of him," he said. "Is he Mafia?"

"Kinda-sorta. The Feds say he's not actually a made guy, but he works for the New Orleans outfit from time to time. He freelances too, and he has his own rackets going. Anyhow, the girl is supposed to be in Dallas visiting her family right now."

"Oh, she's here all right. But she's not visiting. She's come home to stay."

"How did you happen to know that?" I asked.

"Informants," he said with a laugh. "How else do you find out anything in this business? She and her mother are setting up to run an outcall massage service out of the old man's domino parlor. He got crosswise with another bookie a couple of years ago and wound up with a twenty-two hollow-point right in the center of the forehead, but the family still owns the building. They've signed on a few local girls, all hookers. I've been meaning to get by there and jerk their chains a little just to let the old lady know we haven't forgotten about her. I'll put that on the front burner this morning."

"That's an awful big favor on your part," I said.

"No favor to it. It could be that Arno is financing the operation, and if a guy like him is moving into Dallas I need to know about it. Anything specific you want me to ask her?"

"Anything about Arno you can pry out of her. It's been my experience that these old boys like to brag to their women. Pillow talk, whatever he's been up to or what he's planning. His hopes and dreams."

"Oh, I can tell you all about his hopes and dreams, and I've never even met the man. Silk suits, flashy cars, and big-titted women. And that's about as far as it goes. But I'll do my best and get back to you."

"Thanks a bunch, my friend. I do appreciate it. Let me give you my cell number too."

I was about ten minutes back into my paperwork when I got a call from Billy Don Smith telling me that Arno was having lunch at the Caravan.

"Did he just get there?" I asked.

"No, I saw his car and checked the place out. He's eating. Do you want me to arrest him now?"

"No, just keep an eye on him. I'm on my way."

When I pulled up in front of the restaurant I saw Billy Don waiting outside. I stepped from my car and walked over to where he stood.

"He's just now paying his check," Billy Don said. "If we wait a couple of minutes we can take him out here and avoid disturbing folks inside."

I nodded agreement. Soon Big Paul came through the door, bouncing along on the balls of his feet like a prizefighter. He was wearing a black nylon wind suit and a pair of designer running shoes that would have probably cost a mill foreman a week's pay. He saw me and hesitated for half a step, then started to walk on past.

"Hold it," I said.

"You talking to me?"

"You know I am," I said. I was standing with my hand on my .45 and my body quartered away from his. "A bad attitude could get you killed this morning, Arno. We don't fool around when we have reason to think a man is carrying a weapon, and that permit of yours makes me think you may be."

"My piece is in the car," he said.

"Good. Turn around, spread your legs, and put your hands on the wall."

He complied, but he wasn't happy about it. "This is embarrassing," he said.

"Maybe so," I said. "But it's better than having an old man sitting in the middle of your back whipping on your head with a slapjack, now isn't it?"

Billy Don searched him, and we cuffed him and loaded him in the back of my cruiser. Ten minutes later he was seated in front of my desk and I was taking my own good time about getting down to business. I signed a few letters Maylene had left on my desk while I was out, and then I made a couple of phone calls I didn't really need to make and jotted down some notes about things I didn't need to remember. Big Paul was getting impatient. "You know, I got things to do today," he said.

"Well, you may not get them done, then," I said without looking up. "It appears to me that your ass may be headed for jail."

"Jail? What for?"

"Murder."

"Who?" he asked.

"A woman named Amanda Twiller."

"For the love o' Mike. You can't really think I had anything to do with that."

"I'm a lot closer to thinking it since your alibi caved in. Willie Day gave you up."

"Who?"

"Willie Day," I said. "That young computer wizard at the South Winds Motor Hotel in Lake Charles. He's in jail in Bermuda. Altering a motel or hotel record is a federal offense, you know. The cops down there put the screws to him yesterday, and he cracked like an egg. They've got signed and notarized statements and everything."

"That slimy little shit . . ."

"How much did you pay him?"

"Three bills. And he rolls over on me."

"Three hundred?"

"Yeah, the twerp."

I laughed out loud. "That kind of bonus money will sure buy him a lot of daiquiris lying around down there on the beach," I said.

"Beach?" he asked stupidly. "I thought you said the cops had him."

"I was lying."

"Shit . . ."

"If you weren't involved in the Twiller murder, why did you go to all the trouble to set up an alibi?"

"I'm not saying nothing more without a lawyer."

"You know, I could go upstairs right now and get a warrant and charge you with this killing. This time you'd stay jugged because murder for hire is not a bondable offense. I think we have enough to get an indictment. I doubt that we could prove it in court, but we can cause you some very expensive trouble. But truth of the matter is that I really don't think you did it. So if you could just give me something to hang my hat on . . ."

"Like I said, I'm not talking without a lawyer."

"You should have dummied up and asked for an attorney

when I first mentioned Willie Day. But like a fool, you showed your hand. Now when you could tell me something that would help you, you've got nothing to say."

"So?"

"So I think you're just about the stupidest son of a bitch I've met this whole year."

He didn't like hearing that. His eyes were full of fire, but he knew there was no percentage in getting tough. "I still got nothing to say," he said sullenly.

"Are you planning on leaving town anytime soon?"

"I've got business here that will keep me around for a few days."

"What kind of business?" I asked.

"Private business."

"Okay, get lost."

"You mean I can go?"

"Until the next time I need to talk to you."

"Some people might call this harassment."

I gave him an honest laugh. "Do I look like I give a shit what anybody calls it?"

I called Tom Waller to fill him in on what I had on Arno. He agreed with me that while we might get an indictment, conviction was doubtful. I told him I was putting any action against the man on hold. For some reason Big Paul as Amanda Twiller's killer just didn't gel for me. I know it's unscientific, but I've been at this business long enough to pay attention to my hunches, especially when they told me somebody was innocent. Not that I was worried about any injustice that might be done to Arno. He was a killer several times over, and whatever charge he went down for was merely a matter of bookkeeping. But I wasn't content just to clear the case.

"How does this tie in with Dennard?" he asked.

"I have no idea. I guess Dennard could have hired Arno to do it, or even done it himself, maybe after getting Doyle to deliver her to him. Then a couple of days later he killed Doyle to shut him up."

"Do you believe that?"

"I have trouble with it," I said. "Dennard is smart and a lawyer himself. The Bureau has nothing that would tie him to Sipes or any other skulduggery. The only possible motive I can come up with is to protect his marriage."

"That's been behind many a murder," he said.

"If it was in this case, it was more likely he was trying to protect himself financially from a bad divorce judgment. This state now has alimony, remember?"

"Oh yes. I'm very aware of that."

"Do you think the grand jury would indict on what we have?"

"Maybe and maybe not," he said. "I'm still wondering why Sipes's bail bond company took such a flier on Raynes."

"Sipes claims Zorn vouched for the kid's innocence. Why, I don't know, but it's not a crime, so . . ."

"By the way," he said, "the judge set Dennard's bond at a half million dollars. Noncapital murder and he's a substantial citizen."

"That's still a stiff bond," I said. "Has he made any effort to come up with it?"

"Not a bit. MacGregor won't accept anything but cash or surety from a licensed bonding company. Dennard doesn't have that kind of liquidity. He could probably come up with the fifteen percent a bail bond company would require, but that's seventy-five thousand dollars that he wouldn't get back. It looks like he's either innocent and confident or guilty and pessimistic. Either way, why waste the money?"

We hung up and I thought for a few moments, then dialed Hotchkiss on his cell phone. He answered on the second ring. "What's up, Doc?" he said.

"Maybe we ought to find out where Emmet Zorn lived before

he came to Sequoya. He's been here about five years, and I know he did some rodeo promoting before that."

"No problem. The first thing I'll do is check the national computer for any minor criminal charges and check the addresses to go with them. Actually, we should have already done that. I'll get back to you."

Next I fished Roland DeMour's card out of my wallet and started dialing. None of his numbers answered, but I left a message on his voice mail asking him to call me. Almost an hour later Maylene buzzed and told me DeMour was on the phone.

"How can I help you?" he asked after I said hello.

"I recall your cousin Camille saying you work organized crime. Is that right?"

"It sure is."

"If you've got a minute I'd like to ask you a few more questions about Paul Arno."

Just before noon Linda came in with a report on another case that I needed, and I motioned for her to sit down. Before I could tell her what was on my mind, Hotchkiss called. I lifted the receiver and he started jabbering away without even giving me a chance to say hello. When he finished a couple of minutes later, I said, "Thanks, Hotch," and hung up.

"What?" Linda asked.

I gave her a coy little smile and raised my finger to my lips to silence her. "Be patient," I said. "I've got to make one more call."

It took me five minutes and some heavy threats to get patched through to Lester Sipes on his cell phone. Finally he answered. "Hello, Sheriff," he said. "I don't know why I'm talking to you, especially in light of the insulting things you said to me when we met in Nacogdoches."

"I'll give you one good reason to talk to me. Answer a couple of questions truthfully and I can eliminate you from a list of possible suspects in a murder case. That should be worth a few minutes of your valuable time."

There came a long pause. "Fine. Speak your piece."

"I think that one night last week you were scheduled to come up here to Sequoya. I think you were supposed to arrive around midnight. I also think that something happened that prevented you from coming. Am I right?"

"How on earth did you know that?"

"Never mind how," I said. "It was the night Amanda Twiller was killed, wasn't it?"

"Yes . . . yes, it was. But I had some important business associates came into town on the spur of the moment."

"From South America?" I asked.

"Where they were from doesn't matter, but I promise you I have several respectable witnesses who will place me here in Houston until well into the next day."

"I'm sure you do, and I would believe them in a heartbeat. But I've got even stronger proof that you were never here that night."

"And what might that be?"

"You're still alive," I said and hung up the phone.

Linda's eyes were wide with surprise. "Are you going to tell me what *that* was all about?" she asked. Then she answered her own question. "No, never mind. You'll just say something about my young and tender ears, and I'll get pissed off all over again."

I laughed at her. "I want you to hear this, but I don't want to have to tell it twice. Call Toby and see if he's interested in eating some barbecue in a half hour. My treat."

CHAPTER TWENTY-EIGHT

It took Toby the better part of an hour to finish his call and get back to town. Linda and I met him at Seabrook's, and while we were ordering at the counter my cell phone buzzed. I listened for a couple of minutes, then said, "Thanks, my friend. I owe you a big one."

"What was that?" Linda asked.

"You're too damn snoopy," I said.

"Come on, Bo. That call had you grinning like a possum, so what's the story?"

"Icing on the cake. Let's sit down and I'll give you the whole story."

We managed to get the back corner booth once again. "What's cooking, boss?" Toby asked as soon as we were seated with our iced tea in hand.

"Arno's off the hook on the Twiller murder."

"How so?"

"The problem I've had all along with him as the killer was the way the body was dumped in public. That's just not a mob hit, and Arno's a mob guy. When they move a victim's body, they take it out to a gravel pit or somewhere and bury it to make it less conspicuous, not more so. Yet we still had the fact that he was here and went to the trouble to try to establish an alibi. And now I know why. A little while ago I had a phone conversation with a Louisiana State Police organized crime investigator named Roland DeMour that Hotchkiss and I met yesterday down in Lake Charles. I asked him if it was likely that Arno would come all the way up here and do a hit for the kind of money Zorn could pay. He said not unless he was hurting for money pretty bad. He also said there was no reason for him to be hurting since he's got a couple of rackets going in Lake Charles that are pretty lucrative."

"If he didn't do the Twiller killing, then why's he here?" Toby asked.

"I don't know why he's staying around, but he came up here in the first place because he was after a bigger fish, one worth the risk."

"Who?" they both asked.

"Lester Sipes."

"I don't get it," Linda said.

"We've assumed all along that Arno was hired to lean on Sipes by the people down in South America. We thought that because we know he's worked for them at least once in the past. But that wasn't the case at all. Yesterday I remembered something that Parker Raynes said when I interviewed her at the Sawmill Club the day Amanda Twiller was killed. She told me that Doyle had mentioned to her the evening before that they were leaving the club early that night because Zorn was meeting his partner at midnight. That meant nothing to me at the time, largely because I was focused on Doyle. Then I understood. Charlie Morton has been working with Zorn on selling the Pak-a-Sak, and he's seen all the paperwork on the place. Up until about six months ago, Sipes was half owner. So I figured he had to be the partner Doyle was talking about. With that in mind, I asked Hotchkiss to run down Zorn's previous addresses, and guess what? For a couple of years before he moved up here to Sequoya he lived in New Orleans."

"Which means he could have met Arno," Toby said.

"He did meet Arno," I said. "They were busted together in a gambling raid. Minor stuff. Hotch says some guy running a card parlor in the French Quarter got behind in his protection money and they gave him a rap on the knuckles. Eleven guys paid misdemeanor fines, and Zorn and Arno were both on the list."

"But why was Arno going to whack Sipes?" Linda asked.

"Because he and Zorn were going to sell the coke to that drug dealer up in St. Louis and split almost a million dollars. Arno is a lot more likely than Zorn to have contacts like that, and I bet he was the one who got in touch with the St Louis people in the first place. If you'll remember, Peet said it was some guy who knew both Zorn and his boss up north."

"That's right," he said.

"Remember how much money we're talking about here. That's a half million apiece for each of them, but they knew it wasn't going to be a good idea to screw Sipes that badly and leave him alive. He's a little man with a long memory and a short fuse. I just talked to Sipes a little while ago, and he admitted that he'd been planning a trip to Sequoya that night, but something came up that kept him in Houston."

"But who was that who called when we were standing in line?" Linda asked.

"Sergeant Wolf of the Dallas PD. He visited with a girl named Brandi Springer this morning. She was Arno's girlfriend down in Lake Charles."

"And?"

"This gal and her mother are in the process of opening a call girl operation in Dallas, and Wolf was concerned that Big Paul might be backing it financially. But it turns out that Brandi came home to Dallas to get away from the guy. He was trying to get her to marry him, but she was afraid of him and didn't want any part of it. And he bragged to her a couple of weeks ago that he was working on a project that would bring him enough money to build her a big, fine house."

"So all this means . . . what, exactly?" Linda asked.

"It means we've eliminated the prime suspect, and I'm happy with that because I never bought him for the Twiller murder anyway. Now we won't be wasting any more time in that direction. And it means we have a clearer picture of what's going on with these people. It also means we need to take a closer look at Emmet Zorn."

"Good," Linda said. "I don't like the guy, anyway."

"Why not?" I asked. "Has he been hitting on you?"

"No, but since he's hit on every other woman in town under fifty, I think he could have made at least one pass at me just to be polite."

"Probably the uniform puts him off," Toby said. "I don't make him for a cop groupie."

"Don't let it worry you," I said. "You're way too good for him."

"Thanks, Bo. Any more compliments you want to throw my way while you're in such a good mood?"

"You bet," I said, laughing. "You're a hell of a peace officer, and so is Toby. I'm proud to have you both on my force."

"Well, well," she said. "As long as you're being so cooperative, I'd still like to know why you can get Gog and Magog to behave when nobody else can."

"That story's just not for your young and tender ears," I said, and quickly moved my legs just as she kicked at my shins under the table.

CHAPTER TWENTY-NINE

I got back to the office to find my desk phone ringing. I picked up the receiver, listened for a moment, then said, "Thanks." Next I called Hotchkiss. He answered on the second beep.

"I know I promised you a day's notice on busting that bookie I told you about," I said. "But you seemed awfully eager the last time we talked. What do you have on the burner this afternoon?"

"Nothing terribly important. You want to do it now?"

"You bet. He's writing at this very instant. They got several big preseason games coming up this weekend, and my snitch says he's going at it hard."

"Can you get the warrant this quickly?"

"Hell, I've had the warrant for a week."

"Let's go then."

Linda and two of my other deputies, along with two city cops, got themselves all decked out in face shields and flack gear and did a SWAT team number on the front and rear doors of the house. Quinn obviously wasn't expecting any problems. We caught him, dumb and happy, working away at his kitchen table like a busy accountant going over his weekly figures. Three cheap cell phones lay on the table alongside his paperwork. He must have thought that by avoiding landlines he would leave less of a paper trail.

Hotchkiss and I watched as Linda cuffed the man, slammed him back down in his little rolling desk chair, and proceeded to stand over him with the stern frown of an avenging angel.

He was a nondescript, pudgy fellow of medium height in his early thirties who would have been utterly unmemorable if the substructure of his face hadn't still shown the effects of the terrible beating he'd taken a few years earlier. As it was, he looked like something put together by a clumsy child. A bowling pin can be a fearsome weapon.

I motioned my deputies out of the room and stood looking down at Quinn. Finally he snapped, "What?"

"You've been a naughty boy," I said.

"Big deal. A chickenshit gambling charge even if you can make it stick. I'll be bailed out by sundown."

"Not this time," Hotchkiss said.

He looked up at the young agent. "Who the fuck are you?"

Hotchkiss flipped his ID open in Quinn's face. "FBI. Federal Bureau of Investigation to the uninitiated. Only you're not uninitiated. You've been down this road before."

"Huh?"

"Federal charges, nitwit. Interstate gambling."

"Oh, no you don't. You've got no records of my phones."

Hotchkiss sighed and shook his head, no doubt amazed as I myself had been dozens of times at the monumental stupidity of criminals. "Fool, cell phones leave computer records just like landlines. Besides, the statute has been changed. All we have to do is prove you laid off one single bet on a single out-of-state game and your ass is fried."

"Aw, shit . . ."

"*Aw, shit,*" I said mockingly. "That's a fitting response if I ever heard one, since you've really stepped in it." I pointed at Hotchkiss. "You need to listen to this young man so you'll know what the future has in store for you."

"Right," Hotchkiss said. "With your prior record, even the greenest assistant on the federal prosecutor's staff could get you a couple of years in the slammer. Only you won't draw the greenest guy on the block. The verdict will be guilty, of course, and I'll make it a personal point to feed plenty of juicy information to the guys doing the presentencing report. You can count on it. So maybe you ought to figure on five to seven, just to be safe."

"What have you got against me?" Quinn whined, a standard criminal complaint I'd heard a thousand times. Bust them and they think you have targeted them out of some personal vindictiveness. They can never understand that you're simply doing your job.

"We don't have a thing against you personally," I said.

"Bo's telling you the truth there," Hotchkiss said cheerfully. "I'll admit that I don't like gambling, but you're nothing special. Just a means to an end for us."

Quinn rolled his eyes. "Why me?"

"You're the only bookie in town," I said.

"So?"

"But you don't have to be the one left holding the bag."

"I don't?"

"Nope," Hotchkiss said. "There's another way this whole thing can end. Want to hear it?"

Quinn shrugged morosely. "What have I got to lose?"

"At least five years of your life," I said. "That prospect would get my attention in a hurry."

"Okay, okay. No need to rub it in."

Hotchkiss smiled. "You give us a name and a signed statement and you can walk on the whole deal with nothing more than a fine."

"What name?"

"The guy you're laying off bets for," I said. "Your boss, Weyland."

"Who?" The man seemed authentically puzzled.

"Sam Weyland, over at Fillmore," I said.

"Never heard of the guy."

I gazed at Quinn's face. He was either a consummate actor or he was telling the truth. "Then who are you working for?" I asked.

"This is my own operation," he muttered.

"Bullshit," I said. "You're dead broke and we know it. Give it up. Who's backing you?"

It was then that Hotchkiss did something that almost floored me. First he stood and regarded Quinn thoughtfully for a few moments, apparently pondering something. Then he leaned down so his face was only a few inches from Quinn's and said, "Your boss is Lester Sipes, isn't he?"

Quinn twitched like he'd been hit with a mild electric current. I probably did too, and I know I felt my mouth dropping open once again. Hotchkiss persisted. "It *is* Sipes, right?"

"God help me," Quinn muttered. "Why can't you guys just haul me in and charge me?"

"You're the little fish," Hotchkiss said. "We want the big fish. The guy at the top of the food chain."

"Listen," Quinn said, "even if I was working for Sipes, and I ain't saying I am, do you know what he would do to me if I ratted him out?"

Hotchkiss nodded like a wise old philosopher. "I see your point. I really do. But the grim truth is that you really don't have the choice of not giving him up."

"Oh yes, I do."

"Oh no, you don't. You either roll on Sipes or we'll just go ahead and bust him tomorrow on a federal warrant naming him as your co-conspirator on an interstate gambling charge. Which will, of course, make it appear that you rolled on him even though you didn't. He'll get bonded out quickly, and so will you because he'll have his Coastal outfit go your bail. And like you said, you know what happens to people who rat him out. You've heard the same stories I have."

"You can't do this to me!"

"Oh, but I can. And I will too, if you don't get cooperative."

"So I'm screwed no matter what? Is that what you're telling me?"

"No," Hotchkiss said. "You give up everything you have on him and you can go into the federal witness protection program."

"Jesus!"

"What's the problem? Do you have family you don't want to leave behind?"

"That's a laugh. I got a girlfriend, though."

"Then maybe she can go with you. At any rate, witness protection is better than getting fed to the crabs off the Galveston jetties."

Quinn shivered and looked as miserable as any man I had ever seen. I turned to Hotchkiss. "We need to talk," I told him quietly.

"Sure," he said with a nod.

I called Linda back in the room to ride herd on Quinn and steered Hotch out on the front porch. "What's going on here?" I asked. "What gave you the idea he was working for Sipes?"

"You think he is too?"

"I don't see how there's any doubt about it. He damn near turned green when you mentioned the man's name. But what I want to know is *why* you mentioned it. What did you know going in here today that I didn't know?"

"Nothing, Bo. I swear. I just made a lucky guess."

"Lucky guess, my ass—"

"No, really. Some recent intel we have on Sipes says he has about a dozen guys running book for him all over the eastern part of the state. Actually, what he's done is muscle in and take over a couple of other operations. Maybe even this guy Weyland's. When Quinn didn't seem to know Weyland, I just took a wild shot in the dark."

"Let's say for a moment that's true—"

"It is, Bo. Think for a minute. If I'd known, why would I have waited for you to bust him when I could have done it on my own?"

I pondered this for a few seconds and then conceded the point. Besides, the boy had been straight with me so far. "But why in thunder is Sipes into gambling all of a sudden?" I asked.

"If I had to guess, I'd say he's trying to generate some quick cash."

"To pay the Colombians for the missing cocaine. Right?"

"Must be. Besides, it's a lucrative sideline, and he *is* a gangster, you know."

I nodded. "Okay, but at this point I want to give you some unsolicited advice about this witness protection business. Don't you ever promise something you can't deliver if you're going to stay in law enforcement. To be effective as a lawman you have to have the reputation of keeping your word and treating your snitches right."

"I can deliver."

"Are you kidding me?" I asked, peering closely at his face. "You mean you can really get the guy into the program over a gambling charge?"

"Sure."

"And Mack will back you up?"

"He'll fall all over himself to do it, Bo."

"But why? Quinn is a two-bit nobody and you're willing to put him on the government tit for a lifetime?"

"The RICO statute. Under RICO interstate gambling adds a bunch more years. One more nail in his coffin."

I shrugged. "I hope it's worth it to you. I hope it's worth it to the taxpayers."

"It will be. We want Sipes to walk out of that courtroom wrapped in chains and staring down into the better part of a century of hard time. In that first debacle he made us look bad and he made the attorney general's office look bad. Hell, he crapped on the whole criminal justice system."

I could have told him that all the crap fell on the Feds, and that the state and county boys came out looking fine. But there was no point in rubbing it in since they hadn't really been at fault.

Quinn rolled and rolled big. He'd been dealing directly with Sipes, and at one point the man had even foolishly given him a personal check. You would think a banker would have known better. But if I have learned even one thing about hoodlums in my three decades of sparring with them, it is that what they lack in judgment they make up for in arrogance. I suppose Sipes's first acquittal made him feel omnipotent.

But what Quinn told us proved we were wrong about one thing: this was no recent move on Sipes's part. He'd been into gambling for well over a year. In fact, he'd had a couple of college kids writing for him down in Nacogdoches for several months. Quinn had simply moved the operation to Sequoya when he signed on because he had inherited the house where he was busted from his grandmother.

"You live and learn," I told Hotchkiss. "With a guy like Sipes your information is always going to be incomplete no matter how good your snitches are."

"I guess you're right. But keep in mind that our informant knows more about the drug side of the operation."

"Well, this is something new for this part of the country. Generally the gamblers stick to gambling and the drug people stick to peddling drugs."

"Things change, Bo."

"Do they really?" I asked with a laugh. "I never noticed."

We installed Quinn in the tank at the new jail where we lodged federal prisoners. Hotchkiss called Mack Reynolds, and he dispatched a couple of agents up from the coast to take him back to Houston. Neither of us waited around for them to arrive. The kid went to his motel room and I drove home, brooding the whole way. I couldn't help but wonder how far the Feds were willing to go with their witness protection offers.

CHAPTER THIRTY

I was at the courthouse early the next morning before the day shift punched in. I was still puttering around in the outer office when Maylene cruised in with Hotchkiss only a few steps behind her.

"You are a timely young man," she told him.

"How so?" he asked.

"Well, I see that Bo has the coffee made and . . ." She smiled, set a large canister down on her desk, and removed its top.

"More cookies!" he said, the delight clear in his voice. "May I?"

"Have at 'em."

"You're a wonderful cook," he said around a mouthful of oatmeal raisin.

"And how is our Mr. Quinn doing this fine morning?" I asked, motioning him into my inner office.

"He's at the federal building in Houston giving statements and signing papers even as we speak. He'll be in protective custody until after the trial, then he'll vanish. I hope you don't mind losing the state gambling bust."

"I don't mind a bit. Getting a bookie shut down was my main objective. As long as he's out of my county I don't care who gets the credit."

"I'm glad you feel that way. It's for the greater good."

I had my doubts about that, but I didn't say so. Instead, I asked, "So what else is on your mind?"

"Yesterday evening I made some phone calls. One of the Bureau's agents in Houston has been doing a background workup on Zorn, and I thought you might be interested."

"Sure. Let's have it."

He reached in his inner pocket and pulled out a notebook and flipped it open. "The man was born August twentieth, 1962, in Kerrville, Texas, which makes him forty-eight years old. His parents were of German descent, and owned a successful hardware store there in Kerrville. He graduated from high school and did one year at Southwest Texas State at San Marcus before dropping out."

"That's a big party school," I said.

"I didn't know that, but it fits his personality. After that he odd-jobbed around for a while, then enlisted in the air force. Came out in three years with an honorable discharge. Pretty good military record, though he was called on the carpet once for making sexually suggestive remarks to an officer."

"Female, I assume."

"Right. Then a couple of years later he somehow emerged as the agent-manager for a pretty well known bronc rider from Midland, and from that gig he went into rodeo promotions, whatever in the hell that means. That's where he met Lester Sipes. When Lester started to hit it big, he took Zorn on as his agent."

"He should have made some decent money with that one."

"He did, but he flitted it all away on high living. You know the story. Big cars, fancy apartments—"

"And high-maintenance women."

"No doubt. Then about the time Sipes quit the rodeo circuit, Zorn's mother had a major stroke, and he wound up taking care of her for several years down in New Orleans."

"Why New Orleans if they were from Texas?" I asked.

"His only sister lived there and she helped out."

"Anybody talk to the sister?"

"No one could since she died of cancer a couple of years ago. They did contact her husband, and he says Zorn managed a bar part-time and did a good job with the old lady. When his mother died, Zorn and his sister split what little was left of the family fortune, and he drifted up here to Sequoya."

"Any criminal record?"

He shook his head. "Nothing substantial. Just a couple of minor liquor violations here in town and one down in New Orleans. And the gambling charge I mentioned the other day. Everybody my contact interviewed thought he was a pretty decent guy, friendly, a lot of fun at parties."

"Hmm . . ."

"What's your analysis of the man, Bo?" he asked.

"If I had to speculate, I'd say that his decency probably comes more from habit than conviction. And like you said that morning at the Caravan, he's a guy who's spent his whole life nibbling at the crust while others were getting the pie. Had to be some envy there. Then something happens. A midlife crisis, maybe. Who knows? But he wakes up one morning and sees himself facing the remainder of his days wrangling with salesmen over a quarter discount on a case of beer. Tedious. So when opportunity presented itself in the form of Lester Sipes's cocaine deal, he jettisoned what little ethics he had and signed on. Before he knew it, he was in over his head, and things start to snowball."

He nodded in agreement. "For what it's worth, his brother-in-law liked him, but he claimed the man just cannot leave the women alone. When one caught his eye, he had to have her or bust a gasket."

"That's true." I said. "He was after my niece until I told him I'd put a knot on his head if he didn't leave her alone."

"The brother-in-law also said that, one way or another, some woman would be his downfall.' "

"Amanda Twiller."

"Could be."

After Hotchkiss left, I spent some time thinking about the case and reviewing what I had, which was little of substance beyond Zorn's involvement in the cocaine trade. How Nobel Dennard factored into the equation, which already had too many unknowns, I had no idea. He was still sitting complacently in the jail, saying nothing and making no attempt to make bond. An enigma.

Sherlock Holmes used to say that once you had eliminated all the suspects who couldn't have committed the crime, what you had left was the guilty party no matter how improbable it seemed. I had eliminated Paul Arno, which left one of the other six billion people on the planet as the killer. That meant I needed a name, not a smug slogan from a nineteenth-century pulp detective.

So for lack of anything better to do, I headed for the Sawmill Club. The joint held a dozen or so tired-looking blue-collar guys, three curvy college girls, and a pair of honky-tonk heroes who were trying hard to put the make on them and apparently getting nowhere. Parker Raynes was once again behind the bar, and this time she was decked out in a pair of cherry-colored Wranglers and another of her wiggly-squiggly blouses.

"Well, if it ain't Marshall Dillon," she said. "Have you come to court Miss Kitty?"

"No, ma'am, I can't say that I have," I replied with a laugh. "But if I do decide to ever go courting again, Miss Kitty will be high on my list."

"That's good enough for me. You want another one of them Coca-Colas?"

"Yes, ma'am, and with plenty of ice."

She set the glass in front of me on the bar and said, "Well, if you ain't here to make an assault on the high walls of my virtue, you must want information."

"I don't know what I want. I'm at loose ends."

"Hon, I been there myself more times than I can count."

"I meant to come to Doyle's funeral," I said. "Mainly because I wanted to see if there was anybody there who looked suspicious."

"There wasn't much of a funeral to speak of. Me and my preacher and the fellow from the funeral home was all the folks that showed up. I had him cremated and put in the columbarium at the city cemetery beside his momma and daddy."

"You mean none of his friends came?"

She shook her head. "Pitiful, ain't it? But you and I both know his running buddies weren't the kind to have a strong sense of obligation toward a fallen comrade."

"Probably not. Do you know anything about them?"

"His friends? Not really. I wasn't that close to the kid. Mostly I didn't see him unless he needed a little money or some help of some kind."

"And you always came through, didn't you?" I asked.

"Of course. I'm a pushover, which is one reason you need to keep my name at the top of that list."

"I'll do it. Do any of his buddies stand out in your mind? Anybody special?"

"Oh, from time to time I'd see him talking to a few of the younger bozos that hang out in here, but none of them seemed to stick with him. I think the truth is that Doyle was a pretty lonely kid."

"Did anybody contact you or send condolence cards or anything like that when he was killed?"

"One whiny little nitwit named Tia something-or-other came in here and said she didn't come to the funeral because she wanted to remember him the way he was rather than seeing him lyin' in a casket. Damn fool. You hear more and more of that kind of crap these days, and it's nothing but an excuse people use to get out of doing what they know they ought to do. Anyhow, I told her there wasn't nothing to see but a box of ashes, and we didn't look at them."

"Could she have been his girlfriend?" I asked.

"Girlfriend? You got to be kidding."

"Why would I be?"

"Doyle was gay, hon."

"You don't mean it. . . ."

"Oh, but I do. He was queer as a two-headed penny. I thought everybody knew that. He came out of the closet right after he dropped out of high school."

I laughed and picked up Parker Raynes's hand and gave it a gentle kiss. "Miss Kitty, you sweet thing, I think you may have solved this murder case for ole Marshall Dillon."

"Huh?"

I drained my Coke and threw a couple of dollars on the bar. "You can read about it in the funny papers, darlin'," I said as I turned to leave.

"Where you going this time?" she asked.

"I got to catch me a killer."

She shook her head sadly. "I do believe you're the most sudden man I ever met."

An hour later I had Toby and Linda in my office with the door closed. "What I'm about to tell you two stays in this room," I said. "Just the three of us. Understand?"

They nodded.

"As of now I have reason to make Scott Kimball for the Twiller murder. And before you object that nobody we've talked to has seen him around town in months, just remember that we haven't asked that many people about him."

"Whoa," Linda said. "How did you get on this track?"

"A little confidential information, and I was able to put two and two together. I'll tell you all about it later. Now we need to get moving."

"So what do you want us to do?" Toby asked.

"To start with, keep this strictly to yourselves. Go to every informant you've got and try to find out if they've seen Scott around the county. But do it as casually as you can. Ask them about other things too, and just throw this in. Talk to his friends and try to find out if any of them have seen him. We aren't going to fool people long. If we haven't gotten a good lead in a couple of days, he'll get word that we're looking for him. Then he'll flush on us for sure. If nothing has turned up by then I'll try to get a warrant on him and put it out statewide. What we have is thin, but Judge MacGregor hasn't gotten annoyed with me yet. If you don't mind working late, I'd like for you each to put in a few hours tonight. I'm going to be out there doing the same thing, so . . ."

"How about that Dennard guy?" Toby asked. "Does this bust him loose?"

I now had a pretty good idea where Nobel Dennard fit in the story, but it wasn't something I was about to tell them, now or ever. That was one piece of the puzzle I'd deal with myself when and if the time came. I shook my head. "Not yet," I said. "Let him stew awhile longer."

CHAPTER THIRTY-ONE

I was running the roads until almost midnight, stopping at taverns and liquor stores all over the county. I hit known weed peddlers and compulsive snitches, petty thieves and ex-cons. I drew a blank everywhere I went. I got into bed at one and rolled out at sunup the next morning and started over again, this time inside the city limits. I ground away at it all morning with no better results than the night before. After a quick sandwich for lunch, I decided to drop in on Emmet Zorn at the Pak-a-Sak. When I pulled into the parking lot he was cutting up cardboard boxes and dropping them in the Dumpster beside the building.

When he looked up and saw me, he shook his head in annoyance. "What now?" he asked.

As I drew closer to the man I could see that his face was taut and drawn. "Don't be that way," I said cheerfully. "I might have dropped by to tell you that you're completely off the hook on the Twiller killing."

"Am I?"

"No."

"Sheriff, I did not kill that woman!"

"No, but you could have hired it."

"But what possible reason could I have had?"

"That's an interesting question, isn't it?"

He leaned back against the Dumpster and pulled a thin cigarillo from his shirt pocket and lighted it with a fancy gold lighter. When he did, his hand shook just a little and there were worry wrinkles around his eyes.

"You seem a mite nervous," I said.

"Have you ever had the cops on your ass for something you didn't do?"

"Don't believe that I have. By the way, I found out that your buddy Lester Sipes was your silent partner in your business here, but he got out a few months ago. Mind telling me why?"

"He only came on board when I started up to help me get the store rolling. He always intended for me to buy his half."

I gave him a sympathetic nod. "That was nice of him. I hope you've repaid his kindness."

His eyes narrowed a little at this. "Sheriff, like I asked you the other day, what do you want from me?"

"A confession."

"But I haven't done anything."

"Oh, we've all done *something*."

"I need to get back inside."

"You do that," I said and stood watching as he walked across the parking lot, all the while puffing furiously on his cigarillo. My stop had accomplished one thing. It had told me that stress was eating the man up. I wondered how much longer he could hold it together before he cracked.

I went back to the office with the notion of attending to some pressing paperwork and getting it out of the way as quickly as I could. As soon as I walked in Maylene handed me a dirty scrap of paper with some illegible scribbles on it.

"What in thunder is this?" I asked.

"That's a hand-delivered note from Lew Feemster. Some kid brought it in and said Lew wants you to meet him at Jeeter's Tavern at nine this evening."

Feemster was one of my oldest informants, an ex-con who'd gone down to Huntsville at the tender age of nineteen behind an armed robbery and shooting that he still claimed he hadn't committed. My dad, who was certainly no fool, maintained that they hung that beef on Lew to get a rich boy from Lufkin off the hook. Whether that's true or not, it's a matter of record that he entered the penitentiary as a wet-behind-the-ears kid back in the days when the Texas prison system meant business. When he came out almost two decades later, he was bitter, cynical, and as mean as a rattlesnake. In his view, society had unjustly branded him as a criminal, and a criminal he would be content to remain, though he managed to avoid further incarceration. For the most part he gambled and bootlegged and dealt in corn whisky back when moonshining was a viable business. He was the best dice switcher I ever saw, and what he couldn't do with a deck of cards could not be done.

In the early years of our relationship, I paid him for information by going easy on his bootlegging activities and overlooking the nighttime crap games he ran in various deserted sharecropper shacks around the county. I did this because the people I nailed through his information were always a far greater threat to society than the drinkers and gamblers. But in the last decade he'd begun to demand cash, and as he grew older he became ever more cantankerous and difficult to deal with.

"Was he expecting an answer?" I asked Maylene.

"No, he just said for you to be there and he'd make you a happy man."

———

A little after five I was almost out the door on my way home when a phone call from Hotchkiss brought me back to my desk. "What's up?" I asked.

"I just thought you might like a little update on Sipes."

"You thought right. Fire away."

"As you've probably guessed, we're monitoring his bank transactions pretty closely."

"Can you do that without him knowing?"

"Sure. It's so easy now that all this business is computerized. My records, your records, everybody's records . . . We just slip in on little cat's feet and—"

"Spare me, please."

He laughed, and his laughter was good-natured but a little mocking. "I'm just trying to get even with you for not telling us about that hiding place in Emmet Zorn's floor."

"I don't know about any hiding place," I said, lying smoothly. "And if there is one, how did you find it?"

He giggled. "Creepy-crawl, creepy-crawl . . ."

"Hotch, have you been drinking?"

"I may have had a couple."

"Old Hoover would have your hide for a rug, boy."

"He probably would, but he's dead. Anyhow, I called to fill you in on Sipes. As we suspected, he's been in something of a cash crunch lately, but in the last couple of days he's hustled around and managed to come up with six hundred thousand dollars, which he deposited in one account. Then it went offshore by wire transfer."

"Some of that gambling money he's been hustling."

"Part of it must have been."

"That means he must have paid off the boys down in South America," I said. "You know, if you think about it, we made a damn lucky guess on this one. Based on Arno's presence here in Sequoya, we assumed that the South Americans were fronting the coke. We were wrong about why he was here, but we were right about the conclusion it led us to."

"I was thinking about the same thing myself last night."

"I guess this means Sipes is off the hook with his suppliers, then?"

"Maybe and maybe not. The people he's dealing with are real animals, and they don't like screwups. No matter how it shakes down, he's going to be on thin ice with them."

"And this is bad?" I asked.

"It could be. He's not the only rich, high-profile bastard involved in the drug trade."

"So?"

"We want to send the message that even the mighty can fall. That means we need Lester Sipes on his way to federal prison with plenty of publicity. Not beheaded and dumped in a swamp somewhere."

"Beheaded?"

"That's how that bunch he's dealing with gets rid of people. It's their signature method of execution."

"Sounds like he's running with his own kind. I keep thinking about the guy Sipes and his goons fed to the crabs."

"Birds of a feather," he said. "Beheading is supposed to have more emotional impact than shooting."

"Well, it damn sure makes me perk up and take notice."

"Me too," he said, his voice suddenly deadly serious. "Especially since they don't draw the line at federal agents. Remember when it leaked out to the press last year about those two DEA guys that disappeared down in Colombia? We know about it through informants, but we've never found the bodies so the government hasn't released any official information yet."

"But they were . . ."

"Yep, with machetes."

CHAPTER THIRTY-TWO

Jeeter's was an oldtime, rural honky-tonk a few miles out of town off Route 9 South. Nestled in a small clearing in the woods at the end of a rutted gravel lane, it dated from an era that ended decades before country became cool. When the long-departed and now half-mythical Ed Jeeter built the building back in 1940, he installed a huge neon sign on the roof that spelled out "Jeeter's" in fancy baroque script, and even though the place has gone through several subsequent owners, none have seen fit either to remove or change it. Now ancient and in its death throes, the sputtering old sign still cast a pale, greenish glow that on moonless nights could be seen for a couple of miles back along the lonely road.

When I pulled into the parking lot that evening there were a dozen or so cars ringed around the small building, and the bar-room was about half full. The club's current proprietor was a stolid man called Tub who reigned over his small fiefdom from behind the bar and dispensed his beer with a maximum of steady efficiency and a minimum of talk. The furnishings were sparse. Aside from a short row of squeaky bar stools, the room held nothing beyond a dozen or so tables of chipped black Formica, a pair of languid, dust-encrusted ceiling fans, and an ancient Wurlitzer jukebox. The pulpy floor was unfinished pine, and the bare, unadorned walls were covered with plywood long darkened by several coats of cheap varnish and decades of tobacco smoke.

As I threaded my way between the tables, no one paid any attention to me. As dives go, Jeeter's was a relatively peaceful place. Only a few times over the years had my department answered disturbance calls there, but sometimes I stopped by to have a beer simply because I loved to watch the regulars. They were a ghostly, interchangeable crew of tired, listless women with haystack hairdos and defeated faces, and weathered, khaki-clad men of indefinite age and vague occupation who drank their beer straight from the bottle and smoked their unfiltered Camels with the calm intensity of those who know they are doomed and can't quite summon the energy to care. Misanthropes and loners, Jeeter's patrons said little to one another, and what conversation there was to be heard above the faint hum of the wall-mounted air conditioner was a soft, murmured litany of failed marriages, ungrateful offspring, and leaking trailer houses.

Lew Feemster was a regular and looked the part as he sat at the back corner table drinking a Shiner longneck and smoking a hand-rolled cigarette. In his late sixties, he was a pencil-thin man of medium height with a crown of unruly white hair and a nose that had been flattened and bent to one side, probably in a long-ago barroom brawl. That evening he wore a shirt of faded gray checks and a pair of rumpled khaki pants.

When I approached his table he looked up and gave me a sour frown. "If you want a damn beer you better go back and get it," he said. "Tub don't give no table service."

I took a chair opposite him and said, "You're sure ornery tonight. What's the occasion?"

"I'm the same way I always am. It's my hobby."

"I've suspected that for years. What have you got for me?"

He smiled, and I wished he hadn't. Lew's smiles were the kind you'd expect to see at hangings. "I know where you can find Scott Kimball," he said. "Or at least I'll know where he's gonna be a little while after noon tomorrow."

I was surprised but shouldn't have been. There were times when I thought the old buzzard knew more about my business than I did. "How in hell did you know I was hunting Scott Kimball?"

He cackled and then took a long pull on his beer before he answered. "Well, for one thing you've been rooting around under every bush in Caddo County asking if anybody has seen him. And in the second place, before he went to Houston he was running with that boy you arrested for shooting the preacher's wife. It don't take no Einstein to put it all together and figure out that you think Scott's the one that pulled the trigger."

"And you really know where he is?"

"I will tomorrow, I told you. I know for a fact that he's in town and has been for several days."

"Why don't you know where he is tonight?"

Just as he often did, he flew off the handle for no apparent reason. "Because my source won't know until tomorrow, damn it!" he snapped. "Kimball's selling him a little something, and the kid's being real coy about meeting with him."

"Drugs?"

"No, some stolen money orders he got down in Houston. Just a few thousand dollars' worth. He thinks my source is going to meet him and give him a quarter on the dollar for the damn things, but we're willing to set him up for you. And that, by God, is all I'm saying. Are you interested?"

I knew I couldn't probe any deeper without running the risk of having him get up and walk off. "Sure," I said. "What's it going to cost me?"

I could almost hear the wooden cogs creaking over in his old iron ball of a head as he calculated how much he could stick me for. I knew he didn't care all that much about the money, but I also knew he wanted to gouge me as deeply as he could just because he was Lew Feemster and that's what he did. "I've got to take care of my source too," he said.

"How much, Lew?"

He ruminated a few seconds longer, then said, "Two fifty."

"Done," I said without hesitation and reached for my wallet.

"Hell's bells!" he yelled. "I knew I could have got more."

"Shut up and take the money," I said. "Most snitches are content with enough to buy another bottle of cheap whisky or a little weed."

"I ain't most snitches. I know stuff they don't know, and I've never steered you wrong."

"That's all true, but you could have made it easy on me and called in and not had me come all the way out here after a hard day. You know I'm good for it."

He snatched up the money and slipped it into his shirt pocket. "I don't want to make nothing easy on you nor nobody else," he snarled.

"Why not?"

"Because I hate the goddamned human race, that's why!" he said, his voice rising to the high, clear register of rage. Several people turned and looked at our table, then shrugged and went back to their beers.

"Settle down, you fractious old bastard. Now give me the particulars."

He took his time about it, first building another of his hand-rolled cigarettes and finishing off his beer. Then he rose and went to the bar and got another longneck, and while he was there he indulged in a lengthy, heated, and no doubt pointless argument with Tub after first paying for the beer with change he laboriously dug piecemeal out of several pockets. Eventually he made his creaky way back to the table and sat down. He started to speak, but stopped and fished in his pockets for a light. Finding none, he began to rise again when I reached over and put my hand on his shoulder and pushed him firmly back in his chair.

"Cut the crap and start talking, Lew," I said. "Or I might decide to run your skinny ass in and lock you up for fraud. You've got the money, and now I want my information."

"Ha! I'd like to see anything you could do in that Tinkertoy jail of yours that would get my attention. Why, down at the Ramsey unit I once spent three months in the hole and—"

"Hush. I've heard it all a dozen times before, and I don't aim to hear it again. Now talk."

All the while he'd been searching once again in his pockets. He came up with a kitchen match, which he struck on the underside of the table and touched to the end of his cigarette. Then for no reason I could see, he burst out in a high-pitched, braying laugh and then got strangled and coughed and snorted. Once he got his breath back, he sucked on his cigarette and drank a big swig of his beer. Finally, he looked across the table at me and smiled, enormously satisfied with himself for being such a jackass.

"Scott Kimball, Lew," I said firmly. "Either start talking or I'm going to take my money back and be gone."

He snorted one final snort and began to talk. "Ain't hardly nobody noticed that he's back in town. That's because he's changed his appearance a right smart. For one thing, he's shaved his damn fool head. Not only that, but he's growed himself one of them goatee beards. He's got some little gal with him too."

"A girl, huh?"

"That's what I said, ain't it?"

"Do you know her name?"

"Hell no, but any female running around with Scott Kimball is bound to be an idiot, so it don't make no difference what they call her."

"Have you seen her?"

He shook his head. "They tell me she's blond and pretty good looking. And she's got a little kid."

I had no idea who "they" were and didn't ask because it would just set him off again. It really didn't matter since his information had always been good. "How long has he been in town?" I asked.

"Beats me. From what I understand he was here for a while, then he went back to Houston for a day or so. When he came back he had that girl with him."

"Did anybody see him in Sequoya around the time Amanda Twiller was killed?"

"That, I don't know," he said.

"What's he been doing since he's been back this time?"

"Lurking around in the shadows and acting like an asshole, I guess. Ain't that what he does best?"

"Come on. You must have some notion of why he's in town."

"Well, he's kept a pretty low profile, but I did hear that he's been trying to drum up some money. A pretty good chunk of money, in fact. The story is that he's got some gambling debts. Ain't that stupid? A punk kid like him running up gambling debts."

"What's he driving?"

"How in hell should I know? All these damn cars they're making nowadays look like something squeezed out of a duck's ass. I can't tell one make from another."

"Anything else?" I asked, rising to my feet.

He didn't answer. His mood seemed to shift as it often did of late, and he gazed off across the room. I sat there looking down at him for a few seconds. He was not a pensive man, and I'd never seen him at a loss for words before. "What's on your mind, old fellow?" I said.

He looked up at me. His rheumy, corpselike eyes actually held a little sadness, and when he spoke, his voice was soft and serious. "You really think Kimball shot that preacher's wife, don't you?"

"I don't know if we'll ever be able to prove it in court, but yes, I do. And I feel even more certain of it now that I know for sure that he's been back in town."

"They were nice folks. They treated me decent."

"The Twillers, you mean?"

"Yeah."

"How on earth did you meet them?"

"Well, don't let your damn teeth fall out of your head, but sometimes I go to them Thursday night community suppers they have there at the Methodist Church."

"I didn't know that."

"I get lonesome every now and then. I don't like people, but I can't wean myself off of them altogether."

"There are times when I feel the same way, Lew."

"Mrs. Twiller was a sad lady, wasn't she?" he said. "I'd heard about the dope and all that business."

"It's not just her that I'm concerned about. I think Scott killed Doyle Raynes too, and he was another sad case. Just a pitiful little old gay boy."

"Doyle was queer?"

"According to his aunt he was."

Lew Feemster might have been grumpy as hell, but he was no fool. "That explains a lot," he said.

"It's what got me onto Scott in the first place. So I can expect you to call around noon, right?"

He sighed and nodded. Then he reached in his shirt pocket and pulled out the money I'd given him and laid the bills carefully on the table. "I can't take no pay for helping you get a guy like that out of circulation."

My face must have shown considerable surprise. "What about your source?"

"I'll take care of him. Hell, he owes me money, anyhow."

"That's awful decent of you, Lew."

"Now don't go getting sentimental on me," he snapped.

I laughed. "You're the one that's sentimental, you old buzzard, telling me how nice the Twillers were. You keep on like this and I'm going to have to put you up for membership in the Rotary Club."

"Screw you, Bo Handel," he said without conviction and took a long pull at his beer.

"You be sure to call me tomorrow," I said.

He nodded. "It'll probably be some time between noon and two."

At the door I turned and looked back where he still sat at the corner table, carefully rolling another cigarette. I stepped outside into the hot night air. The ghostly green glow of the ancient sign on the roof turned the cracked and buckled asphalt of the parking lot into an eerie island surrounded by dark, towering walls of silent forest. Just before I rounded the first turn down the road, I looked in the rearview mirror and caught a quick glimpse of the moon where it hung, red and baleful, just above the dilapidated old tavern.

CHAPTER THIRTY-THREE

As I was having my coffee the next morning the weatherman on the radio said the area had been without rain for sixty-seven straight days. I hadn't counted, but I was willing to take his word for it. I knew it was drier than I ever remembered. Reservoirs across the state were reporting record low levels, and there had been almost a dozen weather-related deaths since the drought began, the last two coming during the previous week.

I got to the office and read the sheet from the night before. Domestic squabbles and car wrecks and more of the same. I whiled away the rest of the morning on paperwork and administrative duties. Since I had skipped breakfast, I called the café across the street for a hamburger as soon as it opened.

I finished my lunch, and finally Lew Feemster phoned a little after one and gave me the address. "He's supposed to be waiting there," he said. "He told my friend to come by about two and bring the cash for the money orders."

I thanked him and hung up and found myself faced with a logistical problem. Calls had been coming in so thick and fast that day that I fretted all morning long about having a backup available for the raid. Now the time had come and I didn't. The curse of small departments is that we have to cover too much territory with too few people. Linda was at the doctor's office, Billy Don and Otis were on calls at the north end of the county, and Toby was working a big wreck out on Route 9 South where a tank truck carrying hazardous waste had turned over when it swerved to miss an old man on a tractor.

I called the city PD and found them in much the same shape. Every day-shift patrol officer they had was on a critical call and couldn't be pulled in except for extreme emergencies.

That left Bubba Cates. Bubba had been with me from the start of my law enforcement career, and back when he was younger he'd been my best deputy. Now almost seventy, half deaf, and with eyes dimmed by incipient cataracts, he only worked part-time. The last two years I'd kept him assigned to guard the district court when it was in session because Judge MacGregor preferred him to anybody else. Both men were pipe smokers with large collections of pipes from around the world. During long recesses and jury deliberations, the two of them smoked and played chess and argued about everything under the sun. Three years earlier the commissioner's court, responding to the nationwide lemming effect, had instituted a smoking ban on all county property. This was done, of course, with considerable publicity meant to assure the voters that their elected officials were doing their duty as guardians of Caddo County's health and morals. Then they quietly overlooked the fact that the town's most popular officeholder was quietly ignoring their smoking ban. Just as they overlooked the bottle of forbidden whisky in my desk drawer.

I hated the idea of putting Bubba back into the line of fire, but I could see no other choice. I threw two flak vests over my shoulder and grabbed a Remington riot gun and a bandoleer of three-inch Magnum buckshot. After passing up the elevator as too slow, I vaulted up the rotunda stairway to the third floor and was almost to the door of the district courtroom when Charlie Morton emerged from the commissioners' office.

"What's going on," he asked. "Why all the hardware?"

"I'm going to get Bubba to back me up in a raid."

"He's not up to it, Bo."

"I know that, but I've got no choice."

He gave me an ironic grin. "Hell, you'd be better off with me."

Something in the tone of his voice got my attention. "You were in the army, weren't you, Charlie?"

He shook his head. "Second Marine Division, Tenth Regiment, Desert Storm."

"You've been in combat?"

"You bet I have."

"Would you be willing to cover a back door with this shotgun, or were you just joking?"

"Sure. Who're you raiding?"

"I'll tell you on the way. You are now officially deputized."

I handed him the shotgun and one vest, and once we were in the car I filled him in on Scott Kimball and the tip I'd gotten. "At this point I'm pretty sure that he killed Amanda Twiller," I said. "And the Raynes kid too."

He shook his head sadly. "That damn boy's never been any count. I feel sorry for his mother if it's true. I feel sorry for her anyway."

"I hope you don't get hurt today, Charlie," I said. "I called the city police, and all their people were tied up too."

"I expect I can handle myself under fire better than any of those kids could, Bo. I don't think a single one of them has ever been in a shooting scrape, and I've been in a bunch."

"Were you scared?"

"Hell yes, I was. I'm scared right now. Aren't you?"

"You better believe I am."

The house was a small cottage that had been built in the 1930s only a few blocks from the garage apartment where Doyle Raynes had been arrested. I drove around the block and dropped Charlie off to cover the back door, then I parked around the corner from the front and walked slowly up the sidewalk.

I slipped my .45 auto from its holster as I went up the steps. When I knocked on the door, I heard heavy feet running somewhere inside. It was no time to stand on etiquette. I took one step back and kicked the door in, then plunged into a cluttered living room that held a fancy flat-screen TV and a sprung and battered sofa that held a young woman with a toddler clutched in her arms. The kid was howling and the woman's eyes were full of panic. "Stay put," I told her.

A pair of open double doors led to a messy dining room. The silhouette of a big man in a fancy wind suit appeared on the other side of the dining table and sprinted across the room. I ran after him just as he disappeared through an open doorway. A moment later I heard a screen door slam. Then I heard Charlie shout something I couldn't make out. I raced through the kitchen and out on the back porch and kicked the screen door completely off its hinges.

Paul Arno stood in the middle of the backyard, a pistol in his hand. Charlie crouched behind an old-fashioned picket fence to the left side of the yard, the riot gun at his shoulder. "I said, drop the gun!" he yelled.

"You heard him," I shouted. "Drop it!"

Arno appeared confused for a split second, then turned my way. I saw eyes that were coke-bright and crazy and a hand that was pointing a pistol in my direction. A tiny flash of light appeared at the pistol's muzzle, and splinters flew off the door facing a foot from my head. That's when I decided it was checkout time for Big Paul. My 230-grain Norma hollow-point caught him in the center of his chest just as Charlie's charge of Magnum buckshot slammed into the right side of his head from a distance of no more than thirty feet. The two shots came so close together that we would never be able to decide who fired first. Not that it mattered.

A half a minute later the shakes hit us both, then came the laughs. We trembled and laughed and slapped each other on the back and congratulated ourselves for being alive. It's not pretty to watch, but it often happens at such times. Not everybody can be John Wayne. If fact, John Wayne wasn't really John Wayne.

The whole incident took less than a minute from the time I kicked in the door. The aftermath took the rest of the afternoon. Hours later Charlie and I were back at my office enjoying a drink from that bottle of whiskey Maylene disapproves of so strongly. The body had been sent off for autopsy, which was getting to be a habit, and the house was being thoroughly searched by my deputies and a DPS forensics team, which was also becoming habitual. I had called Bob Thornton, the local Texas Ranger, and he'd taken a statement from each of us, which is a mandatory procedure I'd set years ago for my department in such incidents. But I knew there would be no problems for either of us. It was a justifiable shooting if ever there was one, and I thanked Charlie profusely.

"Does this get me off the hook, Bo?" he asked.

"Why, hell no, it doesn't. You ought to know me better than that."

"I didn't figure it did."

"But I will tell you something that might make you feel better when you go to bat for me. When I was first elected, the department had three riot guns, and all three were Winchester model ninety-seven trench guns from the First World War. Fine old guns in their day, but they were pretty well worn out when the county bought them as military surplus back in the 1930s, so you can imagine what they were like forty years later. Think about that a minute. How would you have liked to have been standing behind that house this afternoon with one of those babies instead of that nice Remington you were holding? Which, by the way, I had to fight like hell to get the commissioners to buy."

He nodded and gulped down the remainder of his drink and held out his glass for a refill. "I see your point."

CHAPTER THIRTY-FOUR

The search of the house turned up a half ounce of cocaine. Arno had already been facing one possession charge, which was a possible explanation why a normally level-headed hoodlum like him might have fled. I personally confiscated his identification and ordered his name withheld pending notification of the next of kin. I really wasn't all that concerned about his relatives, but at the time it seemed like a good idea to play my cards close to my vest.

But the raid had created more questions than it answered. For example, why did I find Paul Arno in that house when I was expecting Scott Kimball? What was their connection? And where the hell was Kimball and why hadn't he been there? The girl almost certainly knew the answers, but so far she'd proven unwilling to talk. I had lodged her and her kid temporarily in one of the holding cells off the outer office.

Her name was Trina Newland, and the two minutes I'd spent with her back at the house convinced me that while she might be blessed with a body that wouldn't quit, she was also cursed with a brain that wouldn't start. From the slight swelling of her belly it was also obvious that she was going to have another child.

She was about five foot five with short, honey-colored hair

and a face that would have been very pretty if it hadn't been marred by her perpetually sullen expression. I told Linda to bring her and her child in.

"I want to go home," she said in a whiny voice as soon as she was ushered into my office. "I need to feed my baby."

"You're not going anywhere for a while," I said. "We can get him something from the café across the street."

"He likes Tater Tots. With ketchup. And real sweet iced tea."

"How about a little protein?" I asked.

"Huh?"

"Fried starch and sugar water aren't very good for him."

"It's what he likes. I don't see nothing wrong with Tater Tots."

I had Maylene order the Tater Tots and a broiled chicken breast. Then I turned to the girl and asked, "How far along are you?"

"Along what?"

"You're pregnant, right? So how many months?"

"Three and a half."

"Is Scott Kimball the father?"

"That's none of your business."

"Is he?"

If looks could kill, I would have been in my grave. "Yeah. So what?"

"Lovely," I muttered. "And is he the father of this child here?"

"Why are you asking me all these nosy questions?"

"I need to know who to notify about your baby when I lock you up for cocaine possession."

"What? I didn't possess nothing. I was just there in that house waiting for Scott to get back."

"By the letter of the law you're guilty," I said. "Now is the father the same man?"

"No."

"Does this little boy's daddy pay you any child support?"

"Sometimes."

"Were you married to him, by any chance?"

"Why don't you leave me alone?"

"Were you?"

"No."

"Are you currently living with Scott Kimball?"

"Yeah."

"Where have you been staying here in town?" I asked. "At that house where we found you?"

"Yeah."

"Where's Scott?"

"I don't know," she said.

"Why wasn't he there this afternoon?"

"He said he had to go get something."

"What?"

"I don't know."

"Look, young lady," I said, trying to sound as fatherly as I could. "You can get some serious time in the penitentiary for cocaine possession. You tell me what I need to know, and you can walk out of here today, and we'll forget all about that dope we found."

"I'm not saying nothing against Scott. He takes care of me."

I laughed and shook my head. "Scott Kimball has never taken care of anybody except himself in his whole life. He treats his mother like a cur dog, and his brother is dead because of his damn foolishness."

"I don't believe any of that. Scott told me about his brother, and he said it wasn't like that at all."

"Then tell me if he's so concerned about you why he left you and your baby in the house with a coked-up Mafia hit man?"

"Maybe he didn't know he was a hit man, even if he was. All I got is your say-so on that, anyway."

I was getting nowhere. I decided to use a little pressure from another direction. "Don't you realize you will probably lose custody of this child if you're charged with cocaine possession? To say nothing of the possibility of going to prison and losing him permanently? Does any of that mean anything to you?"

"I told you I'm not saying nothing to hurt Scott. I love him."

"I would guess you loved the other one who got you knocked up and then deserted you. Did you ever think that maybe you're not too good at picking men?"

She stared at me with eyes that were burning with resentment and hostility. "Kiss my ass, Mr. Smarty."

I motioned to Linda and Maylene. "Call Child Protective Services and have them come get this baby. Then take this little gal out to the jail and book her in for reckless endangerment of a child. That will hold her until I can get the paperwork done on the drug possession charges. And be sure to tell the jailers to put her in the female felony tank. Maybe a night with the big girls will get her heart right."

"I told you I didn't have no drugs," the girl said.

I didn't bother to reply. Maylene took the baby from Trina Newland's arms, and Linda cuffed her and pushed her gently toward the door. "Keep your hands to yourself, you dyke bitch," the girl snarled.

After they left, I turned to Maylene. "It's above and beyond, but would you feed that poor child when the food gets here?"

"Sure, Bo."

"Thanks, sweetheart. You're worth a million dollars."

After weighing my options for a while, I grabbed the phone book and looked up Lulu Wilson's number.

I'm a peace officer, not a social worker. Yet there have been a few times over the years when I've taken flyers on people based on nothing more than a gut instinct that told me they were redeemable. Lulu was one such individual. She was about five-eight, slim, wiry and tough, with creamy chocolate skin and a face that could have made the cover of *Vogue* if she'd gotten a few breaks. She landed in Sequoya a decade earlier badly strung out on heroin and under the thrall of a pimp named Titus Nash who had a long criminal record and a short memory. By that I mean he'd forgotten how much he'd hated the Texas prison system the first time he'd gone down behind two dozen caps of Mexican Brown and an illegal handgun. Which is about what I caught him with after the desk clerk at a local motel called late one evening to report a disturbance that turned out to be Titus beating Lulu half to death.

Something in Lulu's eyes that night told me she wouldn't have become what she was if she'd had any choice. So I gave her that choice: testify against Nash for his Sequoya business, plus a couple of armed robberies the Rangers wanted to nail him on down in Houston. In return I agreed to get the DA to drop everything we had against her, get her into rehab, and see to it that she found a job when she got out. I also promised to lend her enough money to get her a place to live and make it through to her first paycheck. She made the right decision and went into the ninety-day drug treatment program at Rusk State Hospital. Meanwhile, the DA hit Titus with the bitch, by which I mean he convicted him under Texas's habitual criminal statute, which allows a jury to prescribe life for a three-time felony offender it they are in the mood to do so. And East Texas juries usually are. The last I heard, Titus was picking cotton in the Brazos River bottom and would be until about 2030. Lulu had been clean for ten years and was now holding down a good job as the manager of a local convenience store. Somewhere along the way she'd joined Nelda Parson's father's Rising Star Baptist Church, and she'd even found a decent boyfriend, a divorced gentleman a few years her senior who coached the boys' basketball team at the local high school.

When I called she was happy to hear from me. "What have you got on your mind?" she asked.

"Lulu, do you remember how you've said so many times that

you wished there was some way you could repay me for going to bat for you? You do remember? Well, that's great because I think it's about time for you to make your acting debut."

A few minutes later I put the phone down, laced my fingers behind my head, and leaned back in my chair to stare up at the ceiling fan with a smile on my face. "Dykes," I said and laughed.

CHAPTER THIRTY-FIVE

I decided I wanted a real meal for supper that evening, but I also decided I didn't want to stay in town. I picked up the phone and dialed Carla's cell number. "Let's go over to Nacogdoches tonight for Italian," I said as soon as she answered.

"Do you think that's wise?"

"I don't care if it is or not. Me and Charlie Morton killed a guy this afternoon, and I want some company."

I heard her sharp intake of breath. "God, Bo! Who?"

"That Paul Arno character. Haven't you heard about it?"

"Don't you ever look at the schedule? I'm off today. I've been home all afternoon with the TV and radio off and the house phone unplugged. Soft music on the stereo and housecleaning. Sometimes I just have to get away from all the craziness."

"Well, today I've been in the middle of the craziness. Pick you up about seven?"

"Sure, Bo. If you need me."

"Dammit, I'm beginning to suspect I'll always need you."

I hung up the phone and muttered to myself, "Now why in the hell did I go and say something like that?"

No fool like an old fool.

Carla wore a pair of black slacks and a simple blouse of coarse gray silk. Besides her gold watch, she wore no jewelry except for a single strand of creamy pearls that contrasted with the tanned skin of her neck and made her look edible. I felt myself sinking even deeper.

My favorite restaurant in Nacogdoches is Auntie Pasta's, a great Italian joint down by the railroad tracks in an old building that was built back in 1892 as the first refrigerated warehouse west of the Mississippi. We had just ordered and gotten a glass of Chianti when an old friend named Ben Ruggles appeared at our table. Ben was one of those rare football coaches who had real brains. Besides coaching the backfield at Sequoya High School for years, he'd taught accounting and business law. He was tall and not overly bulky, as befitted a man who'd been a star full-back at Texas A&M many years earlier. Ben had short gray hair and a face that was full of good humor.

"Sit down, Ben," I said, pointing to a chair. "You know Carla, don't you?"

"Oh yes," he said, giving her a warm smile. "But I've just got a minute or two. I'm with some friends and I need to get back to our table."

"Sure. What's on your mind?"

"Amanda Twiller's murder."

I felt the hair on the back of my neck stand up. Ben Ruggles was not the sort of man to engage in idle gossip. If he had something to say, it would be worth hearing. "Go on," I said.

"As you probably know, I've been working part-time at the Pak-a-Sak for about a year."

"I'd heard that," I said. "I also heard that you and Zorn had become buddies, which surprised me."

He shook his head. "Emmet and I aren't really friends. We

could have been, but he tries too damn hard to impress, and I can't stand that. I also got tired of listening to his stories about his love life, and I told him off and quit three days ago."

"How did you happen to be working for him in the first place?"

"I was in there buying some beer one day not long after I retired, and the two of us got to talking. He told me that he knew I'd taught accounting and asked me to help out with the bookkeeping. I was a little bored with retirement and knew I could always use some extra money. So I signed on as assistant manager."

"Is it a good business?" I asked.

"It makes him a decent living. It could be a great business if he'd stay there and take care of things. The beer companies are always offering specials where you can buy fifty or more cases of a popular brand cheap enough to double your margin, but he would never let me make the decisions on things like that. He was always off chasing women or hanging around in these country-and-western clubs."

"He does like the ladies," I said.

"The Casanova of the soap opera set."

Carla laughed. "Doesn't sound like you have much regard for the man, Ben," she said.

"In a way I feel sorry for him. It's like he's always onstage trying to make a big splash, but I finally got tired of hearing his conquest stories. I think the truth is that he doesn't really care all that much about women beyond bedding them and having a good looker on his arm to bolster his ego. But as far as really enjoying their company?" He shook his head. "The man just doesn't get it."

"Did he ever say anything about Amanda Twiller?" I asked. "I mean beyond the obvious."

"Oh, yeah. I heard all about it."

"How in the hell did the two of them ever meet, anyway?" I asked.

He smiled. "There's a sad irony in that, Bo."

"What do you mean?"

"Reverend Twiller got caught up in this return-to-authentic-Christian-practices movement. As you probably know, up until after the Civil War everybody used real wine in communion. Then came Carrie Nation and the temperance movement, and most of the Baptists and Methodists and Presbyterians switched to grape juice. In the last few years a lot of congregations have gone back to real wine and unleavened bread because that's what the early church used. Twiller must have delegated the wine buying to his wife because she came in one morning asking questions about what kind of wine would be suitable. She was a fine-looking woman, and Emmet battened on to her like Velcro. After that, nature took its course."

"Did he ever mention anything about Amanda Twiller having a prescription drug addiction?"

He shook his head. "No, but I'd heard rumors and Emmet bragged to me a couple of times about being able to get drugs without a prescription. I know for a fact that he used some mild amphetamines every now and then. He always claimed they improved his performance in the bedroom."

"Can you remember anything else that he might have said about her?" I asked.

"A couple of days before she was killed they had a little tiff right there in the store. After she left he was really steamed and said something he probably shouldn't have said."

"Which was?"

"'That bitch knows too much about my business.'"

"Yeah?"

"Right. And I didn't get the feeling that he was talking about the store, either."

CHAPTER THIRTY-SIX

The next morning Carla woke me up and then slipped out the door. I put on the coffee and called the dispatcher and told her to have Trina Newland brought down to the courthouse for interrogation as soon as breakfast was finished at the jail. I also called Hotchkiss and asked him if he could meet me at the office. He agreed and was already there when I arrived, installed in front of my desk with more of Maylene's cookies and a big mug of coffee. I filled him in on what I had learned in the last two days.

"So you're convinced that Arno didn't do the Twiller killing?" he asked.

"Yeah, but so far you and Toby and Linda are the only people who know that, and I want you to keep quiet about it. There's nothing to be gained by broadcasting it."

"And you feel pretty strongly about the Kimball kid?"

"I sure do."

"You've known him all his life, haven't you?" he asked.

"Oh Lord, yes. This office has been handling him on minor stuff since he was in junior high school. Ditto for the city police."

"Did he ever seem to fight against his worst impulses?"

"Never a time that I could see. It's like he always knew he wanted to be an outlaw, and that's all he ever studied."

"I wish I knew what causes a person to be like him. All the textbooks say it's environmental influences, abuse and so forth, but still I wonder. . . ."

"Well, in his case the textbooks are wrong," I said. "There wasn't any abuse. Scott's parents were two of the finest people you'd ever want to meet."

"Do you know if he had any record of torturing animals or anything like that when he was little?"

"Not for sure," I said. "But I've heard stories. My niece is pretty close to his mother, and Willa has told her things about the kid that she doesn't want to dwell on."

"Whether he did the Twiller killing or not, he was up to something with Arno, and it had to be bad."

There came a knock at the door. It was Billy Don and Linda with Trina Newland in tow. "Stick around," I told Hotchkiss. "You might learn something."

Linda ushered her in. The girl was already beginning to look institutionalized in her ill-fitting jailhouse coveralls, and the delousing shower had taken all the body out of her hair. I motioned for her to sit down, and then I let her wait while I finished reading my morning's report. Hotchkiss sat silently and munched his cookies and sipped his coffee. I tossed the report on my desk and looked her over good. I could tell that she was humbled but not broken. But she was close.

"You don't look like you got much sleep," I said.

"I didn't. There was this black lesbo that was after me all night long."

"Well, in that case you should have complained to the jailers."

"Yeah, sure. I know what happens to people who snitch in jail."

I shrugged. "Your choice. We can't fix problems we don't know about."

"What did you bring me down here for?"

"I wanted to appraise you of your situation, Trina. Under state law you were in possession of that cocaine by virtue of being in the same room where it was lying there in plain sight. It's a slam dunk for two years right there. But . . ." Here I stopped speaking and gave her a grim smile. "By a quirk of Texas law, this felony can be enhanced by a number of other factors. For example, your past record."

"I ain't got no past record," she said, "except a juvie beef or two, and even I know you can't use them in adult court."

"Right you are. But the possession charge can also be enhanced by any other felonies you committed while in possession of the coke. Such as the reckless endangerment of your child. So you can see that once you're convicted of the possession charge, the rest of it falls over like the next domino in the line. When it goes to trial, you'll get a country jury made up of good small-town Baptists and Methodists and Campbellites with maybe a couple of oldtime Presbyterians thrown in to leaven the mixture. They'll stay in the jury room at least an hour to make it look like there was a little debate involved. Which there won't be. Then they'll come out and hang fifteen to twenty years on your happy little ass. After which they'll go home and have a good supper and then sleep secure in the knowledge that they've done the Lord's work."

"Twenty years? My God! I never did no drugs in my life except a little weed. This ain't fair!"

"I know, dear. Life's rough and then you die. But that's only one way it can all shake down. The other way is that you tell me what I need to know and you walk out of here today free as a bird. All this unpleasantness will be forgotten."

"Do I get my baby back?"

"That's out of my hands. Under state law there has to be a custody hearing within ten days. I can get you hooked up with an interfaith social services agency that will show you what moves you have to make. But I can tell you that if you put forth any effort at all to clean up your act and be the momma that little boy deserves, then you'll get him back."

She thought it over for a minute, all the while chewing her lower lip. "Okay," she said. "I'll tell you anything except where Scott is."

"But that's the one thing I need to know," I said.

"I love Scott, and I won't give him up."

She'd seen the carrot, and now it was time for the stick.

"Do you think he really cares anything about you, girl?" I asked roughly. "Do you actually believe he's going to wait around until you get out of the pen a dozen or so years from now? Shit, he'll be out there pronging the first little twit that catches his eye, if he isn't already. And you'll be locked up in a steel cage and getting older by the day."

"You're just awful!"

I stood up, came around my desk, and jerked her chair around to where she was looking straight at me. Then I leaned down with my face just a few inches from hers.

"I'm worse than awful. I'm the meanest old son of a bitch you ever laid your two eyes on. You think we got bad dykes here in our jail? You ain't seen nothing like what they've got at the women's unit at Mountain View. Some of them weigh two hundred pounds or better and look like they could eat a Jeep for breakfast. You're sexy and you know it, and that's an asset here on the outside. But inside it's a liability because you'll just be fresh meat to those gals. Two or three of the biggest and meanest will pick you out the first week, and then they'll square off and fight to see which one owns you. You've never seen anything like a pair of bull daggers fighting. They go at it like rabid hyenas. I don't even want to think about the winner. Hell, I bet she'll have an iron ring in her nose and tattoos all over the rest of her body. Whatever she looks like, she'll be the she-wolf in that pack, and you'll be her little piggy. Then every night that passes she'll sit on your pretty face and howl at the moon."

That's when she broke.

CHAPTER THIRTY-SEVEN

I had no intention of letting the girl tip off Kimball because of late-blooming second thoughts. Which meant that she would stay in custody at least another day. I called the interfaith group like I'd promised, and they sent a representative down to the courthouse to begin the process of working with her. I also assured her that there was no need to drop the reckless endangerment charge because it had never been filed. We saw to it that she got a good lunch from the Texan Café, and by early afternoon she'd perked up and started to act like a human being again. I think she was even beginning to see the possibility of life after Scott. I hoped she'd make it into the ranks of the decent and the productive, and I told her so. But I had seen too much in my years as sheriff to have much confidence that she would.

I had phone calls to make and details to attend to, but in mid-morning I stopped to have a cup of coffee and a donut with Linda.

"That was a very creative interpretation of the state enhancement statute you gave that little fool," she said. "I've never heard anything quite like it before."

"She was Mirandaized and didn't ask for a lawyer. I don't see that it's my duty to explain every little nuance of the law with gilt-edged accuracy. Besides, it scared her into giving Scott Kimball up, and when she did that she made the right move for herself and her kid. Can you imagine raising a child around that boy?"

She shook her head. "She's sure scared of dykes, isn't she?"

I snapped my fingers. "That reminds me to make a note to Maylene. I want to have her draw up one of those fancy citizens commendation certificates from the sheriff's department."

"You don't give many of those out, do you?"

"No, I do not. I strongly believe that they should be something more than a PR move."

"I just remember two in the five years I've worked for you. Who's this one for?"

"Lulu Wilson. And I'm going to personally send her a big ham at Christmas time."

"Lulu? What did she do?"

I grinned and sipped my coffee. "That's another of those stories too harsh for your young and tender ears."

"Damn it, Bo," she seethed. "You can be such an asshole sometimes!"

Just then Toby came in and took the other chair opposite my desk. "How about telling us how you made Scott Kimball for this mess?" he asked. "I thought nobody had seen him in town."

"Two things. For one, Danny Kettle has a source who says that the coke was stolen from Zorn just like we thought, and that it was Scott who got it. At the time he told me the story, I didn't believe it because Scott hadn't been seen in town in months. But the last time I talked to Doyle Raynes's aunt, she told me that Doyle was gay. Did either of you know that?"

They both shook their heads.

"But you both remember what Scott looks like, don't you?"

"Sure," Linda said.

"When Parker Raynes's told me about Doyle being a homosexual, my mind flashed back to the other day when I was out at Willa's house. She showed me two studio portraits she had made of her boys a few years ago and it all started to fall into place for me."

"I fail to see your point," Toby said. "What have his looks got to do with it?"

"I get it," Linda said.

"I don't," Toby said.

"He and his brother Hamilton were two of the best-looking guys this town ever produced," Linda said. "I had a terrific crush on Hamilton at one time even though he was three years younger than me."

Toby shrugged. "Okay. I'm willing to take your word for it, but what does this have to do with Doyle Raynes? Do you think something was going on between them?"

"I feel sure of it," I said. "I think Doyle was in love with Scott, and Scott was jerking him around every which way. Walter Durbin told me he thought Doyle was protecting somebody."

"Isn't this kinda off the wall?" Linda asked. "I mean, girls were always nuts about Scott, and he has the reputation of being quite the little stud hoss. And then there's this Newland girl."

"Not at all," I said. "There was a juvenile case similar to this that he was involved in the year he was a junior in high school. The records were sealed by the judge's order, but I knew what happened because I did the investigation. Do either of you remember a kid named Jimmy Dale Webster?"

"I've heard the name," Toby said. "But I was in the army at the time."

"I do," Linda said. "He killed himself."

"Maybe he did and maybe he didn't," I said. "It was eventually ruled a suicide, but I had my doubts even back then, and I really have my doubts today. You see, Jimmy was in the closet, and he and Scott did a string of burglaries together. Scott was the instigator of the whole thing, and he was using poor Jimmy's homosexuality to control him."

"You mean he was letting Jimmy blow him, don't you?" Linda asked.

I laughed. "I was going to phrase it a little more delicately, but yes, they were having sex. Scott took the male role, as you might expect. Jimmy Dale copped to the whole thing. Jimmy's dad was a retired air force officer, and at the time he owned a security company that had contracts spread out over three or four counties. Since his clients were the only ones hit, it was obvious what was happening. I leaned on Jimmy pretty hard, and he confessed. The windup of the thing was that both boys got probation because of their age."

"But why would Scott kill him if they were already caught?" Toby asked.

"Revenge. He was mad as hell that Jimmy had revealed their affair. I knew about it, the judge knew, the prosecutor knew, Walter Durbin and Dud Malone knew because they represented the two boys."

"I can see that," Toby said. "For lots of people, queer is queer and it doesn't make any difference whether you're pitching or catching. Most black folks are that way."

"So you're convinced Scott was doing the same thing with Doyle Raynes?" Linda asked.

"I'd almost bet my life on it. I think Scott killed Amanda Twiller and made Doyle help him dump the body. You see, I always had a problem with Arno as her killer because a pro like him would have gotten her off somewhere and shot her and left the body where it fell. Then there's another thing. Agent Hotchkiss and I have thought from the first that somebody was sending a message by dumping the body right out in public like that, and I know for a fact that Scott hates me and he hates this town. So . . ."

"What possible motive could he have had?" Toby asked.

"Either somebody paid him to do it, or the three of them were together and something got out of hand. It could have been unpremeditated. Amanda Twiller and Doyle were both known dopers, and I feel sure Scott isn't averse to trying a little of whatever came along. Put three unstable people together with a bottle of whisky and some drugs late at night, and you've got a recipe for disaster."

"What about Willa?" Linda asked. "Do we need to go see her?"

"I already have. She says she hasn't seen him, and that means she hasn't. All the times I ever had trouble with Scott, she backed me up because she knew I was trying to get him to settle down and be decent. He'll avoid her because he knows she won't hide him or lie for him."

By late afternoon I had assembled my team. It would be a multiagency operation for the simple reason that I didn't have the available manpower to go it alone. Nor was I inclined to do so. The target house was inside the city limits, which gave the Sequoya Police Department a strong claim on inclusion and so did Hotchkiss. Texas Ranger Don Thornton was working the Doyle Raynes case, and I knew I could count on him. From my own force I picked Linda and Toby, with Otis Tremmel as surveillance and backup.

Clyde Morgan over at the city police assigned one of their best young patrolmen—Herbert Stovall, a graduate of the police academy up at Kilgore Junior College. I was one of the few people in town who knew Stovall's first name since he'd gone by "Bobo" practically since birth. So we had a Bo, a Bobo, and a Bob, something that gave me a momentary urge to include Bubba Cates just to confuse the media people if anything newsworthy came out of the raid. But I resisted.

I got everybody together in my office in the courthouse. "First order of business," I said after I had made introductions. "What we have on tap tonight is something we're almost certain is a big drug buy. I'm sure all of you remember Lester Sipes from the newspapers and TV a few years back. According to Agent Hotchkiss, Sipes is now heavily involved in the cocaine trade. One of our local yokels, a liquor store owner named Emmet Zorn, has been muleing the stuff to Dallas for him. On the most recent shipment Zorn decided to screw Sipes, sell the coke, and then vanish. To that end, he got in touch with a drug dealer in St. Louis who wanted the stuff really bad. This St. Louis guy sent an idiot named Willard Peet down here to arrange the transaction, but when he hit town he couldn't find Zorn. Peet freaked out when he failed to make contact, and went around asking people about him and insulting folks and in general acting obnoxious until he came to the attention of two of my deputies. They hauled him in, and largely through the encouragement of Chief Deputy Toby Parsons, he was made to see the error of his ways."

"How did you do that, Toby?" Bobo Stovall asked.

"I appealed to the brother's sense of racial solidarity."

"Yeah, right," Bobo said with a laugh.

"Once Peet saw the light," I continued, "he ratted out both Zorn and his employer up north. But by this time Zorn had developed a major problem. The cocaine, which is valued in the neighborhood of a million dollars wholesale, had gone missing, and everything points to its having been stolen from Zorn by one of our local bad boys, a young rogue named Scott Kimball.

"I'm sure most of you are familiar with Scott. I'm also sure you realize that my main interest in this affair is nailing him because I think he did both the Twiller and Raynes killings. Yesterday, one of my informants called in a tip that Kimball was at a house over on the north side of town. We raided the place only to find that for some reason, Kimball had bugged out just before we got there. We did apprehend his girlfriend, and she has acknowledged her errors and begun to mend her ways. As a show of good faith, she told us about this drug buy. A second consequence of yesterday's raid was that a mob-connected hoodlum named Paul Arno crossed on over Jordan. Kimball's girlfriend told me that Arno was helping Kimball sell something that was supposed to bring him a big chunk of money, so I don't see how it could be anything else. My take on it is that Kimball had the coke, but no contacts with possible buyers. Arno had the contacts but no coke, so they both must have seen it as a match made in heaven."

"Aren't you afraid Kimball will assume the girl tipped us off?" Stovall asked.

"Not really. He's either going to be there or he isn't. The girl claims he's not aware that she knows about it. She heard him and Arno talking when they didn't know she was listening. We think Kimball owes some heavy gambling debts to some bad people down in Houston, and he's probably getting a little desperate."

"There's something else that makes me think he'll be there tonight," Bob Thornton said. "With Arno dead he may not have any way to get in touch with his buyers to reschedule the meeting. So it's now or never."

"Who does the house belong to?" Linda asked.

"It's a rental. One of Kimball's buddies is the name on the lease, but he hasn't been in town for two weeks. He left Kimball the key." I looked around the room. "Any more questions?" I asked.

A shaking of heads.

"Okay," I said. "The house across the street is also a rental, and it's empty. I got the key from the owner, and Otis Tremmel is going to go over there in civilian clothes about seven and go in the back door. He's got binoculars, and there's a streetlight right in front of the target house. He'll let us know if and when the people show up.

"Now remember one last thing. Scott Kimball has almost certainly murdered two people that we know about. He was the cause of his only brother's death, and he never showed a dime's worth of remorse or guilt over that. Ever since he was a little kid he's given every indication that he was developing into a stone psychopath. In all probability, the people he's dealing with on this coke deal are going to be of similar disposition. So I want you to keep in mind that each of you is more important to your families, your community, and to me than any of these people we'll be going up against. So don't take any silly chances, and don't hesitate a second if your life is on the line. I want everybody safe and sound and back down here bitching about the paperwork when it's all over."

Bob Thornton raised his hand.

"Go ahead, Bob," I said.

He turned to face the group. "Folks, Bo is telling you right about that. And something else. Me and him both have been in enough of these old shooting fracases to know they're no fun. When it comes down to the wire tonight you're going to be scared shitless. And I'm not ashamed to admit that I'm going to be scared shitless right along with you. In fact, if you aren't scared you need to get out of police work because a little fear is an asset to this job. Now go ahead, Bo. I've had my say."

"Thanks, Bob," I said and looked at my watch. "It's four-thirty now and we need to meet back here at seven. Go across the street and have a little supper if you want. Or go outside and smoke or whatever. Just be here on time with your flak vests and helmets and all that fancy Dirty Harry gear. Okay?"

CHAPTER THIRTY-EIGHT

At seven we met back at the office and I checked everybody's equipment—Kevlar-lined vests, Kevlar helmets with shock-resistant face shields, and radios with wrist mikes and earpiece headphones much like the Secret Service uses. Bob Thornton had secured an unmarked DPS van, and that gave us two. I assigned Toby, Linda, and Hotchkiss to the rear, and Bobo Stovall to cover the side door that opened from the kitchen. The four of them were in the DPS unit, which was stationed in an abandoned garage on the street behind the target house. Thornton and I parked well around the corner on a potholed side street and waited, sweating like pigs the whole time.

I have never known of a criminal who could consistently be on time for anything. That is, I think, part of their problem. On every stakeout and raid I have ever participated in, at least one of the suspects was late. It was eight-nineteen when my headphone came alive and I heard the urgent tones of Otis Tremmel's voice informing us that a big Lincoln Town Car had just pulled up in front.

"Let us know when they get inside," I said. "Toby, bring your people into position."

Less than a minute later the radio came alive again: "They're in the house and the door just closed," Tremmel said.

Thornton and I stepped from the van and quickly made our way around to the front of the house and started carefully up the walk. We had almost reached the front door when two shots rang out inside, followed closely by a short burst of fire from an automatic weapon of some sort. We stood silently, waiting, then we heard several shots behind the house. A moment later Toby's voice came through my radio earpiece! "It's Kimball, Bo. He was coming out the back door when he saw us. He shot first, and then ducked back inside."

"Hold your positions," I whispered into my mike. "Everybody hold your positions and do not approach."

"Bo, what do you think?" Thornton asked.

"I think if we hit him now he'll flush. I don't believe this boy will ever give up, and if we wait around for him to get his bearings things will just be that much more dangerous when we do have to go in."

"My notion exactly," he said. "And I really don't want this to turn into a three-day standoff."

"Me either. Right through the front door together?"

"Let's knock the damn thing clean off its hinges."

We did. It caved in like a cracker box to reveal a small living room that held some worn but decent furniture, a half dozen cluttered bookcases, and two bodies that appeared very dead. An instant later Scott Kimball materialized in the doorway on the opposite side of the room and fired two quick shots. The first hit Thornton in the chest of his flak jacket and put him down. The second shattered a vase on a bookcase beside my head and threw stagnant water all over the faceplate of my helmet, clouding my vision. I snapped off three shots of my own, only to catch a glimpse of the kid as he vanished into the darkened room beyond. I wiped my faceplate and looked down at Thornton. He had the wind knocked out of him, but his vest had held. He motioned me to go on.

It's strange what runs through your mind in such situations. As I moved carefully across the room, I was very aware that this was a near replay of the day before when Arno was killed. I also found myself wishing that Charlie Morton was waiting outside with that Remington riot gun along with my other people. I knew from experience that Charlie wouldn't hesitate, and I was afraid some of them might, good hands though they were.

I crept up to the doorway and peeked around the door facing. I caught a quick glimpse of Kimball on the other side of the room with a duffel bag in one hand, a pistol in the other, and what looked like an Uzi slung over his shoulder. I jerked my head back just as he fired a shot that splintered the doorway's wooden molding right beside my ear.

"Give it up, Scott," I yelled. "The place is surrounded."

"Fuck you, old man," he called out, and I swear there was a happy lilt to his voice. Then two more bullets slammed into the wall just opposite my head, and I found myself thanking my lucky stars that the house was old enough to have wooden interior walls instead of the plasterboard they use nowadays. I stood motionless for a few seconds, barely breathing until the silence was broken by a long burst of automatic weapon fire from the rear of the house. It was counterpointed by a half dozen or so individual shots that seemed to come from several directions. The earpiece of my radio crackled with static, and I heard, "Trooper down! Trooper down! Linda's hit!"

I ran through the next room and out onto the back porch in time to see Kimball spray one final burst of fire from the Uzi and then dive through the dense privet hedge that bordered the right side of the yard. He made it, but his duffel bag didn't. It hung up in the shrubbery, and I emptied my .45 at the hand that held it. The hand dropped the bag, and I heard footsteps running down the alley beside the house. Just as I slammed another magazine into my pistol, Linda yelled over the radio, "It's just my damn foot! Go get the bastard! Aw, God, but it hurts!"

A motorcycle engine roared to life in the alleyway, and I fought my way through the hedge in time to see its taillight turn out into the street. I ran as fast as my aging legs would carry me and reached the end of the alley just as Toby screeched up in the van. I piled in and we took off after the rapidly dwindling cycle.

As soon as I caught my breath, I said, "Call the city PD and the highway patrol."

"I already did," came the reply. "I wonder what was in that suitcase. Dope or money?"

"Money," I said firmly.

"What makes you think so?"

"Two dead men in the front room of that house back there. Scott didn't come here for a deal. He just decided he'd kill himself a couple of mainline hoods, take their money, and then go sell his crap someplace else. Ain't this boy a piece of work?"

Kimball headed for the south side of town. Twice he cut through yards and down alleys and we almost lost him, but Toby hung on. As we rounded the square, he flashed onto South Main just past the courthouse and blazed down the street ahead of us, weaving his way in and out between cars and pickups and running two red lights in the process. We threaded through traffic and eventually managed to close up half the distance between us and the taillight of the motorcycle by the time we reached the edge of town. "He's heading out State Highway Nine South," Toby said over the radio.

Just as we passed the city limit a highway patrol cruiser roared up beside our van. Toby motioned him ahead, and the cruiser shot past us, its lights blinking and its siren howling. Our van wasn't built for either handling or speed, and it had been a miracle that we stayed with him in town. Out on the highway we gradually began to lose ground, but the DPS car was slowly gaining on him. About two miles outside of town a Sequoya Police Department patrol unit joined the chase, then a couple of miles farther on we saw a second DPS cruiser coming toward us from the opposite direction with its lights flashing. It was in the process of trying to turn sideways to block the highway when the motorcycle swerved to the right onto an oil-topped county road that angled away from the main highway.

The first highway patrol cruiser was going too fast to make the turn and screeched past it with its brake lights shining and its front bumper almost down to the asphalt as the trooper tried to slow his cruiser. The city boys managed to fishtail onto the oil road, and we were right behind them. After a half mile or so, I looked back to see the two DPS units gaining on us. It was a wild ride, one I never want to repeat. Sixty and seventy miles an hour on a winding, one-lane county road in the dead of night is not my idea of fun. A mile or so off the highway the deep woods began, and soon came the sensation that we were flashing down a dark canyon whose walls rose high on either side of us. Three miles farther and the road's oil surface turned to gravel, yet still we sped onward, the motorcycle's taillight a faint red dot far ahead.

We slid through a broad, sweeping turn and roared down a long grade, going deeper into the forest. Then a sign flashed by that said COUNTY ROAD 7, and I realized where we were. "Toby," I said calmly, "get on the radio and tell those city boys to start slowing down. We're coming up to a dead end."

He picked up the mike and spoke, and a moment later I saw the cruiser's brake lights come on. "Then we've got him," he said.

"Nope. We're going to lose him."

"How?"

"Just watch."

Far ahead the motorcycle's taillight bounced a time or two,

then dwindled and vanished. The city police car pulled up into the intersection and stopped, and we swung in beside it. A few seconds later both highway patrol units arrived. We all climbed from our vehicles.

"What the hell happened to him?" Toby asked.

"See that?" I asked and pointed across CR 292 where CR 7 continued on into the woods as two narrow, overgrown, and rutted trails.

"What on earth?" one young city patrolman said.

"When CR 292 was built back in the 1930s, the county decided not to maintain Road Seven past this intersection. Hell, they were just old logging roads, and neither of them were even numbered back then. But they put in a culvert on the far side of 292 so timber company trucks could get across in wet weather."

"So where's Kimball?" one of the DPS troopers asked.

"Gone, my friends. This one got away."

"But where does that trail lead?" Toby asked.

I laughed. "It leads to anywhere he wants to go. The damn thing crosses three more county roads and a half dozen other old logging trails that are in good enough shape for a motorcycle."

"Do you want us to call over to the prison unit for the dogs and horses?" one of the DPS troopers asked.

"Lord, no," I said. "He'll be gone from these woods long before they could even get here. I don't guess anybody got close enough to get the tag number on that motorcycle, did they?"

The young city cop grinned. "I got it with my night binoculars."

"Great work," I said. "Put it out on the radio, but I don't really expect to catch him riding it. This kid is too smart for that. He'll abandon that cycle and steal himself a car someplace."

"Where do you think he's heading?" Toby asked.

"Houston. He's been living down there for several months, and no doubt he's got contacts and people who will help him."

"Looks like this boy is trying to be the John Dillinger of Caddo County," the older DPS trooper said.

"As far as I'm concerned he's done made it," I said. "We exchanged a few words tonight inside that house, and from the tone of his voice it sounded like he was having the time of his life. What can you do with a guy like that?"

CHAPTER THIRTY-NINE

When we returned to the scene of the shootout, it looked like half the town had gathered in front of the house. Two of our cruisers sat out front, along with three city police cars and a pair of DPS units and an ambulance. We parked down the street and ducked under the crime scene tape. Inside the house Agent Hotchkiss was running the show and doing a good job of it.

"First thing, how's Linda?" I asked.

"She's not in danger," Hotchkiss said. "Otis Tremmel talked to her for a couple of minutes before they took her cell phone away. They're prepping her for emergency surgery in the hospital in Nacogdoches. No X-rays yet, but the ER doctor said the bullet broke a couple of bones."

"Have her parents been notified? I don't want them to hear it on TV."

"They have. Tremmel called them, and they're on their way to the hospital. They took it pretty good, he said."

"How about Bob Thornton?"

"Sore and grumpy, but no permanent damage. And we've got the bullet that hit his flak vest. It's a little distorted, but intact. If it matches the Twiller and Raynes murder weapon, we've got a bankable case on Kimball."

"Excellent," I said. "How about the deceased? Have we got anything on them?"

"Hoods out of Mississippi. Names are Robert Quest and Donald Eugene Weeks. The Bureau has files on both of them but it will take a while to get the works."

"We can assume they are both heavies, though?" I asked.

"Absolutely."

"I don't suppose you found any cocaine, did you?"

He grinned. "No, but we found a suitcase full of money with two forty-five-caliber holes in it. We also found an empty Uzi out in the alleyway."

"My age," I said, shaking my head. "I'm getting to where I can't see when it's dark. I'm a good shot in the daytime, but my night vision is gone. How much was in the suitcase?"

"We haven't counted it down to the nickel, but it looks like a quarter million in hundred-dollar bills."

I looked around at the bullet-riddled living room. "Hotch, how do you figure this mess went down?"

"I think that considering how quick it happened, Kimball must have started shooting almost as soon as they were inside and he was sure they had the money. One of the rednecks had the Uzi. We figure that when Kimball shot him, he sprayed the ceiling as he fell. That was the burst we heard right after the first two gunshots. Then Kimball grabbed the Uzi and used it to shoot his way out. We found two magazines for the thing, one that he discarded on the back porch and the other was still in the weapon. My thinking is that since we didn't find any coke, this had to be a straight-up robbery. Quest and Weeks were lured here for what they thought was going to be a buy. Either Kimball and Arno together planned to take them out and steal the money, or Kimball planned to do all three of them from the first. Which do you think it was?"

"The latter," I said. "From what I've seen of this kid lately, I don't think he would have planned to kill two people for a fifty-fifty split when he could kill all three and keep the whole thing."

"We've got fugitive alerts out all over the state and western Louisiana too. Do you think we should stake out his mother's house?"

"No. That's the last place he'll go because he knows she won't hide him. I would bet anything that he's swiped a car and is already on his way to Houston."

We were there until well after midnight. The mobile news unit from the Lufkin network affiliate arrived along with a half dozen print reporters, including Sheila, who showed up in shorts and with her hair still damp from the shower. I was pressured into holding an impromptu press conference on the scene wherein I spread a little creative disinformation. I said that as the result of a reliable informant's tip, a multiagency task force had raided the house in an effort to apprehend a murder suspect and in the process interrupted a drug buy that had gone bad. I revealed that two people had died in the raid, and that their names would be withheld pending notification of the next of kin. I named the officers involved and praised them all, and gave them the details of Linda's injury. Then I said I would answer any questions I could without jeopardizing an ongoing investigation.

"Were either of the deceased killed by police officers, Sheriff Handel?" asked Emma Waters, the pretty blond coanchor for the Lufkin station.

"Absolutely not."

"You mentioned a murder suspect," another reporter said. "Was this in relation to the Amanda Twiller homicide?"

"It was, but I can't give you the suspect's name at the moment."

"Why haven't you released the name of the man killed in

yesterday's shootout?" asked Dan Ryder, a congenital smart-ass who served as the wire service stringer in central East Texas.

"I had my reasons, but I'll be happy to do that right now. He was a mob-connected figure from New Orleans named Paul Arno. They called him Big Paul."

"What was he doing here in Sequoya?" he asked.

"We think it had something to do with this drug deal."

"Were any drugs found?"

"No."

"Then how do you know it was a drug buy?"

"Informants, and from the amount of money that was found at the scene it could have hardly been anything else."

"Money?" he asked. "How much?"

"We're not sure yet, but it was certainly enough to get the attention of a struggling scribbler like yourself."

He didn't like that answer. "Maybe it was a peaceful poker game you raided. Did you ever consider that?"

"Dan, even you should know that people don't bring Uzis to friendly neighborhood card games. But I will admit that in a sense they were gambling, and it looks like they lost."

CHAPTER FORTY

I had a mountain of paperwork to contend with the next morning. In addition to ordering the medical records on Linda for our group insurance, I had to collect and summarize reports from each officer involved. Document, document, document—all at the insistence of the county's attorneys, who were ever mindful of potential lawsuits.

Because of the Arno killing the day before and the involvement of two well-known Mississippi hoods, the shootout had made the national news, and a CNN stringer out of Houston called and wanted to do a profile on me and my department. I told him I couldn't stop him, but that I wouldn't help him either. He got a little argumentative and I had fun hanging up on him. The big national media boys are always so surprised when they run up on somebody who isn't foaming at the mouth to get his fifteen minutes of fame. As an elected official, I have sense enough to cultivate the local press. Which meant Armand Fiske, owner of the *Sequoya Gazette,* Sheila and the rest of the people at the *Sentinel,* and the reporters from the Lufkin TV station. For them I made time. The press folks from surrounding counties got time when I could give it, but the rest could go hang.

The door opened and Carla eased into the room wearing jeans

and a well-worn Stephen F. Austin sweatshirt. She latched the door behind her and came over and stood beside me. As soon as she leaned down to kiss me on the cheek, she asked, "Who was that on the phone?"

"CNN."

"And you wouldn't give them the time of day, would you?"

"Nope."

"You're hopeless, Bo Handel," she said with a laugh.

"Yep."

"But you are okay, aren't you? I mean after last night?"

I sighed a deep sigh. "Yeah, but I don't want another chase like that for a while. This job has gotten awful lively here lately."

"Well, it may get even more busy. You're about to be short a deputy because I'm giving notice."

I felt a sinking in the pit of my stomach and it must have showed on my face.

"It's not like that, Bo. It's something I've been planning for months, and I'm doing it so we won't have to skulk around in the shadows anymore."

"But what are you going to do for a living?"

"I'm buying Nite-Flite Security Company over in Nacogdoches. Plus I'm going to hang out my shingle as a private investigator. I've got some money saved up, and Walter Durbin is going to lend me the rest. As you probably know, Walter's in a situation of his own that he can't really be open about, which meant he was sympathetic to my plight."

"So you're going into business?"

"Yep."

"How do the books look?"

"It's making money, and there is plenty of room for expansion. Walter and Dud will give me their investigative work, and I've got a contract pending with a big drilling company out of Tyler to investigate oil field theft."

I got to my feet. "So this means . . . what, exactly?"

"That we can come out of the closet as a couple. If that's what you want."

"Of course, but I hate to see you have to—"

"It's not just us," she said. "I've always wanted my own business."

She hugged me and she gave me a quick kiss. "I wanted to tell you before the fact, but now I've got to hurry over to Walter's office. We're signing the papers in a little while, then I need to go home and get dressed. I'm on duty at one this afternoon."

"Well, don't let me get in your way," I said with a laugh as she left in a whirlwind. Where was this all headed? I wondered.

Three hours later I met Sheila for lunch at the Caravan. Just as the waitress arrived with our tea, my cell phone rang. It was Hotchkiss with the particulars on the deceased.

"Quest and Weeks both had long rap sheets," he said. "Various heavy charges including auto theft, armed robbery, interstate gambling, and some drug trafficking. A couple of convictions each for middling offenses, but most of the big stuff failed to stick."

"I wonder why?"

"Several times witnesses have either gone missing or changed their stories."

"Were either of them mobbed up?"

"That depends on what you mean. Back in their younger days both of them had some connections with that old bunch of cracker thugs the newspapers called the Dixie Mafia. And according to our notes, in the last few years Quest has been associated with several organized crime figures, including Big Paul Arno."

"Surprise, surprise," I said.

After we hung up, I filled Sheila in on the previous night. "Why were they selling the cocaine for only a quarter of a million dollars?" she asked once I'd finished the whole story. "After all, it's supposed to be worth closer to a million."

"There are several possible reasons that I can see. For one thing, they weren't in a seller's market any longer after we caught Peet and the St. Louis connection fell through. The logic may have been just to grab what they could and be done with it. Or maybe they'd just made a deal to sell part of it. Then it might be that Scott and Arno planned to rob Quest and Weeks from the start, and Scott decided to go through with it after Arno got killed. I don't think we'll ever really know. Even if we catch the kid alive, we can't afford to believe anything he says."

"Do you think you'll get him?"

"Somebody will. Either that, or he'll get wasted resisting arrest."

"Do you really think he was having fun during that shootout last night, Bo?"

I gave her a tired smile. "I can't swear that he was, but he sure sounded like he was making the best of a bad situation. As for me, I can promise you I damn sure wasn't enjoying the proceedings."

She laughed a little, and we finished our breakfast in the near-silence of people who are comfortable enough with each other not to feel obliged to fill every minute of their time together with pointless chatter. I paid the check and was walking her to her car when my cell phone beeped again.

"Bo here," I said.

I listened for a few seconds and said, "Thank you and try to settle down, Miss Bess. I'll take care of it." Then I closed my eyes and shook my head and leaned against somebody's car.

"Bo, what's wrong?"

"This damn thing doesn't seem to *ever* end."

"What?"

"You know Lucy and Bess Porter, don't you? Those two old

maid sisters who used to run that little dress shop down on the square?"

"Sure," she said.

"That was Bess. She was almost hysterical, and Maylene gave her my cell number because she wouldn't talk to anybody but me. She and Lucy decided to drive out to Sycamore Ridge Cemetery a little while ago and visit their parents' graves. They found a body out there."

"Oh my God. Who was it?"

"Scott Kimball."

The boy was easy to find. Dressed in jeans and a black T-shirt, he lay on his back, his glazed and lifeless eyes staring upward at nothing at all. I squatted down beside the body.

"I think we can be sure that he wasn't killed with his own gun," I said as I peered closely at his chest.

"How can you tell?" Sheila asked.

"The entry holes are too big for a nine-millimeter."

There were two wounds in his chest, one in the center of the breastbone and one a couple of inches to the left. I looked up at her from where I was squatting beside the body. "Have you got that little digital camera of yours?" I asked.

"Yeah, it's right here in my purse."

"Good. Get me a dozen or so shots of this body from a bunch of angles."

"Okay. What are you going to do?"

"Procedures be damned. I'm going to turn him over when you get through taking those pictures. I want to see something."

As soon as she finished, I rolled the body over to one side. I was looking for exit wounds, and I found one. "Look at this," I said. "One bullet went all the way through, but the one in the breastbone must have hit the spine. At least we'll have something to start with if it isn't too deformed."

I stood up again and looked around. Then I pointed at the tombstone at the boy's feet. "Right at his granddaddy's grave. I wonder if that means anything."

"He's not armed, is he?"

"No. Whoever killed him must have taken his gun."

A few moments later one of our department cars swung into the cemetery, followed by a highway patrol unit. I knew it would take the ambulance a little longer. The cruiser pulled up beside us and Billy Don Smith and Carla climbed out. I gave orders while Carla took notes. Billy Don chewed tobacco and tried to look useful while Sheila just looked out of place. Once I had the process of dealing with the case started, I turned to Sheila. "I've got to go tell his mama," I said. "She only lives a quarter mile down the road. Why don't you come with me? You can stay in the car if you want to."

"I'll go up to the house with you to talk to her, Bo. You know you'd rather I did."

"I would, but it's my duty, not yours."

"Yes, it is. She's my friend."

Willa took the news of her last remaining son's death stoically and declined our offer to have someone from the church come to stay with her. "It's nothing more than I've been expecting for years," she said. "I've lived through it a thousand times in my mind."

"I wish it hadn't ended this way, Willa," I said.

"So do I, Bo. He could have made something of himself and given me grandchildren and been the comfort of my old age." She leaned against the door facing and stared out across the yard. "My life sure hasn't meant much," she said to no one in particular in a voice that was barely louder than a whisper.

For just a moment I thought about telling her about the child Trina Newland was carrying, but I didn't. I don't know why not, but it just didn't seem to be the right time and place. In the weeks and months since then I've gone over the moment a thousand times in my mind and wondered if the whole story would have ended differently if I had. But that's something I will never know.

We returned to the cemetery and went through the grim litany once again—autopsies and ballistic examinations, blood tests and pathologists' reports. We combed the site for physical evidence and found none. When the ambulance departed with the body, I drove Sheila back to the Caravan so she could get her car and go on to work and file her story. Then I had one more unpleasant chore to take care of.

CHAPTER FORTY-ONE

I stopped by the new jail and had them bring Nobel Dennard into one of the interrogation rooms. I waved the jailers out, closed the door, and motioned for him to sit. He looked ratty and deflated. A few days in jail will do that to anybody.

"We need to talk," I said.

"Bo, it's like I told you the day after you brought me in. I haven't got anything to say."

"Scott's dead, Nobel."

His face froze. "What? . . . How?"

"He was found out at the cemetery this morning. Shot twice."

"Do you know who did it? Or why?"

I shook my head. "Not a clue who killed him, but as to the why, considering the kind of people he ran with, what can you expect?"

He looked down at his hands where they were clasped on the dull gray metal of the table, and I thought for just a moment he was going to cry. Then he got control of himself.

"I know you didn't kill the Raynes boy," I said. "It was obvious, given what I've learned about the Twiller murder in the last few days. Scott called you and asked you to pick Doyle Raynes up and bring him out somewhere on the north side of town, didn't he?"

"Yes, but how—"

"And you couldn't say no, could you?"

He shook his head.

"Where did you and Doyle meet him?"

"That little crossroads store about five miles northwest of town."

"What reason did he give you for not coming to get Doyle himself?" I asked.

"He said the city had a couple of traffic warrants out on him and he was afraid if he came near the jail he'd get picked up."

"So you dropped what you were doing and drove thirty miles to run an errand for a kid most people didn't even know you were acquainted with?"

He nodded. "Yeah," he said, his voice almost inaudible.

"Because he knew you were the one person he could trust to help him, isn't that right?"

He looked up at me with eyes that were infinitely sad. "You know, don't you, Bo?"

"Yes, Nobel, I know. Willa told me years ago, back when Scott was just a baby. A man just can't give up on his son, can he?"

He took a deep breath and sighed a long sigh. "No, a man can't. But I wonder why she told you, of all people."

I shrugged. "We're old friends, and something like that is a heavy burden to bear alone. Did you ever let Scott know you were his father?"

"God, no. I would never have done that to Willa."

"Good," I said and gazed pointedly into his eyes. "And she'll never know that you and I talked about it either, will she?"

"Absolutely not." He sighed and ran his hands through his hair. "I know what I did was wrong. A young woman, lonely and mad at her husband because he's been called to active duty. I took advantage of that."

"It takes two, Nobel. Not that I'm in any position to condemn either of you. But you've never stopped. Amanda Twiller, remember? And how many others?"

He nodded bleakly. "It has its consequences, doesn't it?"

"When did you first contact Scott?"

"Back when he was in high school, right about the time you nailed him and that other kid on those burglaries. Bob Kimball was dead by then, and I could see that Scott was starting to screw up pretty bad. Otherwise I never would have interfered even though it was pretty rough knowing I had a boy out there that I couldn't acknowledge. At the time I thought maybe I could be an older friend and give him some guidance. I still think it was the right thing to have done."

"Of course it was," I said. "And I'll admit that it proves you're a better man than I ever thought you were. One thing baffles me, though. What were you going to do? Take the rap for him?"

"He would have eventually cleared me. I know he would. I don't think for a minute that he killed that Raynes kid."

"He did, Nobel," I said gruffly. "Believe it. He killed Amanda Twiller too. And he killed two Mississippi drug dealers in a big shootout last night."

He looked stunned. "Bo, are you sure?"

"Hell yes, I'm sure. He tried to shoot me too. He's a stone killer, and there's no doubt about it. It's not your fault and it's not Willa's fault, and it's not something I enjoy telling you. Now come on. I'm turning you loose. The DA is dropping the charges, but I'm not going to wait for the paperwork. I'll have one of my deputies drive you home. I thought you might want to go to the funeral."

Back at my office in the courthouse, I made some notes that were meaningless, then stared at the wall for a while trying to think and getting nowhere with the project. I drank a cup of coffee and nibbled a few cookies and reminded myself even as I ate them that I needed to quit between-meal snacks. I made a vow that soon I would do just that as I reached for two more pecan shortbread wafers. Eventually I was able to bear down on my paperwork. I was typing away on the computer in late morning when Maylene stuck her head in the door to tell me that Pappy Clyde was outside and wanted to see me. I told her to send him on in and then to go get the Lysol spray.

In any community all the hard-core drunkards seem to know one another and often congregate together during their squalid revels. In Sequoya, Homer "Pappy" Clyde was their acknowledged philosopher and all-round godfather. He was a year or two past seventy, small, bent, bald, and smelled like he'd been pickled in a mixture of cheap gin and horse piss.

In my seven plus terms as sheriff, I've dealt with plenty of alcoholics. The majority fight against their condition in one way or another. Many get into AA or some other program and eventually make a full recovery back to normal life. But I've known a few who cheerfully admit their disorder and then go right on drinking without any effort to stop. They seem to take the attitude that if God or fate or whatever it is they believe in has seen fit to make them what they are, then it's not their place to try to alter their destiny. Pappy was one such individual, and there were maybe a dozen others like him in the county.

A few times over the years the old man had come to my office in hopes of swapping information for a little money to buy whisky with. But for the most part he steered a wide course around me because he knew that I was apt to arrest him and send him into the detox program over at Rusk State Hospital if I thought his health had deteriorated to the point that his life was in danger. Which I'd done a couple of times in the past. Always before when he dropped by, he'd been either three sheets in the wind or wracked with the shakes and on the verge of DTs. But this morning he looked only moderately hungover.

"What's on your mind, Pappy?" I asked.

"Bad things, Bo."

"Do you need a drink?" I asked.

"I could use one, but I don't feel right taking it."

This was a new turn, and so out of character for him that it shocked me. "Why not?"

"Because I didn't come here to inform and get paid."

"No?"

He shook his head. It had long been rumored that Pappy Clyde had been a preacher before the bottle defeated him. Whether that was true or not, his speech was always colorful and sometimes took wing on the soaring currents of high metaphor, as it did today. "I came to do my civic duty," he said. "Even though it means giving up a good friend into the merciless arms of the law. My heart lies heavy in my breast this morning, Bo Handel. Truly it does, and I hesitate to profit from his misfortune."

I reached into my desk drawer and brought out the whiskey and a glass. I poured a triple shot and pushed it across the desk. "Go ahead, old fellow," I said gently. "Make it easy on yourself."

"I thank you mightily," he said and drained the glass in one pull and held it out for more. I half filled it this time. He cradled the amber liquid against his chest like a long-lost child and took a deep breath and shook his head. Then he sighed and stared morosely down into his drink for a few moments. When he looked up at me he had tears in his eyes.

"What's bothering you, Pappy?"

"I know who killed that Kimball boy. I know it as sure as I know that God in heaven made the very earth on which this courthouse stands. I don't want to tell you, but I feel compelled to. I'm afraid that if I don't, the Lord will never forgive me. I may not be much in the eyes of the world, but I still hold out hopes of His mercy at the end of my days."

"I think we could all use a little mercy, Pappy," I said gently. "So you just go ahead and say what you have to say."

He nodded absently and then looked down at his drink once more. When he looked back up tears were rolling down his cheeks.

"Who did it, Pappy?"

"It was my old friend Jesse, Sheriff. Jesse Kemp."

After I spent an hour getting the warrants, I went across the street to Walter Durbin's office and wound up waiting another half hour until he was finished with a client. Eventually I got in to see him. "Can you take a ride out in the country with me?" I asked. "It's important."

"I guess so. I'm about through for the day, anyway. What's the problem?"

"I want you to represent a man I'm about to arrest. Or at least I want you to represent him until the judge can appoint him a lawyer. Come on and I'll tell you more on the way."

We took the department's Suburban. I stopped on the edge of town and bought a bottle of Windsor Canadian Whiskey. When I got back in the truck I asked, "How much do you know about Jesse Kemp?"

"I know he won't do to mess with. He's an alcoholic Vietnam vet, and he's a little crazy. I also know he's somehow kin to Willa Hathaway."

"Right on all counts. Jesse's a complex fellow, and I've never really figured out what makes him tick. For one thing, he doesn't really believe in racial equality or racial mixing even though he's part white. He just seems to assume the segregated world he was born into was the way things were meant to be, and that all the changes since then are perversions of the natural order. He's smart as hell too. The school psychologist was going back over some old records a few years ago, and he told me Jesse had the third highest IQ ever scored in this school district. And he has dreams and visions. I know several reliable people around town who swear he told them he dreamed about President Kennedy getting killed in Dallas weeks before it happened."

"Do you believe them?" he asked.

I turned and looked at him and grinned. "Hell, yes I do because I'm one of the ones he told. I remember it as clear as a bell."

He pulled a long cigar out of his shirt pocket and stuck it in the side of his mouth to chew on. Then he seemed to ponder a moment before he spoke. "I've dreamed things that have come true a few times myself. Just minor, unimportant things, but it makes you wonder."

"Walter, the rational side of my mind says that with the billions of people in this world sleeping every night, some of them are bound to dream things that come true simply as a matter of chance. But the irrational side says something else."

"Welcome to the club," he said. "What are you going to charge him with?"

"Nothing, I hope. But maybe manslaughter or even murder. I just don't know yet."

"Why don't you tell me the whole story?"

"Pappy Clyde came by to see me a while ago. All these chronic drunks here around town know one another, but he and Jesse have been especially tight for years. He said he went out to Jesse's place early this morning in that old broke-down pickup of his. He'd been up all night, and he thought Jesse might have something to drink. Jesse wasn't there, but he figured he hadn't gone far since he doesn't have a vehicle. So Pappy just decided to sit down there in the yard and wait for him. He hadn't been waiting long when he heard two shots just down the road toward the cemetery. Then about fifteen minutes later Jesse came up the hill carrying a big old revolver. Pappy said Jesse just walked right on past him like he wasn't there and went in that little shack of his. When he came back out he didn't have the gun."

"Scott Kimball," he said grimly.

"Right. The news is all over the county. Pappy wandered into town a couple of hours ago and heard people talking about him being found dead out at the cemetery. Even as addled as he is, he put two and two together and knew what had happened. And I think you can see my problem. I'm convinced Scott killed Amanda Twiller and Doyle Raynes. I know he killed those two drug dealers in that house we raided two nights ago. If Jesse shot Scott, then there's every chance in the world that there were mitigating circumstances and that he was justified in doing it."

"But what possible motive could he have had?"

"More than likely he got it in his head somehow that Scott was going to harm Willa. He's very protective of her. Or at least he's as protective as a drunk with no means of transportation can be. Maybe I should have put a stakeout at her place last night, but I really didn't expect Scott to go home. Besides, it could have caused a hostage crisis, and Willa might have gotten hurt too."

"So you want me to sign on and—"

"If we find the gun and it matches the bullets in Kimball, I want you to talk to Jesse and come up with a plausible defense out of whatever crazy story he gives you. If he acts like he always has in the past, he'll either clam up completely or he'll tell you what happened as he sees it. Whatever he says will probably sound pretty strange because he's obsessed with biblical prophecy. His mother was a spirit lady. You know what that is, don't you?"

"A sort of voodoo practitioner, right?"

"More or less. Over here in East Texas it's called hoodoo, and it's strongly Protestant where classic Louisiana voodoo uses a lot of Catholic symbolism. In hoodoo you've got the priests who actually practice ritual magic, and then you have the spirit ladies, the ones who dream the dreams and have the visions. They're more respected and feared than the priests because people who believe in this stuff think anybody can learn the rituals while the spirit ladies were actually chosen and set aside by God."

"Or the devil," he said.

"Right you are. Nobody who's into hoodoo is ever quite sure where the prophetic gift comes from, and even the folks who consult the spirit ladies are wary of them. So when you're talking to Jesse, you need to keep in mind that not only was he brought up in the middle of all that crazy business, but he's been drinking rotgut whiskey and listening to his good buddy Pappy Clyde expound his own peculiar interpretations of Scripture for thirty years. So don't be surprised if his version of things is riddled with images right out of the book of Revelation."

"Bo, I can't help but be curious why you're going to this much trouble for an old alcoholic."

"Jesse's a drunk, but he's honest and he has a hell of a war record. And as far as I know, he's never hurt anybody who didn't try to hurt him first. Scott Kimball's passing was no great loss to the world, and you and I both know it. I just think it would be a shame for a man like Jesse to have to go down for killing him. I don't believe he'd survive a year in prison."

"Okay, I'll do it. I'll represent him all the way through, and do the whole thing pro bono."

"Thanks," I said with a sense of relief. "You're a good man."

He snorted. "I don't know about that, but I'm a combat vet myself, and I won't stand by and see him turned over to some young pup just out of law school. But we may wind up having to mount an insanity defense, and even if we win, it will still mean incarceration."

"The state hospital would be a hell of a lot better than the pen."

CHAPTER FORTY-TWO

The sun hung low on the horizon when we pulled up in front of Jesse Kemp's cabin. He stepped from the doorway and waited impassively until we got out of the Suburban. Jesse was about five-ten, with the muscular, agile body of a man half his age and skin the color of well-seasoned mahogany. The Kemps had a good measure of Cherokee blood, and it showed in Jesse's features. His eyes were yellowish and slanted over high, flat cheekbones, and that gave his face a distinctly Asiatic cast. That day he was dressed in a T-shirt and a pair of baggy fatigue pants stuffed into the tops of unlaced combat boots. On his head sat an ancient Harley-Davidson leather garrison cap like motorcyclists wore back in the 1940s.

Jesse's manner was always humble and his voice soft, but there was a cold fire in those strange, catlike eyes of his, and I resolved long ago that if I ever got on his fighting side I would be well armed and very alert when I did.

"Hello, Sheriff Bo," he said.

"Hello, Jesse. You're acquainted with Walter Durbin, aren't you?"

"Yes suh, I know Lawyer Durbin."

I reached in the truck and brought out the whiskey. "Could you use a drink, Jesse?" I asked.

"I need one pretty bad. Them men up them trees talked to me all night long last night."

I twisted the cap off the bottle and handed it to him. He turned it up and drank five or six ounces of straight whiskey like it was water. "Are they saying anything now?" I asked.

He shook his head slowly and drank once again. "They only talks at night. It's on account of the moon."

"How's that?"

"Why's blood on that moon. I seen it myself."

"That's just dust in the air, Jesse," I said.

"No suh," he said firmly. "It's blood. It's in the Bible, in the book of Joel. *The moon shall turn to blood, and then the great and terrible day of the Lord shall be at hand.* I dreamed it too, and I seen that day in my dream. I seen the angels of the Lord coming with flaming swords in they hands. They gonna chastise the wicked, and it won't be long now."

He tipped the bottle up once again and drank, then handed it back to me. "I thank you," he said.

"We need to talk to you, Jesse," I said.

"I know you do. I reckon you come looking for that pistol too."

I held up my hand to silence him. "I want you to listen to me carefully. Can you do that?"

He nodded placidly. "If that's what you want me to do."

"I have a warrant here that authorizes me to search your house for a certain handgun thought to be a forty-four or forty-five caliber. If I find it, I also will execute an arrest warrant on you signed by Judge MacGregor this afternoon. Do you understand me so far?"

"I do."

"I brought Mr. Durbin here along with me to see to your rights. As of now, he's your lawyer. He's willing to represent you free of charge, and I strongly suggest you take him up on that offer."

"I don't need no rights, Sheriff Bo. I done it. I killed that boy. I would like another drink of that whiskey, though, if you don't mind. . . ."

I lodged him first at the holding cell in the courthouse, and Dotty Fletcher came over and gave him a shot of Visceril and another of vitamins. What little medical attention he'd had in the last thirty years, he'd gotten from her, and he submitted to her care without complaint.

I didn't even have to search for the gun. He showed me where it lay in the top drawer of an ancient dresser in his cabin. It was a beautiful old Smith & Wesson Triple Lock revolver made sometime between 1908 and 1915. The original purchaser of the piece could be traced through the company's records, but that might take weeks and would mean little since the weapon could have had other owners before it came to Jesse.

One thing about the revolver puzzled me. It had seen very little use, and its condition was near factory original. It was well oiled and showed signs of having been owned by a shooter who gave his guns the best of care. Which was exactly what Jesse wasn't. He squirrel hunted some in the fall. I had seen both his weapons—a Marlin bolt-action .22 and an old Stevens double-barrel sixteen-gauge—and both were disasters. I doubted that either had ever seen a cleaning rod or felt a drop of oil. So why would he own a ninety-plus-year-old Triple Lock that was in near mint condition?

Walter spent an hour with him and learned nothing beyond the fact that he claimed to have killed Scott. He came out of the cell and threw up his hands in exasperation. "He says he did it," he said. "But he can't tell me why, or where he got the gun, or why he and Scott were at the cemetery. He claims he doesn't remember any of that, but he wants to plead out at the arraignment. I've never had a client like this before."

"Can't you stop him from doing that?"

"He has a right to enter a guilty plea if he wants to, Bo. The best I can do is to go over his head and ask for a sanity hearing prior to the arraignment. Which I damn sure intend to do if he doesn't show some interest in saving his own hide."

"Do you think he really did it?"

"Hell, I don't know. He's the most obstinate man I ever met."

"He can't go before the judge until Monday morning. Can you have another shot at him some time over the weekend?"

"Sure."

"We'll have to take him on out to the jail, but I'll leave instructions that you can see him any time you want to."

A few minutes later, as two of my deputies led Jesse off, he gave me a calm smile and thanked me for the whiskey. I left one of the night deputies to finish processing the paperwork and headed home. Just before I got in my truck, I looked up to see the moon where it hung red and foreboding in the eastern sky. I felt a tension across my shoulders, and for just a second the hackles on the back of my neck rose. I knew that something wasn't right about Scott's death, but I had no idea just how wrong it was.

CHAPTER FORTY-THREE

Instead of going home, I decided to drive over to the hospital at Nacogdoches to see Linda Willis. On the way my cell phone buzzed. It was Hotchkiss. "I've got an update on Lester Sipes," he said. "I wanted to let you know that he's reserved that suite at the Fredonia again."

"When is he due to check in?" I asked.

"He's already there, and he's got it booked for a week. It looks like he's planning to spend a lot of time up in this neck of the woods."

"Sounds like he's determined to find his missing coke, doesn't it? Wouldn't you hate to be in Emmet Zorn's boots at this stage of his life?"

"Indeed I would," he said.

"Why don't we go over there and jerk his chain a little tonight? What do you say?"

"Fine with me," he said. "I'm in Nacogdoches right now, as a matter of fact."

"Good. I'm going to the hospital to see Linda. Where do you want to get together?"

He hemmed and hawed for a few seconds, then said, "Uhhh . . . actually, that's where I am at the moment."

I laughed. "That's fine, Hotch. She's a pretty young woman. You're a nice young guy. It sounds good to me."

"I assure you it's just concern for a wounded fellow officer."

"If that's all there is to it, then you ain't got the sense God gave a goose," I said and broke the connection.

I found Linda propped up in bed with her foot in a cast and Hotchkiss sitting in a chair beside her. She claimed to be on some heavy painkillers, which may have been true. But they certainly hadn't taken the edge off her personality. She started complaining the second I walked in the door. The room was full of flowers, and when she finally wound down I asked who they were from.

"The guys at work, Bob Thornton, the highway patrol, the city PD, Maylene, Mom and Dad. And Don here brought the one on the nightstand. The one with the yellow roses is from you. Did you pick it out yourself?"

"No. I would have if I could, but as the day worked out I didn't have time. I just called Tim Formby's flower shop and told him your favorite color is yellow and that he could stick it to me good."

"Thanks. They're beautiful."

I quickly filled her in on what had happened the night before, and on Jesse's arrest. We only stayed a few more minutes. Despite her griping, she obviously needed rest. When we rose to leave I leaned over the bed and kissed her on the forehead.

"Bo, when can I come back to work?" she asked.

"What does the doctor say?"

"Six weeks to two months until he fully releases me. I'm gonna be bored to death."

"Take two weeks and then you can start coming in part-time and helping out with the clerical stuff."

She sighed. "That's better than nothing, I guess. I miss everybody already."

"We miss you too. Nobody has tried to kick me all day long."

Much to our surprise, Sipes agreed to see us without my having to resort to threatening him with arrest. His two goons were hatless, and he himself was wrapped up in a rust-colored silk bathrobe with a cream-colored satin scarf tucked around his neck like an ascot. Once again he was planted in the center of the sofa with one of his big cigars, his feet propped up on the coffee table.

"I don't know why I keep talking to you, Sheriff," he said. "You strike me as a very unpleasant man."

"You keep talking to me because you're just a little bit afraid not to, that's why. You're curious as to how much I know about your business."

"There's nothing secret about the banking business."

"That's not true," Hotchkiss said. "There's a lot that's secret in banking, but it's your drug business we're interested in."

"And who are you? Another of Sheriff Handel's deputies?"

"Special Agent Don Hotchkiss of the FBI. Do you need to see my ID?"

Sipes shook his head.

"Got problems, haven't you?" I asked.

"Everybody's got a few problems. So what?"

"Most people don't have problems like yours," I said. "You're out six hundred thousand dollars for some coke that your good friend Emmet Zorn filched from you. I don't know if you were just fronting for your South American people, or if you were doing business with them on credit, but either way they're not very happy with you at the moment. So you're up here to try to recover your merchandise while you still don't know how long you're going to be able to keep your head on your shoulders. Not a position I'd want to be in."

"I told you before that I don't know anything about any cocaine."

"Sipes, if you had any sense at all you'd forget all about this mess, go back home, run your banks and pray the Feds haven't already got enough on you to make a case. But you won't. You'll never stay straight because you don't understand the value of staying straight."

He stared off across the room and puffed his big cigar in silence for a few moments. Then he laughed a laugh that was harsh and grating and void of real mirth. "I will admit that there have been times when I wished I was free of the curse of ambition. Have you ever felt that way, Sheriff?"

Then he answered his own question. "No, of course you haven't. You were born into comfortable circumstances and you've been content to maintain that. I was raised on the very edge of poverty and had a hoodlum for a father. I wanted more."

"So you're telling us that you became a drug dealer and a killer because you grew up poor?" Hotchkiss asked. "That's a little lame, isn't it?"

"I don't really think you're in a position to judge me, kid," Sipes said.

"Someone is going to eventually," I said. "You can count on that."

"Maybe, and maybe not. Who can know the future? But why in hell did you come here tonight? Just to get on my nerves?"

"Partly," I said. "And partly to let you know I don't have any illusions about why you're in town. You're here to get that damned coke back, and I know it. I've already got three people dead, and I don't need any more. Watch your step."

He nodded. "You've had your say, so why don't we talk about

something more pleasant? I've heard you have an interest in quarter horses. I'm a breeder myself. What bloodline are yours?"

I rose to my feet. "Won't work, Sipes. I couldn't sit here and make casual chitchat with a man like you if I tried. And I don't intend to try."

He looked straight at me, and, once again, his eyes were lifeless rubber knobs at the bottom of deep, dark wells. "Then I don't see that we have anything more to say to each other."

"I noticed you didn't tell him Scott Kimball had stolen the coke from Zorn," Hotchkiss said as we walked down the hall.

"I didn't, did I?" I said with a smile. "Awfully forgetful of me, wasn't it?"

"I know you had a reason, but I can't figure out what it was."

"The minute Sipes finds out he can't get that coke, Zorn is a dead man. I don't want him dead. I want him to answer for the Twiller killing, and the only leverage I have is that I can protect him from Sipes if he comes clean."

"What if he doesn't?"

I sighed and pulled off my hat and ran my fingers through my hair. "Why don't we forget about all this mess for a while? I'll make you the same offer I made Toby earlier this week standing in this very hall. Let me buy you a beer. Or even better, follow me back to my place and we'll have a drink or two of some good whisky."

"Sound great to me."

CHAPTER FORTY-FOUR

Back in the early part of the summer, Sheila had gotten in the habit of coming by my house for coffee on Saturday mornings after she dropped Mindy off for an eight o'clock swimming class at the municipal pool. Until it got too hot in mid-July, we would pick her up at the pool when her lesson ended, and the three of us would go riding out at my dad's old farm where I kept my horses. Sheila was a skilled horsewoman, and I would saddle up my big dun quarter horse for her while I rode a gentle gray with Mindy perched in front of me, holding on to the saddle horn.

After the swimming program ended in August, the two of us continued to get together for coffee most Saturday mornings. A couple of days before I'd stopped at the new boutique bakery that opened a month earlier on the square and bought a pecan coffee cake. We were just finishing a simple but rich breakfast when the front doorbell rang. I went up the hall and opened the door to find Willa Kimball standing on the porch.

"I need to talk to you," she said.

"Of course, Willa. Come on back to the kitchen. Sheila's here. We were just having breakfast. Are you hungry?"

She shook her head and I ushered her to the back of the house and held a chair at the table for her. "Coffee?" I asked.

"I'd rather have a little whiskey, if you've got some."

I took the bottle of V.O. out of the cabinet and poured a couple of inches into a coffee mug. "Do you want ice?" I asked.

"No," she said and took the cup and downed a healthy swig. "One of the girls I work with at the Caravan called me last night. Two city cops were in for supper, and they claimed you'd arrested Jesse for shooting Scott. Is that true?"

I nodded solemnly.

"He didn't do it."

"You sound pretty certain."

"That's because I'm the one that did it," she said. Then she reached in her purse and pulled out a small paper sack and laid it on the table. "That's Scott's gun. I took it from him after I shot him out at the cemetery yesterday morning."

"Willa—"

"I'm going to tell you the whole story, and then I want you to turn Jesse loose. He didn't have anything to do with it."

"Please don't say anything more," I said. "I need to get Walter Durbin or Dud Malone to come down here and represent you before you tell me anything else."

"I don't want a damned lawyer. I just want to tell you what happened."

"Then at least let me read you your Miranda warn—"

"Bo Handel, shut up! I want you to stop being a lawman for once in your life and just be my friend. Can you do that?"

Defeated, I shrugged and nodded. "You know I can, Willa,"

Sheila reached across the table and squeezed her hand. "I'll leave if you want me to," she said.

"I'd rather you stayed, if you don't mind," Willa said. "I think maybe it will seem easier with another woman here." She raised her mug to her lips and finished off the drink. I poured more into the cup and set the bottle where she could reach it.

"You just take all the time you want," I said. "When you get finished, we'll see what we have to work with."

She took a deep breath and began, "Scott was at the house when I came home from work a little after midnight the night of that big shootout that was in the papers. He'd broken in. He had to because I'd changed the locks when he left for Houston. He told me he came through the back way on a motorcycle and left it up in the woods at the edge of the pasture. I guess he walked right by Jesse's cabin, and Jesse must have seen him and known something was wrong.

"He was too wound up to sleep, and so was I. We argued all night long. I think maybe he was taking something because his eyes were funny, and he went in the bathroom every so often as the night wore on. Every time he came back his eyes would seem even brighter. He was mean too. He wasn't trying to wheedle or manipulate me any longer. The time for that was past. He just laid it all out on the table and showed me what he really was. When I told him you were looking for him, he said of course you were because he'd killed Amanda Twiller and that Raynes kid. I asked him how he could do such a thing, and he said Amanda was nothing but a slut and a dopehead and the Raynes boy was a worthless little faggot, and that neither of them had any reason to live.

"Then I started crying because I knew for certain that my son was a murderer. He laughed at me, Bo. He laughed and he told me he'd killed two more people that same night. He said he was going to make me take him to Houston. He said we'd just stay at the house for a couple of days to let things cool down, and then he'd get on the back floorboard of my car and I'd just whisk him right on out of town after midnight. I'd never seen anybody so arrogant and cocksure in my life. He seemed to think he could get away with anything.

"He asked me how much money I had. I told him about fifteen hundred dollars in my checking account. He said when we got to Houston I was going to go to an ATM and take it all out and give it to him. I pointed out that I'd need a little money to get home on. Do you know what he did then? He slapped me. My own child. He reached over and slapped me hard. 'You've got credit cards, you lying old bitch.'

"That's when I started to hate him. Or maybe I'd hated him for a long time and that's when I just began to admit it to myself. But right at that moment I hated him worse than I ever thought I could hate anybody. And I hated myself too, and I hated the world where this *thing* sitting there smirking at me had come out of my body. So I decided to kill him. I told myself that he was only twenty-two years old, and he'd already murdered four people. What would the count be in a few more years? How many lives would I save? But I think that may have just been an excuse. I may have killed him because he was a monster who'd ruined my life."

"How did you wind up at the cemetery?" I asked.

She sipped a little more whiskey and dabbed her handkerchief at the corners of her eyes. "The one decent thing he would always do was go with me to put flowers on his grandfather's grave. Why, I don't know. I think maybe he came as close to loving Dad as he ever did to loving anybody. About sunup I showed him two bunches of fall-colored silk flowers I'd bought, one for Bob's grave and one for Dad's. I asked him if he wanted to go to the cemetery. He said sure, why not.

"When I went upstairs to change clothes I slipped his father's pistol into my purse. He rode on the back floorboard, just like he'd said, and he had me pull way up to one end of the cemetery where the car was out of sight from the road. When we got to the grave I smiled at him and handed him the flowers and asked him to put them in the vase. He did, and when he bent over I pulled the gun out of my purse. As soon as he stood up, I shot him twice right through the center of the chest. It wasn't as hard as I'd thought it would be. Bob had taught me how to shoot years ago, and I knew what to do. After he stopped breathing, I stood there looking at him, and for a few seconds I could see him the way he was when he was a little boy about five."

She looked across the table at me with eyes that were full of tears. I glanced at Sheila, who was crying silently.

Willa sighed a deep, heaving sigh. "I brought him into the world and I took him out of it."

"How did Jesse come to have the pistol?" I asked.

"When I got back to the car, I had the gun I shot him with in my left hand, and I had his gun in my right hand. I must have taken it from his body, but I don't remember that. I don't even remember walking to the car. I just laid them both on the seat beside me and drove home. For some reason, when I got home and got out of the car, I picked up his daddy's gun and left the other one where it was. Jesse was waiting for me there in the yard. He took the pistol out of my hand and said for me to go inside. I told him what I'd done, and he said that he'd been watching when we left the house and he heard the shots.

"First I just sat down in the den and stared at the wall for a long time. Then I went up to my room and lay down and dozed a little until you knocked on the door to tell me the body had been found."

I got up and took the coffeepot and poured Sheila a refill, then topped off my own cup. I asked Willa if she wanted more whiskey, but she shook her head. "Are you going to turn Jesse loose, Bo?" she asked.

"Of course. I hated to have to arrest him in the first place."

She nodded and then lay her head down on the table, cradling it in her arms like a little girl taking a nap on her school desk. "I'm so tired," she said. "I'm just so tired of everything."

Sheila and I drove her home. I knew she wasn't going to run, and I wasn't sure what she was guilty of, if anything, since Scott, who was himself a confessed killer, had forced his way into her home.

"I'll talk to the DA and see what he says," I said. "After all, Scott broke in and was going to rob you. Even if Tom decides to charge you with something, I'll take you in Monday morning and run you through the process. You know as well as I do that Judge MacGregor is going to release you on your own recognizance, so there's no need for you to spend two days in jail when I know you're not going anywhere."

"Can you get in any trouble doing this?" she asked.

"It's my call. If the voters don't like it, they can always elect somebody else. We'll just leave your car here and I'll drive it out this afternoon and have someone follow me in my pickup."

When we got to her place, Sheila got out with her. Willa reached out and took her in her arms and hugged her. They spoke quietly for a moment, and then she turned and went up the steps and vanished in the sprawling old house that had sheltered her family for generations.

CHAPTER FORTY-FIVE

It proved to be a long and dreadful day. First I went by the Pak-a-Sak only to find it closed. I tried Zorn's house but there was no answer to my knock and his car was gone. I told the dispatcher to alert all the deputies, the city police, and the highway patrol to stop him and bring him in. Then I headed home. An hour after I got back to the house my cell phone rang, summoning me to an attempted robbery and shooting at a country store on Route 9 South just at the county line. Fortunately the victim was the robber and not the proprietor, and he was only wounded, but it was mid-afternoon before I was able to go out to Willa's place. I knocked and knocked and got no response. I reached down and turned the knob to find the door unlocked. I stepped cautiously into a house that was silent except for the slow ticking of the old grandfather clock in the hallway. I called her name loudly a half dozen times and got no answer. With a deep sigh, I started up the stairway. . . .

When I pulled into my driveway just after sunset, Sheila's little Datsun was parked in front of my house and she was sitting in the porch swing. Instead of going around back to the carriage house, I pulled in beside her car and came up the steps and sat down beside her.

"What did the DA say?" she asked. "Is Willa going to be charged? Like you said, Scott was a killer and he was—"

"I never talked to the DA, Sheila. You and I are the only ones who know she came here this morning, and I'd like to keep it that way."

"But Bo, you can't cover up a boy's death. You just can't."

"None of it matters anymore. Willa's dead."

"Oh my God, Bo! What happened?"

"I went out there like I promised her I would, and found her upstairs in her bed. From the looks of things, she took a bath and fixed her hair and put on a nice nightgown. There was an empty bottle of Seconal on the bedside table. I don't know how many had been in it, but it was enough. More than enough, probably. A handwritten will was lying on her chest. She named me executor, of all things. The house and the forty remaining acres are to be sold to pay her debts, which will include two funerals and not much else. The rest goes to the town library."

"But if she made you executor she must have trusted you more than anybody."

"I guess so."

"And you let her go home this morning without . . . Oh, Bo! You knew what she was going to do. And she knew you knew."

"I didn't actually know because I didn't let myself think about it."

"You let her . . ."

"I certainly didn't do much to stop her, did I?"

"But why did she do it?"

"I think it was because there just wasn't anything left for her. I think she must have had it on her mind from the time she got back home that morning and realized what she'd done. When

Jesse was arrested it gave her an extra day. She had to see to it that he was cleared."

She began to cry. "There must have been some other way. . . ."

"I don't see what it could have been. At best, if the DA didn't prosecute, what on earth was she going to do? Go back to work at the Caravan and see the reflection of what she'd done in every face that came in the door? And if the DA had charged her, she would have taken those pills as soon as Judge MacGregor released her on her own recognizance, which you and I both know he would have done. Then everybody in the county would have known she killed her own son. She deserved better than that."

"Oh, Bo, it's all so awful. . . ." She was crying freely now.

I handed her my handkerchief and put my arm around her and drew her close. "I'm sorry you were here this morning," I said. "I was thinking about that on the way home. You're awful young to have to digest something like this."

"I'm glad I was, Bo. You needed somebody here with you, and we both know it."

"You're right," I admitted.

She dabbed at her eyes and we sat in silence for a long time. "What now?" she finally asked.

I sighed a tired sigh. I felt weary deep in my bones. "I'm going to release Jesse in the morning and take him home just like I promised her I would. I'll tell him what happened, but he'll never say a word. Keeping secrets is just in his nature. And I'm going to write in the case file that a confidential informant plus new evidence turned up by further investigation cleared him. That old Smith and Wesson forty-four is going to be gone where nobody will ever find it. Pappy Clyde will keep his mouth shut when he's sober, and nobody will pay any attention to anything he says when he's drunk. I plan to put together a press release for you, and I'm going to lay the murders of Amanda Twiller and Doyle Raynes on Scott

Kimball where they belong. My conclusion is going to be backed up by the ballistics report on the pistol Willa gave me."

"It was positive then, I guess?" she asked.

"It will be. It's the same make of gun, and he bragged about using it to kill them both to his own mother. His own death is going down as an unsolved crime, but the press release will mention that according to confidential informants he had owed some heavy gambling debts to some bad people down in Houston. Where Willa is concerned, I think that unless somebody tells them otherwise, most people will assume that she'd gotten to the point where she just couldn't cope with all the tragedy in her life. There are still a few loose ends and unanswered questions. For one thing, I don't think we'll ever know for sure how Scott got in contact with Paul Arno. I don't know how Scott found out Zorn had the coke, either. Probably because Zorn bragged about it, but . . ." I shook my head. "None of that really matters."

"What about Zorn?" she asked. "After all, he started the whole thing. Does he just get away scot-free on this?"

I patted her knee and smiled tiredly in the darkness. "Sheila, let's not talk about him right now. Let's go inside and have some supper."

"I've already eaten. Why don't you make yourself a drink and lie down on the sofa and let me fix you something?"

"That's the best offer I've had all day."

CHAPTER FORTY-SIX

Early the next morning before church, I went to the jail and released Jesse Kemp and took him home. Near the edge of town he asked, "Why you turnin' me loose, Sheriff Bo?"

"Willa confessed," I said as gently as I could. "I know you didn't kill Scott. She came to my house yesterday morning and told me the whole story about how you were waiting in the yard and took the pistol away from her."

"I wish she hadn't done that."

"I know you do, but it's over and done with now."

"Did you take her to the jailhouse?"

I shook my head. "No, I took her home and told her to try to get some sleep. I was going to talk to the district attorney and to see what he said. Scott had killed at least four people, and he was going to make her take the last of her savings out of the bank. He'd broken into her house and he was going to rob her, so I don't know that she was really guilty of anything."

"Where's she at?"

"She's dead, Jesse. She took her own life."

He blinked a couple of times and then leaned back in the seat and closed his eyes. "What happened?"

"She took sleeping pills. I found her yesterday afternoon."

I was surprised by what he said then, but shouldn't have been. I think that with his strange notions and visions, what he called the "other side" was as real to him as the everyday world. "That's good. That's an easy passing."

We rode along without either of us saying anything for at least five minutes. Then he broke the silence. "My momma was a spirit lady. She could read the signs. Pappy Clyde says she had the gift stronger than anybody he ever seen."

"So I've heard."

"That child, Scott, he was born when the stars was bad. My momma saw it, and she told me about it years ago, before she passed. They was ructions in the Pleiades the night he come in the world."

I sighed. "Well, Jesse, I guess that's about as good an explanation for a boy like him as anything the doctors can come up with."

"What started all this killin', Sheriff Bo?"

"Cocaine."

"Say which?"

"You know Emmet Zorn, don't you? The fellow who runs the Pak-a-Sak?"

"I don't trade with him, but I know who he is."

"Well, he stole a bunch of dope from a hoodlum in Houston, and then Scott stole it from him. Now nobody knows where it is."

He tilted his head to one side and sat silently in thought for what must have been half a minute. Then he asked, "How big is this dope?"

"Twenty pounds or better."

He nodded. "I wish you'd said something about it the other day when you were out at my place."

"How come, Jesse?"

"I'll show you when we get there."

That afternoon I talked to Leonard Ott at the funeral home and made arrangements for both funerals. As Willa's executor, it was my obligation. Monday morning I filed her will for probate, and in the late afternoon Sheila and I attended the short graveside service for her and Scott at Sycamore Ridge Cemetery. It seemed like half the town turned out. I'd never seen so many people in the old graveyard. I'd offered to come by and pick Jesse up, but he said he wanted to walk. Much to my surprise he appeared at the cemetery wearing a suit and tie. Both were thirty years out of date and smelled of mothballs, but he looked presentable. Nobel Dennard stood near him, his face ashen.

When the short service was over, most of the people headed back to their cars while Sheila and I drifted slowly toward our family plot in the oldest part of the cemetery near the edge of the bluff where the tall, serene monuments of our forbearers overlooked the town in quiet and timeless contemplation. She knelt for a moment and brushed some sand from the base of her father's tombstone, then placed the small bouquet of silk flowers she'd brought with her in the marble vase at the head of the grave.

Twilight was near. I stood with my back to the west and watched the shadow of the ridge as it moved eastward with the setting sun. Then I looked back over my shoulder toward the fresh grave just as the men from the funeral home began to work the cranks on the catafalques. With hardly a sound, both caskets sank gently out of sight. Jesse stood nearby, his head bowed, looking old and frail.

I reached down and helped Sheila to her feet. "Are you ready to go?" I asked.

She nodded, and we walked silently back toward the car as the last thin crescent of the sun vanished in the west.

CHAPTER FORTY-SEVEN

As soon as I got up the next morning, I checked in with the office to learn that Zorn's store was still closed and his car was still missing from his garage. I hesitated to put out a state-wide alert on the man. Since Willa's death, I had nothing to tie him to the Twiller killing.

With the case at a standstill, I decided to take the day off. I'd seen too much in too short a time, and I needed a break. I went by the office to pick up my shotgun, and left instructions that I was not to be called for anything less than a full-scale riot. Out at the gun club I found a half dozen members I knew, including Charlie Morton. I shot three rounds of sporting clays with plenty of time in between for bragging and horseplay. Any other day it would have been good fun, and I tried to enjoy myself. But my heart wasn't in it.

Charlie and I wound up having a leisurely lunch together at the Caravan. When we finished, he departed for his office. As I drove past the courthouse on my way home Judge MacGregor hailed me. His docket was empty that afternoon, and he invited me up to his office, where the two of us spent a pleasant hour on his tree-shaded balcony. I left him wreathed in a billowing cloud of pipe smoke and drove down to the library intending to check out the recent fiction arrivals. Instead I allowed myself to be seduced by the local history section and was deep into an article in *East Texas Historical Journal* when they ran me out at closing time.

On the way home I stopped by the Dairy Queen and got a milkshake and had only been back at the house about an hour when the phone rang. I put the receiver to my ear and heard Emmet Zorn's voice say, "You've got to help me."

"What?"

"They're outside. I can tell. Just please come over here."

"Where are you?"

"I'm at home. They cancelled my cell phone. I'm on my—" Then the connection went dead.

I called the office to find that Toby was still on duty. After telling him that I would pick him up in five minutes, I climbed in my truck and headed for the courthouse. He was waiting out front. "What's up?" he asked as soon as he was in the cab.

"Emmet Zorn called me. He's back in town and claims they're after him."

"Who's after him?"

"He didn't say, but I don't see how it could be anybody but Sipes. Maybe we can make him come clean on his part in the Twiller killing."

When we got to Zorn's street I circled the block and we saw nothing out of the ordinary. I drove past his house and parked a few feet down from his driveway on the opposite side of the street. We approached with our guns drawn, but the neighborhood was quiet except for the faint hum of an air-conditioning unit somewhere down the street. I knocked on the door and a few seconds later it opened a couple of inches to reveal one of Zorn's bright little eyes. "Are you alone?" he whispered.

"Hell, no," I said in my normal voice. "I brought Toby Parsons. Now cut out the secret agent crap and let us in."

He fumbled around with the chain for a few seconds, and

then the door swung open. After Linda's description, I was curious to see the inner sanctum of a small-town playboy with half a foot of taxidermied hair and what had to be one of the world's largest collection of bolo ties. The furniture was too modern for the architecture, but it was of decent quality, and the fabrics weren't gaudy. The room could have used a smaller pair of speakers than the giant corner Klipsch Horns that went with the overpowered McIntosh stereo. The nudes she'd mentioned were outsize airbrushed numbers that looked like they'd been copied from some men's magazine centerfold. One hung over the sofa and the other was mounted above the entertainment center. Then I glanced down the hall and into the bedroom and saw that round waterbed with its red satin coverlet and black pillows. I couldn't tell if there was a mirror on the ceiling over the bed, but it wouldn't have surprised me a bit. Unbidden, the image strayed into my mind of Willa Hathaway in that bed, and I turned away, a little ashamed of being human.

"Where in the hell have you been?" I asked.

"Out of town. But that doesn't matter. You've got to get me out of here."

"Why did you come back?"

"My bank account's been frozen and all my credit cards have been cut off. It has to be Sipes."

No doubt it was the Feds rather than Sipes, and I could see where they were going with the move. It meant they were within weeks or maybe even days of making their move on Sipes and they wanted Zorn to roll over on him. I didn't fault Hotchkiss for having his own agenda, but it wasn't mine.

"What do you expect me to do about it?" I asked.

"They're gonna kill me."

"For stealing Sipes's cocaine?"

"That's what he thinks, anyway."

"And he's right. He knows you stole it just like he knows you were going to sell to another buyer. But Scott Kimball filched it from you before your customer got here. What I don't understand is why you let that boy know you had the damn stuff in the first place. What were you trying to do? Impress him with what a big wheel you are?"

He gave me a sick smile and shrugged.

"Why don't you just get in your car and leave again?" Toby said.

Zorn shook his head. "I can't do that. With all my credit cards cut off I barely had enough gas to get home. And my phone line's been cut. Here, listen . . ." He picked up the receiver.

"I'll take your word for it," I said.

"And I get a recording telling me that my cell phone account's been terminated. I can't get through to nobody. Yours was the last call I was able to make."

"I don't see how he could cut off your cell phone account," I said.

"He's a banker. Damn bankers can do anything they want to. I know he's still here in town."

"I would be too," Toby said. "After all, you snatched about a million dollars' worth of his property."

"And there's more to it than that," I said. "I think by now Sipes knows that Paul Arno was planning to kill him the same night Amanda Twiller was killed. You and Arno were going to sell the coke and split the money. In fact, Arno is the guy that put you on to the St. Louis buyer in the first place, wasn't he?"

His eyes widened in surprise.

"You didn't have any idea we'd figured that out, did you? If we did, then so will Sipes."

"But I can find the coke for you if you give me a little time," he said. "Then I'll roll over on Sipes. I'll testify against him. You'll have a big bust under your belt. Lots of good publicity."

"What makes you think you can find it?" I asked.

"Something Scott said after he took it made me think he left it with that old nigger that lives out there on his mother's farm."

"*Nigger?*" Toby said.

Zorn was so scared he was oblivious. "Yeah, you know, Kemp. That crazy vet you've got in jail."

"I've already got the cocaine, you idiot," I said.

"You've already got it?" he asked, his voice tinged with wonder.

"Hell, yes. It's locked in the vault down at the courthouse. You were right about Scott leaving it with Jesse Kemp. I turned him loose yesterday, and he didn't even know what the damn stuff was until I mentioned it. It was in the same beat-up old dresser where he stored the gun. If I'd done a thorough search the day I arrested him I would have found it then. Scott asked him to keep it for him because he knew Jesse was loyal to Willa and her kids. So now you've got nothing left to bargain with but Amanda Twiller's murder."

"Amanda? . . . But I didn't—"

"Yes, you did. Scott's dead, Zorn. We found him with two bullet holes in his chest two days ago out at the cemetery. If you'd been in town you would have known about it."

"Dead? But who—"

"Who killed him isn't important right now. What is important is that you were the cause of him killing Amanda Twiller and we both know it. My guess is that she'd threatened to rat you out to Sipes on the cocaine because you were trying to dump her. There could have been other reasons, but they don't matter. You needed to get rid of her, so you hired that little freak to kill her for you. I can't prove it, but I know you did. So don't piss me off any more by lying about it. If you won't confess, then don't say anything."

He acted like he hadn't heard a word I'd said. "You've got to get me out of here. They're going to kill me. You admitted it yourself."

I nodded. "They probably will."

"You can't let that happen."

"Oh yes, I can, and I will too, unless you come clean. Do that and I'll take you out of here right now, safe and sound. It's the only choice you've got."

Zorn took a couple of quick, fitful drags off his cigarillo. "Murder for hire is capital murder," he said.

"You can make a deal with the DA. If you confess and plead out, he won't go for the death penalty. I guarantee it."

He was near panic. A fine dew of sweat beaded his forehead, and the hand that held his cigarillo trembled while his eyes zipped back and forth like rats in a cage. But still he shook his head. "I can't."

"Then that's where we'll have to leave it. Let's go, Toby."

"Please," Zorn pleaded. "Don't do this to me."

"I'm not. You're doing it to yourself."

As we went to the door I glanced around and took a final look at his bachelor pad with its fancy stereo and its satin-covered waterbed and gaudy nudes and felt a wave of nausea rise in me. For a few dreadful seconds I thought I was going to throw up, but then I stepped out onto the porch with relief and drew in a deep breath of the clean night air. I tossed Toby the keys and told him to drive. Just before we climbed into the truck, I turned and looked back. The living room light had been switched off, and I could see Zorn peering nervously out the porch window, his face pasty and ghostlike where it hung framed in the narrow gap of the curtains. Then the window shade descended and I saw him no more.

His house was at the very edge of town. Half a block farther down, the street turned into a narrow county road that stretched away through a stand of dark forest. As soon as Toby cranked my truck, the parking lights of a car came on just beyond where the woods began. He slowed down as we passed, and inside the car I could make out the silhouettes of three men, two in the front and one in the rear. For a moment a cigarette flared on the passenger side, and I caught a glimpse of a lean, hard hand and a bushy mustache.

"It's a black Marquis," Toby said once we'd rolled past. "Shouldn't we go back?"

"Drive on."

"But I thought you were just bluffing him, trying to make him come across . . ."

I shook my head. "Without Scott Kimball we'll never nail Zorn. So we either let him walk, or we stand aside and let the dead bury the dead."

"The dead bury . . . I don't get it."

"I'm talking about Sipes. One way or another his days are numbered. If not the Feds, then the Colombians."

He nodded in understanding, and we said no more. On the way I had him pull in at a liquor store, and I went inside and bought a bottle of V.O. He turned onto South Main and drove slowly until we reached the courthouse. I climbed from the truck and came around to the driver's side.

"Are you sure you feel up to driving home?" he asked as he handed me my keys.

"I can make it. How about you? Are you okay with this?"

"I trust your judgment, Bo."

"Yes, but are you *okay* with it?"

"There's no other way to make it right for that poor woman, is there?"

I shook my head and quickly told him about Quinn and the deal Hotchkiss had cut him. "It had to be the Feds who froze Zorn's finances. They're fixated on Sipes, and I think they're hurrying things along so they can grab him before the Colombians take his head off. They want Sipes so bad that I have no doubt they've already made the decision to offer Zorn the witness protection program in return for his testimony about the coke dealings. Besides, he confessed in an offhand way. Did you notice?"

He nodded. "Yeah, by mentioning murder for hire. Neither of us had said anything about that."

"Right," I said.

His face was hard under the cold white light of the street lamp. "Then I guess I can live with it and not lose too much sleep. You did surprise me, though."

"Sometimes I surprise myself, Toby."

We shook hands and I drove slowly home. After I pulled into the carriage house and locked the truck, I lingered on the patio I'd built many years earlier. A few seconds later Carla came out of the house. "I thought I'd come over and see how your day went," she said, peering intently at my face.

I motioned for her to sit in one of the deck chairs and took the other one myself. "It went," I said tiredly. "That's about all I can say for it."

"Are you okay?" she asked.

"I will be. Want a drink?"

"Maybe later."

I nodded and uncapped the bottle and took a long pull. Carla reached over and took my hand and gave it a gentle squeeze. It wasn't long before I felt the whiskey light a comforting fire in my belly. The town was strangely quiet. For a moment a dog barked somewhere off in the distance, but it soon quit and a hush fell back on the world. We sat there under the towering oaks, aware of nothing beyond the rich, brooding silence of the late summer night and the great red orb of the Blood Moon where it loomed just above the horizon.